Deadly Odds 7.0

Allen Wyler

Deadly Odds 7.0

Other books by Allen Wyler (fiction)

Deadly Errors
Dead Head
Dead Ringer
Dead End Deal
Dead Wrong
Changes
Cutter's Trial
Deadly Odds
Deadly Odds 2.0
Deadly Odds 3.0
Deadly Odds 4.0
Deadly Odds 5.0
Deadly Odds 6.0

Other books by Allen Wyler (nonfiction)

The Surgical Management of Epilepsy

Deadly Odds 7.0 ©2024 Allen Wyler, All Rights Reserved

Print ISBN 978-1-960405-35-7
ebook ISBN 978-1-960405-36-4

Visit Allen online at www.allenwyler.com

Cover design by Guy D. Corp
www.grafixCORP.com

STAIRWAY⹀PRESS
STAIRWAY PRESS—APACHE JUNCTION

www.stairwaypress.com
1000 West Apache Trail, Suite 126
Apache Junction, AZ 85120 USA

CHAPTER 1

Seattle

EXCEPT FOR OCCASIONAL intense sapphire glints from her eyes, low sweeping cedar branches formed an island of impenetrable, layered shadows in a lake of harsh mercury-vapor streetlight, cloistering a petite female in black jeans, black wool turtleneck, black shoes, and a black ski mask over her pale white skin and regimented coif of platinum-blond hair.

She sat cross-legged in a roughly triangular patch of weed-infested ivy, back propped against the scaly red strips of cedar bark. It was her third consecutive night of surveilling Arnold Gold's home from 7 PM to 10 PM.

Precisely.

And like the prior nights, no one appeared to be inside the ultra-contemporary cube despite various lights that turned on at the same time each evening.

Alexa smart switches, she assumed.

Another glance at her watch. Another sixty minutes had just snailed past. Amazing. The time just seemed to…dissipate. Another sixty minutes of her life had evaporated doing…what, exactly? Surveillance. There was, however, a bright side. Those sixty minutes were billable. The not-so-bright side, however, was that the time could never be recaptured.

Oh well, it was a job, and like certain orifices, everybody needs one. If she weren't doing this, she might be wiping tables and slinging hash browns at a Denny's.

She stifled a yawn.

Enough.

She had fulfilled her commitment for the evening.

According to the property records, this was indeed Gold's home. But he wasn't inside during the specified hours on these specified evenings.

Where was he? On vacation? At a girlfriend's? Or perhaps a boyfriend's?

No idea and not her problem, for she hadn't been asked to address that question. Adhering to her well-established reputation as a diligent and rigorous investigator, she intended to write up the exact details outlined in the assignment and that would be that.

Then on to the next job.

She stood, swatted debris from her black pants, did an about-face to ruffle the matted ivy back into some semblance of natural confusion, then stepped back to inspect how well she'd disguised her presence. Not quite perfect. Bending over, she messed up an edge that didn't look quite right. Surveyed her work again and nodded silent approval. Now it was perfect.

Three full strides and she was standing on the edge of the narrow, windy, asphalt side street. Stood still for a moment, scanning the immediate vicinity. No vehicular nor pedestrian traffic. No one in sight.

Off came her ski mask, which she quickly wadded into the back pocket of her jeans, then slid from the concealing shadows up the sidewalk of the deserted street. Turned right at the corner, continued straight ahead for half a block, then another right turn into the alley that again shrouded her in the dense shadows of shrubs and fences.

Silently she navigated an obstacle course of color-coded recycling, garbage, and compost bins, all the while concealed in the darkest areas. With her contracted three hours finished, she was now working on her own time. But true to her reputation for scrupulous thoroughness, she felt it necessary to add a trademark garnish to her report. Lest anyone should ever accuse her work of being shoddy. And besides, it cost only a handful of minutes. Salve for her conscience. This job, after all, had turned out to be less of a challenge than originally thought, so anything to spice it up…

Sneaking along the edges of the rutted compacted dirt, drifting noiselessly from shadow to shadow, she finally came abreast of the security wall along the back of Gold's property.

Another quick scan of the neighboring houses. Nobody at a window or back porch peering into the alley.

Why would they be?

Although that didn't mean some nosy Nelly couldn't be standing surreptitiously at a purposely darkened window, having been alerted by a motion-activated alarm similar to what guarded Gold's house. Well, she didn't know for sure if the strategically mounted cameras on the upper edges of his brutalist domain were motion-activated or not, but she would be amazed if they weren't. Especially considering the other advanced security measures detailed during her prior reconnaissance.

On her toes now, gripping the rough edge of the concrete, she gazed past the inky, shadowy back yard, on through floor-to-ceiling plate glass into Gold's dimly lit stainless-steel and polished-concrete, Gaggenau kitchen.

Nobody there either.

No different than the preceding nights. Leaving her with the distinct impression that Gold hadn't been in the house for a while now, despite having only watched it for three hours each in three nights.

Enough.

She'd completed her contracted work and, in good conscience, finished. After dropping back onto the soles of her cross-trainers, she brushed off her fingers while glancing around one last time. She exited the alley as carefully and stealthily as she'd entered, for she saw no upside to being detected.

Her report would be filed by morning.

Honolulu

As Arnold Gold tossed a chunk of garlic chicken into his mouth—dinner picked up from Gulick Deli on the drive back from taking Chance to his favorite park—the security app on his iPhone began going apeshit. With a sigh of annoyance, he stabbed the chopsticks into the contents of the white take-out container, set it on the side table, grabbed his iPhone. Miss Stealthy One again? A third consecutive night? Yeah, he'd put money on it. He opened the app. There she was. All decked out in black. A carbon copy of the other two nights.

Goddamnit!

He glanced at the dark sky.

What now?

Three consecutive nights? For sure this meant the house was being surveilled. But why? A prelude to a burglary? That didn't make sense because anyone who bothered to look inside the floor-to-ceiling windows—as he knew she had—would see nothing of value inside. No fancy art. No high-end furniture.

So, what the hell was going on?

He swung his legs over the edge of the chaise, stood and made his way from the back deck into the kitchen, on through the living room and into his guest bedroom, home of SAM 2.0, his AI network.

The SAM project began years ago as two tenuously networked PCs and had since grown into twenty-five fully loaded Dell towers working ensemble to form a very potent neural network. As SAM grew more complex and sophisticated, Arnold had begun delegating more responsibility to it, such as managing his ever-changing stock portfolio.

Think of SAM as a super Alexa or Siri capable of working independently. Similar to the infamous HAL in Kubrick's *2001: A Space Odyssey*, but without HAL's disconcerting personal agenda. In addition to managing his investments, SAM also kept a keen eye on the extensive security systems guarding both his

Honolulu and Seattle homes.

After settling into his padded leather gaming chair, he logged into the Seattle security system. At the moment, the woman's heat signature was no longer on the high-def infrared surveillance camera. No big surprise. Odds were, she was long gone by now.

He brought up the recording of the triggering event. Yep. There she was. What little he could see of her. He backed up the recording far enough to watch the crown of her head rise only far enough above the security wall to peer across the back yard into the kitchen. Just enough to trigger the thermal imaging sensors despite that funky black balaclava.

Most definitely a person. SAM's built-in algorithms had long since learned to disregard cats, dogs, birds, and the occasional urban coyote prowling the neighborhood.

What the hell was going on?

Shaking his head in frustration, he saved the video, sat back in the chair to think.

Shit.

He texted Prisha Patel, second banana at Gold and Associates: *Okay to call?*

A few seconds later she called him.

He answered with: "She showed up again. This makes three nights in a row. Any different thoughts?"

Several seconds of dead air, then: "Gotta agree with you, boss. It's pretty clear you're being targeted for something. Not sure what that might be, but scoping your house three nights in a row? Yeah, you're definitely being targeted."

"I think we need to start thinking in terms of *we're* being targeted."

His use of the plural possessive was intended to mean Gold and Associates.

"Why do you say that?"

"On account of there's nothing in there anyone'd want to steal."

"So you said last night, but I dunno, dude. Again, I have to ask why?"

"Can't answer that other than my gut says Mizrahi's up to something," he said, referring to Itzhak Mizrahi, the head of security for Larkin Standish.

"Guess we'll find out one way or another."

The Following Morning

"Enter," Itzhak Mizrahi yelled at the closed office door.

His office door swung open, and the petite woman with the platinum-blond hair stepped into the cramped space, shut the door, then stood before his dented gray Steelcase desk, feet together, arms at her sides. Not really at attention nor parade rest, just standing. Straight.

Mizrahi knew better than to offer her a chair. She was here to submit a verbal report, then leave. Although short on personality, she was as effective at her job as the Omicron variant was at its. And that was all that mattered to him. What she did on her own time was her business, although he often wondered...

"What do you have for me?" he said, knowing that unless asked, she would probably continue standing like that, staring at him with those eerie sapphire-blue eyes until he finally did, and he wanted this over with.

In this respect, she was no different than many of the enlisted men who had reported to him in the military.

"Last night was a carbon copy of the prior two," she offered. "I watched the residence between seven and ten and although a few lights came on, at no time was the target seen in or around the house. At least not from my vantage points. But, as stated in my other reports, so much of the first floor is floor-to-ceiling windows that I'm confident that at no time during those three consecutive hours was the target observed on that floor. If he was elsewhere inside, well..."

She didn't provide the shrug he expected, given her tone.

When he didn't respond, she added, "I have no idea where

he was. All I can tell you is he wasn't inside that house during those three hours on those three evenings." Pause. "Is this it, or do you want me to continue for another evening?"

He considered the question but decided best not to risk it. As it was, he was pushing his luck. If one of the tight-ass accounting gnomes in charge of scrutinizing his surveillance budget decided to question her evening hours, he'd be hard-pressed to justify them.

"No, I think by now we can assume he's not there. At least not during those hours on the evenings in question. Perhaps he has a girlfriend or is on vacation or out of town on business. But I'll tell you what I do want you to do. I want you to get me a copy of the architectural plans for that place. From what you describe, it was built recently, yes?"

Digging up the plans was something he could bury in the hours of a normal business day. Not so with night surveillance. Luckily, he wasn't audited more severely, and had a great deal of latitude.

She appeared to give the question more consideration than warranted, before replying, "It's certainly very different than the surrounding homes." As if not wanting to be pinned down on her answer.

Several seconds of heavy silence ticked past. Mizrahi waited.

"How soon do you want this?" she finally asked.

Again, worried about drawing attention to using her on a case that wasn't firm-related, he made sure his answer was sufficiently ambiguous: "How busy are you?"

Her employment with the firm was unique in that she worked as a per-hour freelance investigator in contrast to its full-time agent. And because her clients included businesses outside of Larkin Standish, he didn't know her schedule or availability.

"That's not hard to do," she answered. "I should have that for you fairly quickly. No problem. Or do you prefer I put a rush on it?"

Which was pretty much her standard response to just about

any request such as this.

"No, no rush...but I'd like to have it sooner than later."

Again, making his reply sufficiently vague that she'd take it to mean sooner. Now, if ever questioned about this conversation, he could truthfully claim he didn't assign a high priority to the task. Mizrahi pulled a black Bic pen from the cup on his desk and began drumming it on the mouse pad, his attention having already boomeranged back to the little rat fucker, Gold. Get the blueprints, study that house, find a way to deliver some major payback. There just had to be a way...

After a moment, he glanced back up at her.

"Tell me again about his security."

She rolled her eyes ceilingward as if resigned to more of a conversation than anticipated or hoped for. She'd already provided this information the prior evening.

"The property appears to be monitored by CCTV. And there's nothing subtle about it either, which, I suppose, is the point if it's intended as a deterrent. Although there's no way to confirm this, I assume the cameras are high-definition full spectrum." She paused a beat as if indenting a new paragraph in her report. "Both the front and back doors require multifactor verification to access. There's no way for me to be certain of this, but it appears to require a numeric code plus either a retinal scan or voice recognition, or possibly both, I guess. Again, there's no way to provide more detailed analysis without being detected. And I have been operating under the assumption you don't want that."

"Unless we can get our hands on the architectural plans," Mizrahi quickly added, suddenly excited by this new flash of insight, convinced now that the house was Gold's Achilles' heel. No one installed that much high-tech, state-of-the-art security unless they were protecting something extremely valuable.

Why hadn't he tumbled to this before now?

Yes, getting his hands on those plans was suddenly becoming critical.

"Oh, one more thing," she added with a bit of a foot shuffle, looking a tad embarrassed. "I forgot to mention it in yesterday's verbal report, but the house has two A/C units." This said in a blasé tone.

"What?" he asked, suddenly aware of her continued presence. "Say again?"

"Your target's house has two A/C units," she repeated, a bit slower and louder, as if addressing someone either hard of hearing or with compromised intelligence.

For a moment, he puzzled over this news.

"So?"

She inhaled sharply as if balancing a politically tricky tightrope, which, given Mizrahi's personality, she was.

"Most houses typically only have one unit. His house has two," she explained in patient, precise statements. "I have no idea why. I don't know that much about such things, but the larger one appears to be what I'd expect for a house that size. What the smaller one does is a complete mystery."

"Huh." Mizrahi puzzled on this. Could be significant. "All the more reason to get our hands on the architectural plans," he added, hoping she'd now kick up the priority without instructing her to. "And while you're at it, find a copy of the building permit as well as the name of the contractor who built the house." Then, with a rotary motion of his hand, added; "Etcetera etcetera. We clear?"

"Yes, sir. Will there be anything else?"

He shook his head, his mind now on its way down another rabbit hole.

After a moment, he realized she remained standing there, arms at her sides in that annoying stance.

He glanced up and said, "Dismissed," with a flick of his hand.

The more obstacles blocking him from learning as much as he could about Gold, the more inquisitive he became. The corollary being: the less he tolerated the never-ending series of dead-end leads. No one—at least no *normal* person—left no footprint in life. But he couldn't find any for Gold. Even the little shit's website yielded nothing. Not even a contact form to fill out.

And now, where the hell *was* the bastard?

Working in another city? On vacation? Shacked up with a girlfriend? Where?

Under normal circumstances, being out of the house would be the perfect time to break in to search for whatever necessitated such over-the-top security. Other than Vladimir Putin or a cartel boss, who the hell needed such extreme protection? What was Gold hiding? The question was beginning to eat into his brain like a parasitic worm.

A knock on the door jerked him out of the rabbit hole: Lorna Glass standing on the threshold, arms folded across her thick chest, sending him a weird look.

"What?" he demanded.

"You tell me, your highness. You summoned me. Remember?"

Leaning back, he waved her in.

"You can cut the sarcasm, Glass. We need to talk and it's important. Close the door" —*behind your fat ass*— "if you don't mind."

"If I don't mind?" she said, turning to do as requested. "Manners. Wow, that's a first. You must want something important."

Door closed, she settled into his only guest chair, leaned forward, elbows solidly planted on her widely spread knees, locking onto his eyes.

"Yes?"

For the umpteenth time, Mizrahi wondered why some dykes seemed to thrive on shoving their preference in your face. Especially the ones with the quintessential butch haircut, rolled-up funky flannel shirt sleeves, radiating an in-your-face don't-fuck-with-me vibe. As if carrying a massive chip on their beefy shoulders because of their great misfortune to be born butt ugly. As if anyone gave a rat's ass. Oh well, not his problem. Found it curious, was all.

Today's agenda item?

The repeat pen-test that he knew was bring directly targeted at him and the six floors he ruled. How did he know this? Because a little over a month ago, the prestigious law firm, Larkin Standish, hired a group of punk hackers to conduct a penetration test to assess the security of their offices and documents, both digital and hardcopy.

Not only did those assholes break into the firm's highly confidential digital files, but they also broke into the managing partner's office. And they did it in an office building marketing itself as a bastion of security. And from the mix of high-value clients leasing office space here, it seemed that the business community bought into the claim.

Both the law firm and the property management company were shocked at the apparent ease with which Gold was able to slip past what was considered hardened security. As a result, the property management company did the expected: they threw a wad of money at the problem. And with those big bucks now thrown, they wanted to see a return on their investment. After all, they couldn't allow their pristine reputation to be sullied over another bad pen-test outcome. Especially if those results were quickly becoming a hotbed of rumors within the local security community.

Lorna Glass was the Director of Security for the building whereas Itzhak Mizrahi was the Director of Security and IT for the six floors leased to the Larkin Standish law firm. As an employee of the property management company, Glass faced the unique challenge of supervising guards who were employees of North Sound Security: a large security firm sub-contractor that provided guards to several downtown high-rise office buildings.

The constant stream of headaches this gave her primarily centered on staff flux, a problem totally out of her control: vacations, sick leave, or the high turnover that came with the nature of the job.

As an employee of the law firm, Mizrahi, on the other hand, supervised a stable crew of three IT techs. A trivial job in comparison.

"Thanks for coming up," Mizrahi said, with molar-grinding civility, having decided that perhaps a more coddling approach this time around might result in her heeding his warning more seriously.

After all, for Gold to have made it all the way up thirty-six floors of allegedly state-of-the-art security, someone other than he had obviously dropped the ball. A point she still refused to acknowledge. And it really pissed him off that blame for Gold's success—perhaps as much as ninety-five percent—was focused on him rather than her.

"Not a problem, Itzhak. What's going on?" she said with disingenuous inquisitiveness.

Drumming his pen on the mouse pad, Mizrahi studied her a beat.

"How's the new technology working for you?"

She shrugged.

"Far as I know, everything's functioning as expected. No technical problems if that's what you're asking. But we both know that's the thing about good security: it grinds away silently in the background until something bad happens. At which point everyone starts pointing fingers and blaming us. Why the sudden interest?"

Mizrahi: "I'm sure you know that with the additional technology in place, our bosses will want to test their effectiveness." He allowed her dimwitted consciousness a moment to process this point, difficult as that might be. "In other words, they'll want to repeat the pen-test. And I, for one, don't want us to look as foolish as last time. I want us to be *proactive*, Glass. I don't want that little shit and his ragtag Tiger Team making another mockery of our security."

Arms crossed, she appeared to process his words, before nodding at him.

"See, this is where we view the same thing very differently, Itzhak. The whole rationale for these tests is to find potential holes in security. When you find one, you fix it, then repeat the test. Last time? Heck, the test uncovered a major weakness that we've now addressed. I'd say that's a very positive result for all of us. Our security is undoubtedly stronger now. But for some reason, you seem to take these tests as a personal threat." She even tossed in a shrug. "They're intended to *help* us, Itzhak."

Shaking his head, Mizrahi peered at her as if inspecting a pool of vomit instead of an individual he should collaborate with.

"You *still* don't get it, do you?" he said.

Hands covering her face, she shook her head, said, "Oh, man..." She dropped her hands to look at him again. "What is this, Groundhog Day?" she said with an eye roll. "*No*, Itzhak, *you* don't get it. We're looking at the same exact thing but seeing two diametrically opposite outcomes. We've been over this *ad nauseum*. North Sound and I see these tests as beneficial. You, on the other hand, see them as some sort of personal affront to your..." She threw up her hands. "...your manhood."

The manhood you try so hard to emulate.

He squelched that last remark before it could accidentally slip out.

Instead, he gave a woeful headshake and said, "Glass, I'm telling you, they're coming after us again. I don't know exactly when, but I *do* know they'll repeat that test and when they do, I don't want us to allow Gold to make fools of us again. If you go ahead and play ostrich and ignore the obvious, I can't be held responsible for the repercussions. Don't say I didn't warn you."

"Fine," she said, standing and turning back toward the door. "I consider myself duly warned." She paused, rotated enough to face him again. "Anything else before I get back to *work*."

Eyes already back to his monitor, he flipped a dismissive wave.

Cunt.

HONOLULU

Chapter 2

Honolulu—Three Days Later

"HE *WHAT?*" PRISHA Patel asked, clearly shocked.

"Exactly what I said," Arnold replied. "He wants to fire Mizrahi and is asking us to replace him."

Now sitting on the chaise, bolt upright, legs over the side, bare soles flat against the sun-warmed weathered timbers of the back deck. He'd called her immediately after disconnecting with Mr. Collier's out-of-the-blue bombshell phone call.

Chance, his beloved Belgian Malinois, was now up too, sensing the tension, ears cocked in anticipation, large brown eyes watching for the slightest hint that his sudden emotional outburst might have something to do with a pooch. A walk at his favorite park, perhaps? The typically deserted view spot where he was allowed roam off-leash to explore shrubs and tree trunks at leisure.

Arnold realized he was once again staring across the ravine to that spot...that relatively flat area of lava and scrub from which his present byzantine life had taken a major turn.

Prisha remained silent, leaving Arnold listening to palm fronds rustle in the breeze and a distant jet making its final approach to Danial K. Inouye airport. Curiosity now piqued, he continued waiting for her to say more, suspecting that, per usual, they'd be in lockstep on this one.

"IT *and* Security?" she finally asked with an unmistakable note of incredulity.

"Yep," he replied in a purposely neutral tone.

Another pause.

"I mean..." she finally said, "I guess we were sorta expecting another shot at going back in if our report resulted in any remedial action, but this...man, I dunno...this's like waaaay beyond that."

After picturing her woeful headshake, he replied, "This is going to require some way serious discussion with the team, but only after we have a ton more information, right?"

"Right!" she answered.

Gold and Associates was Arnold's hand-hewn boot-strapped enterprise, spawned innocuously when his criminal defense attorney—Palmer Davidson—ended up with a nasty virus in his office network. Arnold—who at the time was supporting himself on profits from sports betting—successfully removed said virus. Davidson was so impressed with this that he mentioned Arnold's IT skills to another lawyer in need of IT assistance.

After Arnold successfully resolved his issues, that lawyer mentioned Arnold to another lawyer and before long Gold and Associates was known as a boutique IT service for Seattle law firms too small to afford an IT staff and too twitchy to call in an unknown quantity like, say, The Geek Squad to work on machines loaded with highly confidential records. In other words, he'd developed a nice little niche business with a reputation for ultimate discretion. He'd stumbled into a market.

As business grew, Arnold realized he needed help. And besides, the name Gold and Associates was a bit pompous for a one-banana show. Luckily, he ran into Prisha Patel, a seriously creative IT person, and they hit it off instantaneously. She became his first full-time employee and full partnership associate. The team had since blossomed into three associates and two non-associates.

Then, a couple months ago, the prestigious law firm of Larkin Standish hired them to run a penetration test. Pen-tests— also known as ethical hacking—happen when organizations hire hackers to break into either their computers and/or physical spaces using the same techniques as "Black Hat" hackers or criminals would.

The objective of these tests is to expose vulnerabilities that, if remedied, should improve security. Indeed, Arnold's Tiger Team had uncovered and exploited a few vulnerabilities by first hacking Larkin Standish's computer networks and then by slipping into Mr. Collier's office.

Unfortunately for Itzhak Mizrahi, after penetrating the law firm's firewall, they found an audio/visual surveillance system he'd surreptitiously installed throughout the firm that included conference rooms and partners' offices. Neither Mr. Collier nor the Governance Committee looked kindly on Mizrahi's spy system despite his staunch claim that it was critical for maintaining watertight security.

Instead, they'd told him not only was it an invasion of privacy but that it also violated attorney-client confidentiality.

Arnold said, "Okay then, I'll call him back and set up a conference call. Knowing him, he'll want to shoehorn this into his schedule ASAP. You pretty much free the rest of the day, or maybe even tomorrow?"

"No prob. Just grinding out the routine grunt work."

That Prisha. Always reliable.

"Will get back to you the moment I have something to schedule."

On a bench, leaning against the edge of a weathered wooden picnic table, Arnold's mind drifted from thought to thought as his eyes wandered over an unobstructed westerly view of the deep blue Pacific Ocean as the surf periodically bombarded the solid jagged black lava extrusions below.

Meanwhile, Chance nurdled surround shrubs, sniffer

working overtime. Blissful, satisfying, rejuvenating. His preferred spot for their afternoon break because more than ninety percent of the time, no one else was here, which allowed Chance to roam untethered. Doggie Nirvana.

James Brown shattered his solitude.

Ah, Webster Collier. Excellent. About to take the call, Arnold did a double take at the screen. *Calling from his cell during business hours? Interesting.*

Arnold swiped accept, raised the phone to his ear, said, "Gold."

"Arnold, Collier. Can you talk now?"

The signal carried the vaguely watery quality of a tenuous connection.

"Yes, I can, but can you hold for a moment while I conference in Prisha?"

"No. I want this conversation to be as short as possible," Collier said without leaving any room for debate. "As I'm sure you noticed, I'm on my cell rather than my desk phone. That's because I'm in the stairwell, so I intend this to be quick." Pause. "What's your decision?"

Ah, the stairwell explained the lousy connection. Standing now, Arnold began to pace, torn between pleasing an extremely valuable client and a gnawing obligation to include Prisha in such an important discussion. But this was Mr. Collier and he and Prisha had discussed this, sort of...

"Yes sir, we have. But as you, of all people, should understand, there's a great deal of due diligence we need to do before we can make a fully informed decision, something you should understand."

"Just so I'm clear, does this mean that your company will agree to a more in-depth discussion?"

Which smacked of a temporary reprieve. A warm blanket of relief swathed him.

"Absolutely, but—"

"Excellent," Collier interrupted. "This being the case, we

want an *in-person* meeting ASAP. Any problem with that?" he asked without it vaguely resembling a real question.

More like a given.

"I'd welcome it. As will Prisha."

Well, not entirely. Not with Larkin Standish twenty-six hundred-plus miles away.

But he'd deal with that wrinkle once he had a clearer idea of what lay ahead.

"Just out of curiosity, you said we. Who's *we?*"

After a resigned sigh, as if he really didn't want to waste time with such unnecessary details right now, Mr. Collier capitulated.

"The Governance Committee decided it was imperative to share our test results with both the property managers and North Sound Security. Putting aside our firm's other issue for the moment"—which Arnold interpreted to mean the Mizrahi thing— "we were all understandably upset at the apparent ease with which you appeared to access our offices despite the building's purported security measures. Accordingly, North Sound undertook a comprehensive audit of their security measures and determined that they should enhance certain aspects of their systems. Now that these additions have been put in place, they believe we should conduct another test, in part to assess the efficacy of said enhancements."

From his research leading up to the prior pen-test, Arnold knew that a significant number of offices in the building were legal firms, title companies, and private equity partnerships. In other words, tenants with more than just a passing interest in the security of their offices.

After a brief pause, Collier added, "Needless to say, this carries the potential to generate additional business for your company."

How exactly Gold and Associates might accommodate any uptick in work—significant or not—wasn't at all clear to him. But that issue was for another time. At the moment, he was scrambling to sort through the numerous logistical hurdles involved with attending an in-person meeting within a day or so. Because that's exactly where Mr. Collier was headed and once the lawyer decided on a course of action, he wanted results. End of discussion.

Arnold's only solution was to come clean.

"Gotcha, Mr. Collier. But just to be crystalline, I'm in the Honolulu office." He cringed at how pretentious that sounded. But hey, sounded way better than the truth. "Soon as we're off the phone, I'll lock down the first available flight and text you the details so we can schedule the meeting. That work for you?"

If not, Prisha could begin discussions until he could get there.

Should I be in Seattle more instead of here?

Shocked at the thought, he quickly rejected it, paused, then asked himself, why not? After all, their big jobs were there. And besides, he wasn't really pushing to build the Honolulu business.

At least not the kind of business that required their Tiger Team.

"Excellent. In that case, I'll expect to hear from you within the hour."

"Oh, and Mr. Collier? Until we have a chance to sort a few things out, we *strongly* advise that you not fire Mizrahi." Then a gut-dropping thought hit. "Uh, you haven't already fired him...have you?"

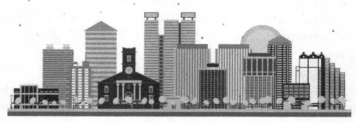

HONOLULU

Chapter 3

"SO, HERE'S THE deal," Arnold told Prisha. "We meet Collier Monday at eight AM, but get this: we're to meet him in the lobby instead of on thirty-four." The thirty-fourth floor—the lowest floor of the six occupied by Larkin Standish—contained their reception lobby. "And the totally weird thing is he called on his cell instead of his office phone. Not only that but he was evasive as hell. Believe me, something's up. Something big, and my money says it has something to do with Mizrahi."

After a sarcastic snort, Prisha replied, "From what you're describing, he's paranoid that that slimeball still has his surveillance system up and running."

"Yeah, that was exactly my thought." Pause. "Oh yeah, almost forgot. I went ahead and called Brian"—referring to Brian Ito, their newest associate and the only other team member (besides Arnold) based in Honolulu—"to update him on this. He's totally chill with letting us negotiate without him since he'll probably not even be involved, and I can't see a reason we'd want to use him. Do you?"

Without the slightest hesitation: "Nope. Besides, we're still dealing with a significant backlog of routine shit, so can't justify any downtime. Best to just keep him there."

That Prisha. Always on top of things. And besides, he totally agreed.

Call finished, Arnold slumped back into the chaise, smiling at the growing cachet that Gold and Associates was meticulously crafting.

Two years ago, his company wasn't even an embryonic concept. Two years ago, his life had no direction other than the SAM project. But now, his company consumed his focus. Though, like most valuable assets, it had come at a cost. In his case, he'd lost Rachael Weinstein, his...his what, exactly?

Girlfriend?

The word ricocheted through his mind, sounding so, well, hollowly sophomoric that he blushed.

Why the embarrassment?

Well, because the word somehow trivialized the deep emotional bond he'd felt toward her right up until the eye-widening realization that their relationship had dissolved without him being aware of it happening. Worse yet was the smashmouth reality that a fresh start was best, that she'd done the right thing by walking away from him.

Although building a business did satisfy a need, it did nothing to replace the delight he felt from anticipating and then fulfilling a partner's needs, of being able to communicate on more than a superficial level, of taking satisfaction in pleasing them in various insignificant actions from day to day. And now—as long as he was being all Mr. Sensitivity, the man in touch with his inner Arnold—that lack of intimacy had punched a gaping hole in his life.

Why can't I have both?

Simple answer, dude: you don't have the cojones to do a damn thing about it.

It'd been, what, about five weeks since their final confrontation and dissolution? Since then, he'd defaulted into his present emotional moonscape of grind it out day-to-day singles life. A situation, he knew too well wasn't in his best interests. At best, a zero-sum game. At worst...

Social and emotional inertia was, however, the path of least resistance. Dysfunctional as it might be.

In the years before Rachael, he didn't know better.

Well, he did now that he had a frame of reference.

And as shackling as his social insecurities might be, his need for someone to fill the intimacy void was beginning to overcome the inertia. His perspective was different now. Perhaps his failed relationship with Rachael might've taught him to be more discriminating this time around and not jump at the first female to pay him any attention.

After all, in a moment of brutal honesty, he'd been forced to admit that they'd bonded solely over mutual grief.

The story went like this: Rachael's big brother Howie and Arnold were best friends. And although Arnold had secretly harbored a serious crush on her, he suspected—even through the haze of social ineptitude—that hitting on his best friend's kid sister might be bad form. Even if he'd had the nerve.

Then, in the days after Howie's cold-blooded murder, he and Rachael had clung to each other for comfort. In truth, other than this mutual grief, they shared little else in common. Initially they were blind to that. But, over time, she realized it. Slowly, she'd started to distance herself emotionally from the relationship until one day she moved back into the apartment she'd continued to rent even after moving in with him. Psychologists have a word for what Arnold had been exhibiting during the final months of their time together: denial.

Smart Rachael, stupid Arnold.

But that was beside the point. Point was, he needed to do something about it.

Shit.

He hated the idea of having to deal with the logistics of sorting through potential prospects, despite knowing it was the price of admission. Months before being murdered, Howie had talked him into trying a speed-dating thing. Three attempts. Three flaming disasters. All such serious self-esteem/confidence gut-punches that he swore to never subject himself to such humiliation again. Ever. Dating apps? NFW. Not with all the false information and other related issues. Strike up a conversation with some little hottie at, say, a bar? Don't hold your breath! No way he could ever pull off something so audacious. And he didn't have friends out looking for him, trying to hook him up with "this terrific girl we just know you'd love."

Moreover, what possible reason was there to expect that his game had improved?

Not a damn one.

How pathetic to realize that at age twenty-eight he still lacked the confidence and savoir faire to pull off meeting a female without tying himself into knots. The mere anticipation of getting back "in the game" was making him feel excruciatingly awkward.

Yet, if he stood any chance of upgrading his nonexistent social life, the embarrassment gauntlet was a prerequisite to be endured. Hopefully, like other skills, his confidence and ability would improve with practice. Unless, of course, he was okay with becoming a very strange curmudgeon with no one to cuddle up to but a dog and an AI network.

How weird would that be?

Pretty damn weird. And really, not a viable option. Not now, knowing how satisfying having a relationship could be. And if you thought about it, the price was worth it.

Yeah, easy enough to say but a real bitch to actualize. Especially for a loner instead of a joiner, a misfit with painfully maladapted social skills.

So where did that leave him?

Totally hosed, that's where.

Too bad he didn't know—

Whoa. Wait a minute. He *did* know someone. And she was, like, molten hot. The little cutie who had sold him the house. Thought about her for a moment. Hmmm...hadn't she mentioned something about a boyfriend?

Yeah, but situations can change. Take his, for example.

Hmmm...do I still have her number?

Arnold cruised through the kitchen on into the guest bedroom, dumped himself into the desk chair, opened the center desk drawer, started rummaging through mechanical pencils, Post-it pads, a ruler, loose paper clips, and finally...ta-da...her business card. Noriko Stokes, Licensed Real Estate Agent.

He rocked back in the chair eyeing the card, flicking it back and forth between thumb and index finger, thinking...*hmmm, why'd I keep it?*

Good question.

Well, because she's hot, and I'd sort of hoped...but never had the nerve...yeah, but things have unquestionably changed, so what about now?

Maybe.

The Rachael relationship had built his confidence slightly. But not enough to feel at ease with what he needed to do. But if his present drab situation was ever going to change for the better...

Another glance at the card. Another moment of indecision. Slowly he typed her phone number into his cell, then stared at it.

Press the green button?

Yes? No?

You know you want to. Go ahead. What do you really have to lose?

Come on, you pussy.

The pussy challenge always seemed to do the trick. Haltingly, nervously, he touched the green icon with his fingertip as the iron-fisted grip of panic took hold of his intestines. Fighting the urge to cancel the call, he closed his eyes and listened to the phone ring.

A female answered on the fourth ring with a hesitant, "Hello."

"Uh, Noriko?"

He cast another nervous glance at the sniper spot on the other side of the ravine.

"Yes?"

"Hi, this is Arnold Gold, uh…"

By now his stomach was doing backflips.

Silence.

Then, "I'm sorry. Who?"

Oh shit, totally forgot.

He'd bought the house under his assumed name.

Will be interesting seeing you wiggle out of this one, dude.

Simply drop the call and try again later? Naw, that would be crazy uncool, especially with his number now permanently embedded in her recent calls log. Besides, why? At this point what did he have to lose?

He sucked a deep breath, said, "Uh that's right, you may remember me as Hans Weiser…I bought the house over off Nohua Drive, couple years back?"

A long pause was followed by, "Oh yeah, now I know…the trust-fund brat?"

Okay, she *did* remember. Wasn't quite the impression he'd hoped to leave her with, but it *was* a start, right?

"Yeah, I'm that guy," he admitted with more resignation than intended.

"Sure, I remember you very well now," she said cheerily, slipping easily back into real-estate-agent mode. "What can I do for you Hans? Or is it Arnold now?"

Just a hint of curiosity in her tone.

And that curiosity inched his hopes up a notch.

"Actually, for the record, my name really is Arnold Gold."

Just hope she's not antisemitic.

She hesitated a couple of beats before saying, "Sorry, I'm still a bit confused, so help me out. You purchased the house under a false name or is Arnold Gold a false name?"

Her voice was now laced with suspicion.

Finger-combing his hair, he grappled with the best way to extricate himself from this tar baby without getting into a discussion. "Oh man…that's a *gonzo* long and complicated story but…" Eyelids scrunched to a wafer-thin line, summoning every

Allen Wyler

fragment of courage available, he blurted, "But I'd love to tell you the story over dinner tonight at Taormina."

As the last word flew from his tongue, it dawned on him just how outrageously presumptuous he must sound, asking out a woman he knew nothing about when two years ago she had a serious-sounding boyfriend. Yes, but that was two years ago, and two years can be a long time. Take him, for example.

Okay, fine, but by now she could be married with a couple of rug rats. Fact was, he knew absolutely zip about her other than she was a real estate agent at the time.

"*Taormina*? Oh, I absolutely *adore* that place!" she replied without hesitation. "Offer accepted. But on one condition, and one condition only."

"Yeah?" Arnold's heart now at full gallop. "And that is?"

"That you tell me the whole unabridged story of why you bought a house under an assumed name. Do we have a deal?"

Was that a note of excitement in her voice?

Arnold's heart stutter stepped in disbelief over what was happening.

"It's a deal," he blurted again in a totally uncool voice. Then began having serious second thoughts. Damn complicated story, that one. Could be a potential turn off depending on...

"What time?" she asked, sounding more like a realtor now, eager to close the deal.

"Unless you hear from me to the contrary, I'll have a table for us at six thirty," he said with a shocking note of confidence. Arnold Gold, Master of the Universe, Man in Control. As a frequent flyer at the Sicilian restaurant, he was counting on them to cut him a bit of slack and grant him a last-minute reservation. After all, a high number of their nightly customers was walk-in Waikiki trade that would never return after one visit. And for those who made a reservation, most came through a hotel concierge. So...

"Perfect. See you then, but just so you know, I have a showing late this afternoon and can never predict how long these may take…so there's a possibility I might be a few minutes late. If it looks like it'll be more than a few minutes, I'll text you. I assume this is your number?"

"That's correct. See you soon."

Butt propped up against the front fender of his silver Mini, Arnold watched Chance nurdle around their favorite view spot, sniffing the usual shrubs, while his mind was a thousand miles away, sorting through questions concerning his dinner date. His first since Rachael.

Little things. Like, what to wear? What to talk about?

How the hell to explain living under an assumed name at the time? Or was there a clever way to smooth talk his way right out from underneath that one? Or, if forced to explain his reasons, how would that make him look?

There were also other more mundane issues to consider, such as, drive or Uber? And if drive, where to park? The closest garages were in the tightly packed large Waikiki hotels with stalls reserved for guests. More than anything, however, was a growing worry about coming across as a total dork.

Because, face it: he was.

HONOLULU

Chapter 4

ARNOLD SLID FROM the red Prius onto the sidewalk in front of the Park West Gallery, moved out into the flow of pedestrians and busied himself giving the Uber driver five stars before adding a nice tip for expertly threading through maddeningly hectic downtown Honolulu traffic in record time, getting him here early.

Immediate tasks finished, he spent another moment checking out his reflection in a plate-glass window. Hmm, not too bad, what with his dress cargo shorts, vintage Def Con t-shirt, and gray Adidas kicks. He nervously adjusted his prized Alium frames, then wiped his lower face as his gut grew exponentially anxious. Crunch time.

As he turned toward the restaurant, a group of two laughing sunburned couples in high-end resort wear flowed around him as if he were a rock in a stream, trailing the scent of coconut suntan lotion with a touch of Mai-Tai thrown in. Within two months of relocating here, that scent had embedded in his hippocampus as synonymous with this area of downtown.

Catching a break in traffic, he streaked diagonally across Lewers Street, on through Taormina's front door to the *maître d'* podium. From there, Kenny promptly ushered him to his favorite table for two by the window, featuring a view back across the street to the spot where his Uber had just deposited him. The surrounding tables were chockablock with customers, the air thick with a mélange of conversations and the aroma of garlic-like umami steam. Made him feel right at home. The downside to this all-too-familiar table was the bittersweet memories it triggered of dinners here with Rachael. Just one more adaptation to singles life that he now needed to power through.

"A glass of your usual?" Kenny asked with his perpetual smarmy smile, referring to Arnold's preference for cabernet instead of their house wines.

He started to say, "Yes," then caught himself.

How would it look to be drinking when she arrived?

Any better or worse than sitting here twiddling your thumbs?

Stop it! Be cool. Aww shit.

He nodded.

"Yeah, perfect. Thanks."

As Kenny glided into the bowels of the restaurant, Arnold slipped his iPhone from his pocket to check the latest CNN headlines. Might as well be doing *something* productive while waiting.

He was knee-deep in a *Seattle Times* article when a voice said, "Hi. Sorry I'm late, but the showing took a lot longer than I expected."

Arnold glanced up just as Noriko slid into her chair with Kenny hovering tableside. It'd been, what? Well over two years since last seeing her, but damn, she was as attractive as he remembered.

Stunningly attractive.

Long, luxurious black hair flowing over broad slender shoulders, long neck, large brown almond shaped eyes set in a flawless untanned light brown complexion; a mixture, he suspected, of perhaps Japanese or Polynesian with Caucasian, considering her last name, Stokes.

Then again, she could've been married, right? Though last time he'd seen her, he'd checked her ring finger and it'd been sans band.

And why, exactly, did you check then?

Well, because she was crazy hot. Still is, for that matter.

He realized he should probably resume breathing.

"Oh, hi," he said.

"May I start you with a drink?" Kenny asked while popping her napkin to float onto her lap, then slipping Arnold a sly approving wink.

When bringing him his wine, Kenny had casually mentioned that Rachael had been in for dinner a few weeks ago and had dropped that she was moving back to Seattle after finishing her contractual obligation to the hospital. Arnold had mixed feelings about the piece of gossip.

"I'll have the same as he's having," Noriko said with a killer smile and a nod at Arnold's wine glass.

"Ah, the cab. Excellent choice. I'll get that going for you. Your server will be over shortly," he added, dealing them menus.

As Kenny levitated away, Noriko returned her attention to Arnold.

Scrambling to regain some semblance of focus after being majorly derailed over how wickedly attractive she was, he asked, "Was it a good showing?"

Why the hell didn't I do this right after moving in?

News flash, dude. You had a few minor distractions going on, like laying low on account of a group of pissed terrorists dead set on trying to snuff you. And don't forget, you were juggling a couple of other minor issues such as settling into a new home, rebuilding SAM from scratch, oh, and adopting Chance.

"Oh, the showing was typical," she replied. "But it's with the couple from hell. They've been looking and looking for over six weeks now." She gave him a roll of her gorgeous brown eyes. "They're in a condo rental at the moment, so aren't in any major hurry to move, but I have the very strong impression they're one of *those* buyers who can never decide on *the perfect* place. You know...always something wrong with this or that or it's just not quite"—in finger quotes—"what they have in mind, although I can't really pin them down on what they do have in mind." She paused, making direct eye contact, and said, "But you're deflecting the conversation from our agreement, so I want to get back to *you*, Arnold Gold, AKA Hans Weiser. I'm just dying to hear the story you promised to tell me."

Uh-oh.

"Story?" he asked, scrambling for a conversational off-ramp before his back was smack up against the wall and he was being forced to answer.

"Yes, *the story*," she said, apparently amused by his confusion. "You know...the one about why you bought the house under an assumed name. That is, if your real name is Arnold Gold."

"Oh, that..." he said dismissively.

Why did he do this shit to himself? Here he sat, totally unprepared to answer although he'd been warned this subject would top the conversation agenda. He stalled by taking a slow sip of wine, mind scurrying through various watered-down pithy iterations of spin. But each one seemed more freaking lame than the last.

With an expectant expression, she continued to patiently watch his deer-in-the-headlights face, which did nothing but amp up his anxiety. He began rocking his wine glass back and forth, frantically searching for a simple explanation to a hyper-complex situation; a story that approximated reality sufficiently to not risk embroiling himself in a lie should the subject ever arise again after tonight.

Alright already.

He set his wine glass on the tablecloth, knitted his fingers together and started in.

"I know this'll sound totally outrageous, but here goes..." A deep inhale. "At the time, I was a CI for—"

"A what?"

"A CI. A Confidential Informant." Pause. "I was working for the FBI."

Another pause.

She waited, one eyebrow raised, her silence compelling him to continue.

"See, what happened is, I stumbled onto a bombing plot by a group of batshit-crazy terrorists. They were, like, planning to blow up an office building in a major West Coast city." He held up a hand. "Don't ask." He paused a beat. "The CliffsNotes version is I blew the whistle on them, so some of them ended up getting caught, but some didn't, and when they figured out it was *moi* who dimed their buds, they wanted to, like, cut my head off, so…" A shrug. "I was forced to, like, go into hiding for a while until things settled down." He gave a no-big-deal superfluous laugh in an attempt to gloss over a chapter in his life that he really preferred to not discuss.

For a moment, she just stared at him, slack-jawed. "Cut your head off? For real?"

"Yeah, like, you know…" he said, drawing a finger across his neck.

"Like, no-joke serious?" Her eyes scoured his face for signs that his far-fetched story was some sort of bizarre joke.

"Noriko, it's not something I joke about," he said with surprising conviction.

She leaned forward, forearms on the table, eyes sparkling with apparent excitement. "I want to hear more."

Suddenly he was trapped in the burning house again, handcuffed to the heavy oak desk, choking on the pungent thick smoke… Then smashing out the bathroom window as Karim continued to kick in the locked door—

"Arnold?"

Hand raised, he stared blankly at the tablecloth, until the wisp of traumatic memory pixilated into restaurant clatter. For a moment, he watched the surrounding diners enjoying this casual, relaxed atmosphere. The high contrast juxtaposition of the here and now to the anxiety-laden there and then shocked him; the incredible high contrast of it all. When exactly had the ever-present incessant stomach-churning dread dissipated? The constant fear that felt like a razor against his neck. Even with the clarity of retrospect, it was impossible to identify an inflection point because the ever-present anxiety dissipated so gradually that there was no definable termination. Well, that wasn't entirely true. Those fears didn't vanish entirely; remnants persisted every time his gaze seemed inextricably drawn across the ravine to that goddamn sniper spot.

Why do I do this to myself?

Like a canker sore you can't stop tonguing despite the pain.

"Arnold?"

Took a moment to refocus on their thread.

He looked up at her again, said, "That's a part of my life I really don't like to dredge up."

Her eyes sobered from the excitement of a moment ago.

"Are you folks ready to order?" A waitress Arnold didn't recognize was now standing tableside, eager to take their order. Keep the customers moving and flip the table. Back to business.

Arnold glanced at Noriko then back to the waitress.

"Could you give us another minute, please? She hasn't had a chance to look at the menu yet."

Noriko flashed her killer smile at him before saying to the waitress, "No need. I'll have the Lasagna alla Romanese." Then to Arnold, "You down for splitting a salad?"

"For sure," he answered, handing the waitress his unopened menu. Two regular customers who knew what they wanted.

"The Insalata di Mela?"

"Perfect," Noriko said.

Arnold added, "And make that two lasagnas."

That Noriko liked this place to the point of knowing the menu by heart, instantly put him at ease. Which he took as a positive sign. At least they had one thing in common. Then again, he was getting way ahead of himself.

Still…

"So!" she said, after her first sip of the cab. "I do want to hear more about you having to buy the house under an assumed name but please go at whatever pace is comfortable. A confidential FBI informant, huh. Wow. Does this mean you're *not* the trust-fund brat I had you pegged for?"

He coughed a dismissive laugh.

"Not even remotely in the ballpark."

He balked at divulging more, for fear it would lead into his personal life, which he wanted to avoid. And besides, he preferred finding out about her. The problem was coming up with a clever way to deflect the conversation in that direction.

"So, what made you jump to that conclusion?" he asked because it seemed like a logical question.

She appeared to consider the question for a long moment.

"Interesting you should ask. I never even gave it a second thought. But now, reflecting back, it seems like it was the way you approached the transaction. Like you didn't even bother to counter the asking price. Plus, your financing seemed to breeze through without a hitch. And now that we're on the subject, mind telling me—" She seemed to catch herself. "I mean, a man your age just walks in and buys…oh, sorry, that sounds so crass," she said, fingertips to lips, "like I'm probing your financial status, but for me, a client like you is, ah, an endangered species."

Wow, how do you deal with a question like that? Ignore it? Was she trying to size up his finances? Sort of sounded like it. If so, it was, well, off-putting.

When he didn't respond, she blushed, appeared on the cusp of adding something, hesitated another beat, then said, "What about the property records?"

"The property records? What about them?" he asked, genuinely unsure what the question meant.

Appearing equally puzzled by his question, she hesitated.

Then: "What I mean is, if the house was purchased under a false name, won't that raise a few issues when you want to sell it? And how do you handle the property taxes and utilities?"

"Oh, *that*." He gave a laugh of relief. "Naw, my lawyer straightened all that out soon as the terrorist thing was taken care of."

She gave a tentative nod, the kind reserved for someone you suspect as being certifiably crazy but really don't want to offend. By now, she radiated the vibe of chalking his bizarre story up to complete bullshit, which was perfectly fine by him. On the other hand, she genuinely seemed to want to hear a few spicy details, especially those involving his work with the FBI. Was she deciding if he was a boaster who reveled in making outlandish false claims about himself?

Wine glass raised to his nose, he inhaled deeply before enjoying a sip, doing the whole wash it over your entire tongue thing. Mr. Wine Connoisseur. Or perhaps a James Bond shaken-not-stirred kind of person. Anyone but Arnold Gold, total nerd. Well, it did buy him a few more seconds of thought.

Head cocked slightly, she seemed to appraise him anew.

"Wow. That part makes you sound so dark and mysterious, not remotely close to how I had you pegged."

"A trust-fund brat," he muttered, replacing his glass on the tablecloth. By now, he desperately wanted to move off the subject of the past as it pertained to him. "I seem to remember something about you being in a serious relationship then?" These last words began reverberating in his mind, making him realize the bind they had just put her in, so immediately amended his question with: "I'm sorry. Strike that." He wanted to crawl under the table, embarrassed.

"But the question's been asked, hasn't it," she stated with a hint of bitterness.

Her face became strikingly pensive as she turned to stare out the window as if debating if or how to respond. A moment later, she returned to him, but now with regret-filled eyes.

"You're very observant. Yes. I was engaged at the time..."

Engaged.

Past tense.

"Jesus, I'm sorry...what happened?"

With pursed lips, she too became focused on her wine glass,

rotating the stem, assembling a response.

A moment later: "We called it off." Pause. "Or, rather, *I* called it off."

And let it hang.

Without thinking, he asked, "Because?"

He immediately realized just how inappropriate it was to probe such a deeply personal issue, especially without knowing her better.

Just one more cringeworthy *faux pas* in the dating life of the new Arnold Gold.

A learning experience.

She returned to staring blankly at the street scene, perhaps debating whether to answer and if so, how much to disclose. After a resigned sigh, she turned her eyes back to him.

"Because he was becoming too possessive. Uncomfortably possessive." Again, head cocked, she appeared to be choosing her words judiciously. "He claimed to adore me." A brief pause. "At first, that felt flattering and wonderful...being adored. But what he claimed was adoration quickly grew into possessiveness that grew increasingly worse. Soon I couldn't do anything without him being super jealous the moment I was out of his sight. You can probably predict what happened next and you'd be correct. Things became ugly."

She paused for a sip of wine, set the glass down on the white tablecloth and stared at it, as if directing her words to it instead of him.

"His suspicions became allegations against me. It didn't matter whether the client was male or female because if it was a woman, he'd claim I was lying. That's when his obsession began preventing me from being able to run my business." She inhaled sharply, eyes growing sad and distant as if seeing sepia-toned memories. "It finally reached a tipping point, and I was forced to make an extremely painful choice. I loved him. I really did. But I also realized I couldn't face his accusations every time I was out of his sight. It got to the point it didn't matter if clients were married or single, alone or as a couple, he always saw things that simply weren't there. The situation became completely intolerable.

"So," she said with a resigned sigh, "I broke off the wedding. Like, about two days *after* the invitations were mailed." She let out a sarcastic snort. "The actual act of dropping those invitations into the mailbox suddenly precipitated an *ah-ha* moment, for it made something that, up to that point, had been hypothetical suddenly very real. Once those invitations dropped..." Shaking her head, she twisted her white linen napkin into a tight rope. "Probably the hardest thing I've ever done."

It still stung, he could see, which made him want to say something soothing. But he realized how disingenuous the words might sound, because, in a way, he felt a twinge of satisfaction in knowing that another couple could also have a disastrous end to an intense relationship, that he wasn't an anomaly.

Instead, he chose simple neutral words that should minimize the risk of saying the wrong thing.

"I'm sorry."

Becoming aware of the taut, white linen rope linking her fists, embarrassment flushed her cheeks.

She dropped the twisted napkin into her lap, glanced up at him again.

"I'm sorry too," she said. "But I take comfort in knowing I did the right thing for both of us. Neither of us could've ever been happy living under those conditions."

Inhaling deeply, she brushed the tip of her nose with a knuckle.

"I totally get it," Arnold said as if speaking from a wealth of relationship experiences instead of only one.

Sitting back in her chair now, she seemed to eye him with curiosity, as if searching for more substance to his words than their casual delivery implied.

"Sounds like you've been down the same path. Recently, or has it been a while?"

Explain about Rachael?

Problem was, compared to what she just described, his reason for breaking off with her was much more vague and way more nuanced. There was no chip-shot, pity explanation. More importantly, he didn't want to turn the evening into a complete downer by focusing on failed relationships. And besides, his emotions were still too raw to handle it. But since she'd asked, she deserved an answer.

"Uh-huh, very recently," he said, fully intending to move on to a more productive topic.

"The love of your life?"

The love of your life?

Those five words seemed to make their emotional bond sound so...what? Trite? Sophomoric? Trivializing.

Then again, perhaps that's exactly what they were. At one time, shortly after she'd moved in with him, when they started grinding out weeks, day by day, he'd begun to realize that he was more in love with his fantasy of her than the actual person snoring softly beside him each night.

Although he knew that enormous differences often span the gap between fantasy and reality, he hadn't really appreciated how true that could be. It turned into a significant life lesson for him.

He assumed Rachael had experienced an analogous revelation toward him after peeling back the outer layers of his basic nerdy personality. Maybe she'd proven herself the smarter one. Maybe she realized he was too weak to be the one to pull the trigger. Retrospect. Always so clear, especially given the benefit of time.

"Oops," Noriko said, reading his reaction. "Sorry. That one's always the toughest, I think. Was she your first true love?"

Her surprisingly compassionate tone struck him as genuine, not pandering.

He directed his stare at the wine glass stem he found himself gripping with both hands.

"Pretty much," he muttered, looking back up at her, face

doing the space-heater thing for being exposed as a relationship retard.

"Yeah, that one…" She shook her head. "That one's always the toughest."

Stomachs full, they lingered on the sidewalk, Arnold with phone in hand, ready to ping Uber, Noriko plowing determinedly through her purse for her elusive car keys. He was frantically scrambling for a hyper-chill way to ask if she would like to get together again but was coming up empty. *Jesus.*

Victoriously, she raised a ring containing a car key with two fobs from the purse. She spoke as if disciplining a naughty pet, then flashed her killer smile at him.

"Ah-ha. There you are."

He, in return, shifted from foot to foot and awkwardly glanced at his phone.

What now?

A moment later, she bailed him out.

"I'd like to see you again, if you're down for that."

If?

He wanted to shout "yes," but realized how seriously uncool that might be, so he settled for "Yeah, I'd like that a bunch." Then he thought about the pending job and quickly revised the statement with, "But here's the catch. I need to fly to Seattle for business and have no idea how long that job'll take." Finger-combing his hair, he let his eyes follow a passing car while trying to estimate the impossible, so ended up saying, "But I'll call as soon as I'm back."

After a quick mental replay, he amended.

"Cancel that. I'll call *while* I'm there, okay?"

"Good. I'd like that." Pause. "Business? Geez, I just realized I hogged the entire evening running on about work and I don't know a thing about you." She appeared to visually reappraise him once again, as if sizing him up more critically. "I have no idea what kind of work you do other than inform for the FBI and be a terrorist magnet."

Ah, man, if you only knew...

At least he had a canned answer ready.

"I run a small IT company," then added, "we have offices in both cities," and immediately cringed at how boastful that sounded.

She glanced off toward one of the larger parking garages.

"I'd love to hear more about it."

Shake hands? Say good night? She a hugger? What?

"Long story. Hopefully to be continued?" he asked, perhaps too eagerly.

She flashed a stunning smile.

"Yes, I'd like that."

"Deal."

C'mon, dude. At least hug her.

After another awkward moment of him just standing there like someone on the autistic spectrum, she turned and headed in the direction of the Halekulani.

Frustrated, he kicked at a cigarette butt on the sidewalk.

Chapter 5

Seattle

ARNOLD RINSED OUT Chance's stainless-steel water bowl, filled it with tap water, then seated it in the platform next to the matching food dish.

By now, Chance's nose was pressed flush against a pane of the French doors separating the kitchen from the back deck, signaling his readiness to trot back inside, having taken care of business in the back yard.

After letting him in and relocking the door, Arnold propped his butt against the kitchen counter and—despite the late hour (Seattle time)—debated opening a bottle of wine.

What the hell, why not?

After all, he'd be here at least a few days, so the issue of consumption wasn't up for debate. He grabbed a bottle of his favorite Rutherford cab from the wine cooler, popped the cork, poured a quarter glass, then leaned his back against the stainless-steel counter again while cupping the glass in both hands to warm the wine.

Although he'd raised the interior temperature to seventy-two before take-off from Honolulu, the house still carried a chill.

Why?

Pondered that for a moment. Concluded that it was his mood rather than the actual air temperature.

Because...?

Because of being here alone?

Naw, that wasn't it. He'd been here alone a couple times during other jobs, so what was it?

But that was then, and this was now. Then he got it. Back then, Rachael was in Honolulu awaiting his return. No longer. Now she was a mere two blocks away, having severed all ties with him.

Really? Was this the reason for his mood? Yeah, he'd bet on it. And realizing this was making him seriously uncomfortable. What would it feel like to simply run into her at any of the places they frequented: the park, PCC market, Nell's restaurant, or simply out walking Chance in the neighborhood? If that were to happen, how would he react? Well, it'd be totally awkward.

And, as long as he was on the subject, the knotty issue of her being their business manager hadn't simply vanished on its own. The group would still be conducting business meetings. How comfortable would it be interacting with her online? He shook his head, knowing that he should deal with the issue instead of just ignoring it, hoping it would go away. This final link needed to be severed. Why keep dragging his feet?

Because you're just too much of a wimp to man up and take care of it, that's why.

Not only that, but he'd been putting off looking for her replacement.

Why?

Same answer: inertia.

Shit.

Time to take care of business.

Yeah, right. But when?

Had to be within the next few days, what with the new job looming. Just wasn't sure how to manage it but replacing her still needed to be done. There are some things in life...

He glanced at the wine glass cupped in his hands. Might as well take it upstairs to sip while reading.

Call Noriko?

He glanced at his watch. Nope. Too late now, what with the early showing scheduled.

Rats.

Chair tilted back, heels of his black Nikes planted firmly on the desk, ankles crossed, Mizrahi was deep into a Charles Cumming read when the harsh ring of his desk phone jerked him from Berlin to the unfortunate reality of work.

Answer it?

Probably should. After all, he was at work. Both soles slapped the linoleum as he rocked forward to pick up that damn thing before it could assault his eardrums again.

"What?" he barked, making no attempt to disguise his irritation at being disturbed.

"And a cheery top 'o the mornin' to you, Itzhak," Glass said in an extremely poor rendering of an Irish brogue.

Glass. Should've known.

Hadn't bothered to check Caller ID.

"What can I do for you, Glass."

"First, let me express my most heartfelt apologies for interrupting your sacred morning solitude, but I thought you might be interested to know that my crew just notified me that our BFFs Gold and Patel just strolled into the lobby, shook hands with your boss, then went straight out the door with him and over to Starbucks."

"They're meeting with Collier?" Mizrahi asked.

Those two assholes meeting Collier wasn't the surprising bit. Walking across the street to Starbucks was. Why not meet in his office?

The obvious answer sent an icy chill skittering up and down his spine. Collier didn't waste precious minutes during his chockablock days sipping lattés at Starbucks over idle gossip. Something murky was underway and he was pretty damn sure he knew exactly what it was.

"He *is* your boss, isn't he?"

He began twiddling a black Bic between his index and middle fingers.

"Just answer the fucking question, Glass."

"Thought I did."

Instead of responding to her snarky remark, he focused on how best to deal with this potentially risky twist of events. His first concern was to make sure Glass didn't know what troubled him about the meeting. She was smart. Probably already suspected the meeting would be to negotiate another pen-test. It was the ancillary drama that he was determined to keep her from knowing.

"Perhaps it's just a continuation of a follow-up session after reading their report," he suggested, struggling to mask his concern.

He referred to the detailed After-Action analysis Gold and Associates had submitted as the final step to the recently wrapped up penetration-test. Easy explanation, but Mizrahi suspected she didn't buy it for even a fractional second. Something else was brewing. And Mizrahi was sure he knew what that was.

Glass confirmed his suspicions by saying, "We both know that sounds like a reasonable explanation, Itzhak, but to meet across the street at a Starbucks? I'm not buying it."

She was right, of course, but that wasn't why he was so annoyed at her. Well, annoyance was actually an understatement. Pissed was a better descriptor. Pissed that his own after-action report hadn't resulted in getting her axed.

After the way she'd disrespected him…he teetered on the cusp of letting go with a real zinger but reconsidered. She was, after all, giving him a heads-up. And he thrived on keeping abreast of the undercurrents and conspiracies snaking their way through the firm. The building too, for that matter. But since he didn't have access to that more general information flow, he needed Glass on his side to provide it; especially now that his attempt to have her fired had failed.

"Perhaps you're right, Glass." He paused long enough to weigh a decision. "Tell you what, think I'll take a little stroll around the block for some firsthand reconnaissance. I'll report back soon as I have a better read on the situation."

Once seated in Starbucks with freshly brewed lattés, Collier told Arnold and Prisha, "I'm sure you wonder why we're meeting here instead of at the firm, so I'll get straight to the point." He inhaled deeply, as if steeling himself for an emotionally loaded subject. "When I informed the Governance Committee of Mizrahi's spying, they were quite understandably outraged at the violation of private attorney-client discussions. Not only did he monitor these highly confidential discussions, but he recorded an unknown number of them. All of which is not only egregiously illegal and a blatant invasion of privacy, but risks serious exposure to the firm and its highly regarded reputation."

He paused for a deep breath, dramatizing the extremely distressing nature of the topic. Then, addressing Arnold: "I hope you appreciate the situation we now face."

Arnold nodded.

"I do."

Then turned to Prisha. She nodded.

The lawyer studied them a moment as if weighing a major decision. "You understand, do you not, that the confidentiality agreement you previously signed remains in effect and binding?"

Prisha said, "I do," and glanced at Arnold.

Arnold: "Me too."

"Good. Because what I'm about to share must go no further than your team. Ideally, it would remain with only the two of you. The risk of word leaking increases with each person who knows."

"Understood," Arnold said.

Mr. Collier studied them a moment longer as if reaching a final determination, then cleared his throat.

Allen Wyler

"At this point the situation becomes a bit tricky, so a bit of background will help. Upon learning of his spying, the Board of Governors voted to terminate Mizrahi immediately. He was called into the meeting and informed that the firm no longer required his services and that he was to surrender his keycard and that I would escort him from the building. He was also informed that all personal items from his office would be returned to him within twenty-four hours."

Mr. Collier inhaled deeply before continuing.

"He simply laughed and said that we could, quote, go fuck ourselves, unquote. That he wasn't going anywhere. He threatened that if we pressed the issue, he would release several recordings that would, and I quote, cause extreme and irreparable damage to the firm's pristine reputation. His exact words. To give his threat credibility, he mentioned a recording made during an extremely sensitive meeting with one of our high-profile clients. For obvious reasons, I'm not at liberty to share further details."

The lawyer shook his head and glanced at the untouched latte on the table in front of him.

"Back to the tricky part," he continued. "This is where you come in. Ostensibly, we want to hire you and your Tiger Team to conduct a follow-up pen-test to determine if security has been strengthened. Nothing wrong with that, is there." Clearly a statement. "But in the process of conducting the test we want you to do two additional jobs for us. First, destroy his surveillance system. Second, destroy every recording that sonofabitch has in his possession. Is this understood?"

Arnold glanced at Prisha.

She returned a barely noticeable nod, so he said to Mr. Collier, "It's crystalline, sir."

Mr. Collier's face softened.

"If you succeed in neutralizing Mizrahi for us there's a twenty-five-thousand-dollar bonus for you."

Wow.

"That's quite an incentive," Arnold admitted, caught off-guard. Mizrahi must either have some dynamite material or the Board of Governors has a collective guilty conscience. He glanced at Prisha.

Uh-oh, her face was deadpan.

Prisha said to Arnold, "It is, but let's not lose sight of an important component of this: you're asking us to make it possible so you"—she pointed to Mr. Collier—"can axe the man who runs your security and IT. That's going to create a hole that I seriously doubt we're prepared to cover. What about the techs? Are they aware of any of this?"

"Far as I know," Collier replied, "nothing's been said to anyone outside the Governance Committee. Unfortunately, we don't have a good read on their allegiances, but we are aware that Mizrahi has a—how shall I put this—a rather gruff management style that can be off-putting. But he *is* their boss. Simply put, we don't know if they're loyal to him or not."

"In other words, we have no idea if they'll stick around *when* he's fired, right?" Arnold said.

"You are correct. But realistically, given what we've been able to glean from various reliable sources, we believe the odds favor them remaining with the firm." Mr. Collier licked his lips, looked Arnold in the eyes, and said, "I hope you now appreciate the gravity of our situation. You're the only ones we can trust to help us navigate this very precarious position."

This was said with enough oratory flair as would be used in a closing argument.

Yeah, and I can part seas too.

What a mess.

He glanced at Prisha. She flashed him an impassive face that said, *Hey, boss, it's your monkey, your circus*, without uttering a word. Arnold found their flow of non-verbal communication— almost as if sharing some sort of weird cosmic telepathic pipeline—a bit unnerving.

What he'd assumed was to be a discussion with Mr. Collier about his frantic phone call to help cover their IT needs had suddenly transitioned into a follow-up pen-test as a smoke screen for sanitizing the firm's gonzo legal exposure. No wonder they were willing to cough up 25K to get the job done.

Larkin Standish's IT needs aside, the job suddenly became exponentially more complicated and riskier. In part because it would transition the playing field from the firm's digital and physical office space to Mizrahi's personal domain. And Arnold knew nothing about the man's capabilities.

Would they be poking a sleeping tiger?

And say they succeeded in greasing the skids for him to be axed? What kind of additional load would that put on the team? Sure, they'd factored a possible repeat pen-test into their workload, but they hadn't counted on managing the whole freaking IT department. No way could they do that without seriously pissing off their present hand-culled clientele. Then again, Larkin Standish was, well, Larkin Standish. You didn't want to piss them off either. What a mess.

Looking the lawyer in the eye, he said, "Let me be totally upfront with you, Mr. Collier. We're happy to do a follow-up pen-test that includes the parameters just outlined. *But*...and here's the deal: we simply *don't* have the manpower to permanently replace him, *especially* if the techs walk out with him. But we'll cover his duties *temporarily* until a suitable replacement can be found." Without looking, he raised a just-a-moment finger to Prisha because he could *feel* her giving him a heavy dose of suspicious-eye. He'd been waiting for an opportunity to slip in the totally off-point question, and this was it. "On an entirely different issue, does the firm have an investigator?"

He'd be surprised if they didn't, and he suspected that the black-clad female who'd cased out his house worked for them. If so, was she an employee? And if so, why the hell was his house under surveillance?

Mr. Collier crinkled his brow, hesitated, asked, "Why do you ask?"

Arnold took Mr. Collier's hesitation as a tell.

"Curious, is all. Well, do you?"

Collier appraised him a moment longer.

"Your tone suggests the question is more relevant than idle curiosity, so again, why do you ask?"

Arnold briefly considered telling him but decided it would detract from the main point of the discussion.

"Trust me. It's a topic for another time."

A smile flickered across Collier's face.

"As you wish." Pause. "In that case, can we count on you to do the job just outlined?"

"Yes, but with no guarantees," Arnold said before looking at Prisha for concurrence.

She nodded.

Before the lawyer could say anything more, Arnold added, "*But* you need to understand a few critical points up front. The most important is that getting back into your network is going to be way more difficult and problematic this time. Why? Because Mizrahi knows the tricks we used last time and has undoubtedly taken appropriate countermeasures. After all, that's the rationale for doing these tests, right?"

Mr. Collier nodded.

"This also means that if we can't get back into your network, we can't neutralize Mizrahi because his surveillance system is totally dependent on it. Do you understand the importance of what I just said?"

Again, the lawyer nodded, but this time with a grave expression.

"In other words, there's a very good chance we'll fail. And if we do, you need a serious backup plan ready to go to deal with the situation. I'm dead serious."

Meaning things could turn ugly very quickly.

"I understand," Collier said. "But this is exactly why we're putting so much faith in you and your team." He glanced around nervously, as if someone might be overhearing. "When can you start?"

Arnold turned to Prisha.

"What do you think?"

She shrugged. Again, his show, his decision.

Arnold told the lawyer, "Soon as I get home, I'll draw up a new SOW to email you for approval. You should have it sometime in the next hour or so."

SOW being the Scope of Work.

Collier said, "In that case, we have one more very important issue to discuss."

Chapter 6

THE MOMENT THE pedestrian light turned green, Mizrahi was moving across the intersection, the Starbucks directly ahead. He slowed upon setting foot on the opposite sidewalk and cut left to pass the front windows of Starbucks, the sun angling in perfectly, spotlighting the tables closest to the windows.

And boy, did he luck out: there they sat, Collier, Gold, and Patel huddled around a table for four, apparently engrossed in a serious conversation.

Mission accomplished.

He sped up before one of them happened to glimpse him breeze past. The sooner he was out of view, the better. After all, his suspicions were now confirmed. Still, seeing the three of them so intently huddled together unleashed a deluge of additional disturbing questions.

Why meet in Starbucks instead of Collier's office? Why so intense and serious? What could they be discussing other than conducting another test?

Him? Had to be.

Shit.

Being unable to listen into their conversation was a serious drawback. Just thinking about the inconvenience was pissing him off. Taken in its totality, Gold and Punjab Swami conferencing with Collier offsite could mean only one thing: they were discussing him.

Sure, that only made sense, especially if Collier suspected that his surveillance system was still intact. And that could mean only one thing: they were plotting to get rid of him. Yeah, that had to be it. From day one, Collier had never liked him. In fact, Collier outwardly disdained him. Although he wasn't sure why, he suspected that Collier had tried to block hiring him.

If forced to guess the reason, he suspected that Collier hated Israelis. Not only that, but Collier loathed not having iron-fist control over *every* facet of the firm, so it made perfect sense that being forced to delegate computer security to him would rub the bastard the wrong way. Collier relished his role as Dictator, the Managing Partner of The Firm.

And Gold? Gold was no better.

Gold despised him too, although he had no idea why. What had he ever done to warrant that? But his disdain was obvious. Yes, they were clustered around that table plotting against him. His worry grew with each step he took. Well, he would just have to keep one move ahead of them. That was the only way to beat those bastards. And if push came to shove, he would go with the nuclear option just to show those assholes who had the real power. He'd release select recordings that would drag that white-shoe firm through a steaming pile of hog shit. Yes, he still held the power, and knowing this comforted him.

But back to more immediate issues: among other things, the three assholes huddled around their lattes must also to be plotting another pen-test. Which he knew would come. He just wasn't sure when. But it now looked imminent.

He stopped in the middle of the sidewalk to reflect on this. *Why so sure of this?*

Was he just overreacting? Being overly sensitive? After all, pen-testers always discussed their results with their employers, so the meeting *per se* could be easily explained as nothing more than that. No, there was something else niggling at him.

What?

He began moving again, more slowly now, working through this new wrinkle. At the corner, he stopped to cross back over to the building. What was so disturbing about the meeting? Why so convinced they were plotting against him?

He worked back through his previous logic and found that it remained solid. The only reason for Collier to meet them in the building's lobby then cross over to Starbucks was if he worried about his conversation being monitored. And the only reason to hide the conversation was if it involved him. So yes, it all made sense now: they *were* plotting his downfall. His initial impression was rock-solid.

What their pea-sized brains seemed incapable of grasping was the fundamental law that strong security relies on the accumulation of timely critical intelligence. After all, this was a group of high-powered attorneys who were purported to be brilliant when it came to legal issues.

Why did they have a problem understanding matters of basic security?

Waiting for the pedestrian light to change, free-floating anxiety began to roto-till his stomach lining. However, he derived some comfort in knowing that he was one step ahead of those conniving sonsofbitches huddled in a pathetic group around a coffee-shop table. He knew what they were up to, but they, in contrast, were oblivious that he knew. For once, he owed Glass for giving him the heads-up. The irony of this reversal was not lost on him.

Now, he was forced to face a pivotal and difficult conundrum: dismantle his surveillance system or keep it intact? Certainly, this time part of Gold's assignment would be to determine if it remained operational. Was its value in gathering vital information—especially pertaining to attack planning— worth the risk? Especially, if it helped him be the victor?

Tough decision.

Chapter 7

WEBSTER COLLIER SAID, "The Board of Governors was, to say the least, quite disturbed at how easily you apparently transited the building to access my office. So alarmed, in fact, that we shared a copy of your report with Frank Smith."

"And he is?" Arnold asked, wanting complete clarity on each detail Mr. Collier mentioned.

"Frank? Frank's the CEO of North Sound Security." As if this were common knowledge. "We were particularly concerned over the porosity of their security. You apparently had little problem moving floor to floor through what is alleged to be a very secure building." He drummed his right index finger on the table next to his untouched latté. "Frank was as troubled by your report as were we. Especially considering our mix of the tenants."

Arnold knew from previously researching the tenant mix that the renters included a large number of law offices and financial firms, including a few private-equity-management partnerships. In other words, people for whom tight office security was a major priority.

Out of the corner of his eyes, Arnold caught Mizrahi walking past the window, pausing long enough to glance directly at them, then speeding up out of view. Arnold tracked him without moving his head.

Simple coincidence?

He just happened to cruise past that particular window as they were meeting?

Highly unlikely. Especially zeroing in on them like he did. No, that was no accident. No, he was *looking* for them. Meaning he'd been tipped that they were over here and came to see for himself. He suspected the chain of events went like this: a guard saw them meet Mr. Collier in the lobby and leave. He notified Glass immediately, who then notified Mizrahi. That made a hell of a lot more sense than simple coincidence.

Arnold believed it was also safe to assume that Mizrahi just figured out they were planning a follow-up test and filed away this tidbit to hash over with Prisha during their postmortem discussion. Although he couldn't verbalize why, seeing Mizrahi skulk past the window simply strengthened his suspicion that he was behind the mysterious female stalker. Although he couldn't think of why Mizrahi would want anything to do with his house. But there was no other...

...unless. *Holy shit.*

Did he have it all wrong? Did she have nothing to do with Mizrahi and was actually a remnant of the terrorist cell remerging to settle an old score? Was that even possible?

Yeah. Possible. Perhaps.

Should he check with Agent Fisher, the FBI Special Agent he'd worked with? Worth consideration. But for the moment he needed to pay attention to the meeting.

"—as a consequence," Collier was saying, "we both updated our security measures."

"For example?" Arnold asked, suddenly refocused on the conversation, hoping Mr. Collier might slip up and divulge an important detail or two.

Laughing, Collier wagged a finger at him.

"Oh, no you don't. You taught me a good lesson last time, Mr. Gold. I refuse to repeat that mistake. That information is classified." He cleared his throat, his less-than-subtle way of changing subjects. "I'm sure you see where I'm headed with this but to allay any ambiguity, Frank is now eager to determine if their upgrades will keep you from accessing our offices again. This means that North Sound and Larkin Standish will be co-signers on the new contract. However, they are not to know about our issue with Mizrahi. That will remain solely between us. Are we absolutely clear on this?" He locked eyes with Arnold, then Prisha.

"Understood," said Arnold.

"Good." He finally raised his latté for a first sip. "The proof of penetration will remain the same."

To avoid any mistaken communication, Arnold emphasized the point: "I assume you're referring to the photos of me in your office, right?"

Which had been a selfie of Arnold holding the silver-framed picture of Mr. Collier's wife next to his head.

"Yes. As well as an appropriate picture to verify the time and date."

Made sense.

Then, out of curiosity: "Who else knows about that picture other than the three of us?" making an inclusionary sweep of his hand.

Mr. Collier replied, "No one. Why?"

"Not even the Security Committee?" Prisha asked with a note of disbelief.

Collier considered that for a moment.

"Well, yes, but after the fact. Why do you ask?"

"As you may have noticed, we intentionally didn't include that piece of information in our report. Just in case you might want us to conduct a follow-up test, as we're now discussing."

Frowning, Collier shook his head.

"I'm not sure I see your logic in that."

This surprised Arnold.

"Well, to address the concern about Mizrahi," and let it hang, to see if he would get it.

A wry smile formed on Collier's lips.

"Ahh...I see."

Prisha jumped in.

"So, what *is* the status of the Security Committee? More specifically, the mole?"

The lawyer's smile changed to a frown.

"That issue is still hotly debated. The problem, of course, is there's no way to determine whether that information was leaked by a committee member or was a result of Mizrahi's eavesdropping microphones."

Good point.

Arnold kicked himself for not having thought of it.

But as long as they were on the subject; "Does North Sound know about Mizrahi's internal surveillance?"

He preferred that term over "spy system."

"Not unless he shared that information with Ms. Glass. As far as we know, no one outside the Board of Governors is aware of it. Considering the potential blowback on the firm's reputation, we've been extremely careful to keep this, shall we say, under wraps."

Yeah, I bet you have.

Arnold glanced at Prisha. She returned a barely noticeable head shake.

"Well then," Arnold said, "I think you've answered all our questions for now, but I'm sure others will arise."

"Excellent. Now that this is settled, we need to set up a meeting with Frank ASAP. I really want for this test to get underway so all the associated issues can be resolved."

Did he hear a word he's said about the likelihood of getting in this time?

Arnold resisted the urge to shake his head.

Chapter 8

MEETING OVER, PRISHA and Arnold escorted Mr. Collier as far as the building lobby where they shook hands, then split up, the two of them peeling off toward the elevator to the parking garage while Mr. Collier continued on to the elevator stack serving the Larkin Standish floors.

Arnold held off discussing the meeting while Prisha navigated her Toyota through the labyrinth of angled cars that eventually took them to the pay-to-exit red and white striped gate, then onto a side street where they climbed the steep hill to turn north on Sixth Avenue, heading for Aurora Avenue.

Once settled into the flow of traffic, Arnold asked, "Thoughts?"

Prisha shot him a quick side-eye.

"About what in particular?"

Arnold chuckled.

"Well, let's see...wow, there're so many topics to choose from. How about we start with Mizrahi."

"Yeah? What about him?" Then, after a beat: "As in, do I think he dismantled his surveillance system?" She shook her head. "NFW. You?"

He nodded agreement.

"Totally. Okay, so what're your thoughts on the job?"

She tossed a dismissive shrug.

"Far as I'm concerned, we committed to repeat it the moment we signed the contract for the first one. Least, that was *my* understanding." She shot him another side-eye. "Why? You have a different take?"

"Naw, that was my understanding too. Which I suspect we can assume was Mizrahi's take on it as well."

She drove in silence for a bit.

Then: "But something else is bugging you about it. Is it the, uh, ancillary work involved?"

"Naw, not really, but it does have to do with our friend."

After refreshing her memory about the black-clad visitor, he described how he'd noticed Mizrahi slink past the front window at Starbucks and immediately lock onto them. He wrapped up by making a strong circumstantial case to link that incident with his house surveillance.

When Arnold finished laying out his case, Prisha continued to drive in silence.

Figuring she either didn't buy his connection, or was still processing the logic, Arnold turned to stare out the side window at the blur of passing buildings. He was already concentrating on prioritizing critical steps for reentering Larkin Standish within Mr. Collier's egregious time expectations which, although yet to be defined, would be unreasonable given the issues they would be facing. Something Mr. Collier would have no frame of reference for. Especially given the tight coordination between the law firm and North Sound Security.

Case in point: Mizrahi's surprise pop-up outside the dirt-streaked pane. Hardly an accident. No, the Israeli knew they were there because of a pipeline from the guards to Mizrahi via Lorna Glass. An otherwise unlikely alliance fueled by Mr. Smith's heightened concern over building security.

On the other hand, Arnold would bet real money that neither Glass nor Mizrahi truly trusted each other. Period.

Would there be a way to leverage this distrust?

Also, from reading their After-Action report, Mizrahi knew that they had accessed the firm's networks by suckering an employee into plugging a malware-infected thumb drive into a computer. To keep this from happening again, he'd undoubtedly intensified his safe-computing training and updates throughout the firm and that would include how to spot and repel typical social engineering scams.

Bottom line: it would be a waste of time to try using a variation of that approach. Major bummer. Social engineering was the easiest and likeliest way to steal a network.

And then there was the issue of North Sound's security "enhancements."

What were they?

How could they find out what they were? Realistically, there were only a limited number of options available, making it logical to anticipate what they might be. He began by breaking the system into basic components. The building's entire security system was focused on access control, and it went like this: Building access—whether off the street or through the garage—required entering the lobby, which created the first choke point. Lobby foot traffic was monitored by security guards and by CCTV.

There were only two ways to access floors above the lobby: elevators and stairwells. Both routes were strictly controlled by keycards. One of the rare exceptions was the Larkin Standish reception lobby, because clients needed to be able to access the firm without enduring the hassle of hunting down a security guard to fob them up.

During non-business hours—6 PM to 6 AM—lobby access was restricted to a single street entrance. Period.

The question now became, how could North Sound tighten keycard control? A few obvious solutions came to mind, but just how sophisticated these might be depended on factors Arnold had no knowledge of, like how much money had building management been willing to throw at the problem or just how sophisticated was their system before the decision was made to enhance it?

Bottom line: finding out specifics on those enhancements was going to be problematic. Unless...unless he could come up with an alternative way to access the target floor without having to worry about the keycard? Hmmm...this was an interesting thought worth pursuing....

"We can pretty much guess what Mizrahi did to tighten his security, but we need to know what North Sound did to strengthen theirs," he finally muttered more to himself than to Prisha.

"Totally," she agreed. "But I suspect they're keeping that information under wraps."

"Yeah, but you never can tell...maybe we'll get lucky when we meet Smith and he'll slip up."

After a long period of silence, Arnold said, "Well, it *is* a job. And it's always good PR to be working for Larkin Standish, right?"

"Right, but we need to know a ton more before we even broach this with the team."

"True that."

Head propped against the side window, eyes closed, Arnold began braiding various strategic threads into a coherent plan of attack. Mr. Collier's anxiety over the damage that Mizrahi could inflict on the firm was becoming contagious, causing his palms to sweat. Wiping them on his thighs, he realized how protective of the law firm he'd become.

Why?

Well, for one, they were a prized client. But more than that, there was the Mizrahi issue. First, as of today, Mizrahi knew for sure another pen-test was in the works and it wouldn't take much of a leap to figure out that this time his job was on the line. Second, Arnold was growing increasingly suspicious that he was responsible for the house surveillance.

Could these be related?

Sure, that was possible, but how? That part remained enigmatic.

"What?" Prisha asked him.

He turned toward her.

"Huh?"

"You just sighed as if the weight of the world just landed on your back."

Had he?

Yeah, perhaps. Sorta described his feelings at the moment.

He shook his head.

"I don't know...nailing that pathetic excuse for a human being before he goes nuclear is going to be tough."

"Agreed. But what choice do we have?"

Chapter 9

ARNOLD WAS ANGLING across the PCC Market parking lot with a tuna sandwich for lunch when it dawned on him that this gig would undoubtedly keep him here for more than just a few days, so the smart thing to do was to text Noriko to let her know not to expect him back in Honolulu for…?

Hmmm, good question.

Assuming, of course, she hadn't changed her mind and was down with seeing him again.

As Chance occupied himself with whatever it was that doggies get off on when sniffing shrubs, he dictated a text, sent it to her, then paused to reflect on how much he'd enjoyed their one evening together.

Was the enjoyment mutual?

Hoped so. Hoped she would cut him some slack over his social bumbling and nerdy awkwardness. A handicap she outwardly appeared to graciously ignore. But what did he know? When it came to reading people—especially those he cared about—he needed a guide dog and cane.

His phone dinged. A text. Started to reach for his pocket, realized the phone was still in hand, so simply glanced at the screen.

Noriko: *Sorry, looking forward to your return.*

Seriously? His heart leapt.

See? Life can continue without Rachael.

Let's not get ahead of ourselves. Don't get your hopes up. You have a tendency do that on matters like this. Besides, you know nothing about her. What if she becomes the girlfriend from hell?

Perhaps something with Noriko might work out, perhaps not. But the key point from his date with her was that he'd taken the first ginormous step at reestablishing a life outside of work.

He just needed to polish up his act a little, was all.

Well, maybe a lot.

He checked on Chance, who still seemed very content sniffing shrubs.

Hmmm...long as he was going to be in town a few days, what about Kara? She was attractive and friendly. Well, a little more than just attractive. Truth be told, he had harbored a few fantasies about her, but had never pursued them on account of being with Rachael, so yeah, why not call, see if she was interested in dinner or a drink?

What did he have to lose?

Well, for one thing, time. This job being a full-court press and all.

True, but all work and no play...

Instead of wasting time flailing through the Cain, Tidwell, Stowell phone tree, he dialed her direct line in full anticipation of having to listen to a recording telling him to leave a message.

Instead, she picked up on the third ring with, "Arnold?"

Catching him totally off balance.

"Kara?"

"You sound shocked. Or is this a butt dial?"

Massaging the back of his neck with his free hand, Arnold licked his lips.

"No, no accident. Just didn't expect you to be at your desk, is all."

"Neither did I, but the deposition this morning took way less time than we anticipated, so yeah, I'm here trying to swim upstream. What up? Back in town?"

That Kara, always on top of things.

"I am. Got in last night. Look, sorry this is so last-minute, but are you free for dinner this evening?"

"I'm always down for dinner, but are you, like, asking *me* to have dinner with *you*? As in a date?"

His face started in on the space-heater impression.

She quickly added: "Just jerking your chain, man. Sure. What do you have in mind?"

Again, caught flat-footed, having not thought this far ahead, he defaulted to a hip-pocket answer.

"How's pizza sound? There's this really killer place not far from my house that puts out some of the best product in town. Flavio's. Know it?"

After a palpable hesitation, she asked, "Weren't you supposed to call me back last time you were here?"

Oh, shit.

He was. But didn't. His gut sank. Then again, he'd been in the thick of the Rachael thing...finger-combing his hair, he licked his lips.

"Yeah, I was. But I had, like, a ton of shit raining down on me all at once and had to bounce back to the island, so, you're right, I didn't. But," he added in a hopeful tone, "I'm calling now."

"Flavio's? Never heard of it. I'll take your word that it's good. And it's just a short walk from your place?"

"Roger that."

"In that case, why don't I just come straight from work, and we can walk over?"

Hmmm, not a bad plan. Simplified things.

Especially since he didn't have a car here.

"Perfect."

And besides, she lived over by Woodland Park, which wasn't that far from him.

"I'll text when I'm leaving the office. I should get to your place around sixish or a little after, depending on traffic."

"I simply don't believe you," Mizrahi told the petite investigator as she stood just inside his office door, both arms straight down her sides.

Totally deadpan, studying him with her trademark robotic stare, her bright sapphire eyes boring straight into his. Radiating a specter of defiance. Inexplicably unnerving. Gave him the creeps is what it did.

"Fine. Since you don't believe me," she said challengingly, those sapphire lasers never unlocking from his eyes. "I suggest *you* waste nine hours checking out the property. Perhaps then you'll believe me."

"Maybe I'll do that," he shot back, before dropping his eyes to the Bic on his desk just to get away from her irritating stare.

What the hell was it supposed to mean?

Shifting positions in the chair, Mizrahi began to drum the Bic on the mousepad.

"Just so there's no ambiguity on this, you're telling me there's no possible way to break into that house? Absolutely none at all?"

With her stare unwavering, she said, "Mr. Mizrahi, you know that's not even a reasonable approximation of what I said. Anything's *possible*. What I *said* is: there's no way to get inside Gold's house without being *detected*. Hey, there's always the option of smashing out a pane in the French doors, reach in and unlock them. No question that'll get you in, but if you intend to get in and out without being detected—which I presume is what you'd prefer—that's just not going to happen. Especially if his perimeter security is any indication of what goodies might be inside. In case I wasn't clear before, every square inch of the property appears to be covered by full-spectrum CCTV."

Meaning cameras capable of capturing images along the entire spectrum from bright sunlight to dense nighttime shadows.

She continued.

"It only stands to reason the interior is tricked out with its own problems."

"Why can't you pick the front or back door locks?"

She shook her head.

"Perhaps you'd understand why not if you actually took the time to read my report instead of just the executive summary. Both front and back doors have numeric keypads on top of what I suspect are retinal scanners. Have I made myself clear this time?"

Cunt.

Mizrahi switched from tapping the Bic pen to drumming his fingers, thinking. He trusted her, but also believed she had to be overlooking something. Every home security system had at least one flaw, an exploitable weak point to defeat. She was usually very skilled at sniffing out such flaws. But not this time.

Why was she failing him now? Did she too have it in for him?

Just like Collier and Gold. Yeah, that had to be it. He could see it now in the way she eyed him relentlessly. From day one, she'd never liked him.

Or, for some reason was she protecting Gold?

Could that be it? Was she trying to double-cross him?

She continued to stare at him with that disconcerting expressionless face for several more silent seconds, before abruptly pivoting and walking from the office without so much as offering a goodbye or the good manners to close the fucking door.

It was obvious to him now: because she disliked him, she was purposely misleading him. There could be no other explanation.

His fingers continued their monotonous rhythmic tattoo as his dyspepsia continued to erode his gastric lining. Fucking Gold. That enigmatic little shit. Just thinking about him now was jacking up his desire for revenge. Exhaustive web searches had turned up not one speck of personal information about him. Even the investigator could find nothing. What kind of freak left no social media footprint? At least, not under his legal name.

In present-day society, such a high degree of invisibility required considerable effort and planning. Starting years ago,

Allen Wyler

when the kid first got online. That was simply unbelievable. Who
did that? No one. Either that, or Arnold Gold wasn't his
legitimate name. Was that it? Was he chasing a pseudonym?
Regardless, such secrecy suggested that little fucker was hiding
something in that house. What?

Well, there was that article in *The Seattle Times* a few years
back about a fire that consumed the original structure—which
explained the new construction—but it didn't contain a word
about the present home and property owner, Arnold Gold.

As a Mossad intelligence analyst, after graduating with
honors from Tel Aviv University, he had considered himself a
canny judge of character. Yet nothing helped him get a handle on
Gold. The only useful piece of information he had dredged up so
far was the property records. To his amazement, he discovered
that Gold not only owned the home free and clear, but that the
property taxes were paid in full. Digging deeper, he learned that
Gold had owned the original home before it went up in flames a
few years ago. What kind of kid Gold's age—which he estimated
to be north of twenty-five and south of thirty-five—could afford
to own a home in a city with a stratospheric tech-fueled property
market?

Where did Gold get that kind of money? Certainly not from
his pissant Gold and Associates business.

Questions, questions, questions with nothing even
approximating an answer. This dearth of knowledge about Gold
was brutally pissing him off but it was an irritation he was about
to rectify.

The evening was probably mild enough to eat on the back deck
had he been sufficiently on top of his game to remember to drag
the deck furniture out from the garage to inaugurate the *al fresco*
dining season, but no, he'd been too consumed with devising a
killer plan for getting back into Larkin Standish to even think
about it.

Too bad. Arnold decided what the hell, they could make do

68

with devouring their eats in the kitchen. Speaking of which…he briefly debated calling in their order but had decided it would probably be smoother to let her choose. See? He was learning, right?

She arrived twenty minutes later looking as cute and put together as ever, what with her red hair, freckles, and sparkling emerald eyes.

After a quick hug, Arnold said, "I'm starving. How about you?"

"I'm ready for some serious eats."

"Good. We can take a shortcut by ducking out the back door and cutting through the alley."

"Cool. But let's bring it back here so Chance can be with us."

"Perfect."

It was a thoughtful suggestion, one that immediately upped her stock in his eyes. What she didn't know was that he'd already planned on carrying the pizza back. Nor did she know that Flavio, the owner, was totally chill with Chance being inside the joint—claiming to anyone who might take issue, that he was a service dog—so nada problem.

Kara, Chance, and Arnold scurried out the back door, slipped through the security gate into the uneven dirt alley bisecting the block, then quickly covered the two blocks to pizzeria.

Arnold and Flavio had bonded a few years ago, back when he was first honing SAM's ability to profitably predict point spreads for sporting events. At that time, he'd focused SAM primarily on predicting the outcomes of horse races. The network became so accurate at nailing winners that sports betting became Arnold's sole income source, picking profitable horses at a rate of sixty-one percent, more than enough to generate some serious cash flow.

About the same time Arnold began to slip Flavio an occasional tip on a race. It was also about this time that SAM became proficient at predicting the outcomes of football games.

Then, once things became serious with Rachael, she dropped the hammer by telling him that if they were to have any chance at a serious relationship he would have to completely walk away from sports betting. Period. Non-negotiable. No wiggle room.

Although he detested ultimatums, he was in love, so ended up deciding that if giving up sports gambling was what it cost for her to be his girlfriend, then so be it. By then, he was already deep into developing stock-trading algorithms so, in truth, it didn't take much to transition from sports betting to stock trading. Realistically, however, he was still gambling. Only now it was with common P/E ratios and arbitrage instead of point spreads or track results. Still profitable, just a less iffy collection of characters playing in the sandbox.

Flavio glanced up from the workspace as they cruised into the warm interior of savory scents: yeasty dough, garlic, cheese, and grease, the combination goosing Arnold's salivary glands into overdrive.

Before Flavio could ask if he wanted the usual, Arnold raised a silencing hand, nodded at the menu on the wall, and told Kara, "You choose."

Cupping her chin between thumb and index finger, with cute little furrows of consternation crossing her brow, she perused the selections.

After a moment: "I'd have to go with a medium sausage provolone with extra mushrooms. Oh, and a few anchovies?" Then, to Arnold, "Uh, you're not one of those people who hates anchovies, are you? I know people that do."

Aiming a finger gun at Arnold, Flavio laughed.

"You set this up just to mess with me, didn't you." Not a question.

Up went both hands in surrender.

"Swear to God, I didn't."

"What?" Kara asked, alternating a bemused glance between the two men.

With a laugh, Flavio told her: "Girl, that's his favorite."

She flashed Arnold a wide-eyed look of astonishment. "Truly?"

A head nod.

"Truly."

"In that case," she said with a grin, "I'm pretty sure I can put a stop to that." To Flavio: "Throw in a kale salad." Then, to Arnold: "Guys hate kale," as if it were a universal truth.

Both Arnold and Flavio busted a gut over that one.

"What?" she asked, hands on her hips.

Miss Pouty. The obvious butt of an inside joke.

Arnold nodded for Flavio to break the news.

Grinning, Flavio asked Arnold, "Extra parmesan, right?"

"Yep."

Kara shook her head mournfully.

"In that case, *I'm* buying." She seemed to reconsider her words, then amended it with, "Am I right to assume you have beer at home to go with this?"

Grinning ear to ear, Arnold spread his hands.

"Anchor Steam."

Her eyes grew even wider.

"No freaking way!"

"Got another packet of those peppers?" Kara asked Arnold from the opposite side of the kitchen table.

Arnold had the French doors ajar so Chance—who was presently stretched out on the deck enjoying the familiar neighborhood scents wafting past—could wander in and out ad-lib. Dining in the kitchen wasn't as cool as being out on the back deck but came in a close second.

Arnold tossed a packet of pepper over the pizza box to her, then shoved the shaker of parmesan cheese to her side just in case, saying, "Yeah, I totally agree. Schneider and Carroll were right to trade Wilson when they did."

The room settled into contented silence as Kara bit off a chunk of pizza. Arnold slumped back in the chair, for the moment content to sip beer and reflect on how ultra-comfortable the evening was unfolding. Especially nice was being able to kick it with someone with whom you shared a ton of trivial preferences. A situation he hadn't experienced since...well, for a long time now. The contrast was a bit shocking.

A moment later, he became aware of an uneasiness worming its way into consciousness, nibbling the edges off the easy glow of contentment, becoming disconcerting.

What the hell?

Thought about it and was shocked to realize he was feeling subtle pangs of guilt.

Guilt?

Yeah, guilt. Over what, exactly?

Well, because you're really getting into Kara, while you want to know Noriko better. If that's even possible.

Thought about this a moment. How ridiculous. He and Noriko had been together socially a grand total of once. That hardly qualified as significant. And even if he wanted to see her again, so what? Was there an unwritten rule that said he couldn't be interested in two women at the same time? They were both smart, career-oriented, entertaining, and easy on the retinas. What's not to like?

And what about Rachael's dearly deceased brother Howie?

That guy was constantly juggling a handful of women. Hadn't Arnold fantasized about being like him? Absolutely. Just about all the time.

But more than that, a remnant of Rachael remained embedded in him, making him feel that enjoying the company of another female was somehow being unfaithful to her.

How crazy stupid was that?

He was moving on with his life, which was all the more reason to savor the companionship.

On the other hand, there was a more pragmatic reason to be nervous about getting close to Kara, one completely unconnected to the Rachael thing. Dating a paralegal from Noah Cain's firm was, like, total insanity. Mr. Cain was, after all, his primary word-of-mouth megaphone to the local legal community, his best referral source. There must be close to a hundred hackneyed admonitions about not defecating where you dined. Piss her off and...

Time to jettison any thought of progressing past the beer-drinking, pizza-sharing, buddy stage.

Easy to say. More difficult to enact. Especially given the undeniable flickers of mutual attraction they'd been tangoing around since the ransomware job he did for Mr. Cain.

All true. Still, she intrigued him. Nothing wrong with getting to know her a little better, even if to remain just friends, right?

Dunno, dude, this is some tenuously thin ice your blades are on.

Crap, what now?

He began scrambling for a totally neutral topic to discuss before this lull settled into something more comfortable.

Setting down his beer, he asked, "Your name. Does it have family significance?"

Still working on a mouthful of pizza, she tore another paper towel from the roll on the table, wiped her lips and fingertips and eventually swallowed.

"Not really. It's an Americanized spelling of the Italian word *cara*, which means beloved."

"Wow, I never would've pegged you for Italian, what with your red hair. I always think of Italian women with black hair."

"That's typically the case, but a small percentage are redheads. Plus, my father's Irish so that probably messed with the odds."

The sudden shift of focus put him more at ease. Had he allowed his fantasies to carry him away? Maybe, maybe not. Still, there was that undeniable tango...

"So, if I stick with the stereotype," he continued, "I'd guess you're Catholic."

Blushing, she said, "In the eyes of the Church, I am. But

that's only because my family baptized me before I had a say in the matter. My parents—both die-hard staunch church goers—forced me to do the confirmation thing, which I agreed to do just to keep the peace." A distant look came over her eyes as if reflecting back on days buried in the past. "I grew up in a primarily Catholic neighborhood on Capitol Hill. Our house was an easy walk to St. Joseph, which was probably intentional on their part. I mean, you could walk to church every Sunday regardless of the weather. They even sent me to Holy Names Academy." Referring to a nearby all-girls college-prep school. "I stopped attending services somewhere in my early teens. I never go back except for the occasional funeral or marriage."

Sitting back in the chair, beer in hand, Arnold found her story interesting in spite of having tossed out the question as a mood changer.

"Sounds like you're not very religions. But I think it's sometimes difficult to shed beliefs our parents instilled in us early on."

Apparently puzzled, she studied him a moment.

"Sorry, was that a disguised question or a simple statement?"

After considering his words again, he clarified the question.

"Guess it started out as a statement, but now that you ask, let me rephrase it. Does that mean you're not a practicing Catholic?"

"Practicing Catholic?" she asked. Then, with an emphatic headshake. "Far from it."

"Wow, no doubt in those words. Does that mean you're anti-Catholic?"

She glanced away, as if assembling a response.

"I wouldn't use the word anti because I personally don't care what other people choose to believe or how they choose to worship whatever it is they deitize. Organized religion just isn't my thing. Yet, I am spiritual...if that makes any sense. Does it?"

Before he could answer, she pressed on.

"Let me rephrase that. Your name is Jewish. Does that mean

you're a practicing Jew?"

Touché.

"Okay, yes, genetically I'm an Ashkenazi Jew, but I don't practice Judaism or go to temple."

"So where does that put you on the religious scale?"

"Oh man…"

He began finger-combing his hair, considering his answer while multitasking in a few totally tangential flashes, like he and Rachael never had this type of conversation. The kind that delves into personal beliefs. Their talks had been, well, more functional. Topics such as who would pick up what for dinner or do the dishes. Trivial day to day discardable subjects big on relevance but short on substance. How very strange. Stranger yet was why was he only realizing this now?

After a prolonged moment, he said, "I don't ally with an organized religion. Period. And I don't have a childish mental image of some white-haired white dude kicking back on a fluffy white cloud waving a golden scepter while deciding who's headed for eternal paradise or who ends up walking on glowing embers. And I don't believe in an afterlife." He paused, digging up the appropriate words for his next thought. "However, I do marvel at that moment when a sperm and ovum combine DNA and the combined genes kick-start a completely unique metabolic factory for however long that factory lives." He paused to let his last words sink in. "What I'm saying is, instead of having strong spiritual beliefs, I have a ton of questions that I don't have answers to and probably never will." Another, briefer pause. "That really doesn't answer your question, but to put it another way, I don't know where this puts me in the taxonomy of spiritual beliefs."

The room fell silent as Kara appeared to contemplate his words.

Finally, she asked, "Hey, what's going on with you and Rachael now?"

The question was pointedly and completely out of context.

The mellow glow he was basking in hit a cement wall doing,

like, sixty miles per hour. He stared at her for a moment, then spoke.

"Whoa. What prompted that?"

Brushing a swath of red hair to the side of her forehead, she flashed a coy smile. "You're so different tonight...we've never shared an evening like this. The few times we've been together outside work—including the time we met for a drink in the Market—you've been, like, super uptight. Tonight, you're totally chill. It makes me curious. Something's going on and I'm curious to know what that is."

She was dead-on, of course.

Was she seriously that good at reading people or was he just pathetically transparent?

Then again, did it matter? No, not really. But he made a mental note to never play poker with her. At least not face-to-face.

"We broke up," he answered in a factual tone that amazed him, as if, here you go, no big deal, when in fact it had been a huge deal.

Probably still was. After all, he was still wrestling with the Life-After-Rachael fallout.

A dark cloud of heavy awkwardness suddenly enveloped the room. She busied herself with another bite of pizza while he opted for another sip of beer, the deafening silence making him want to elaborate on the seemingly unfinished topic, but in truth, what else was there to say? Why was any further explanation necessary? And truthfully, he didn't want to discuss it.

Finished with the bite of pizza, she said, "Rumor has it you guys ran a pen-test over at Larkin Standish. Any truth to that?"

Thank God! A change in subject.

Apparently, word *had* leaked.

Who spilled the beans?

For sure, not anyone from his group. And he seriously doubted word came from Mizrahi or Glass. Perhaps whispers had begun percolating down through the lawyer grapevine via the

Deadly Odds 7.0

security staff. Did Mr. Collier know about this? Specifically, did they include word of Mizrahi's cache of recordings? If so, did this risk triggering blowback on the firm? His high-profile client.

Well duh! Why do you think Mr. Collier's worried sick about this?

Kara was looking at him, waiting for an answer.

An idea budded: was there a possible way to involve her this time? Especially given her connections within the paralegal community. Definitely worth serious consideration...

His phone dinged.

Aw shit, the security alarm again.

Raising an index finger, he said, "Hold that thought," then picked up his phone from the table, glanced at the screen, expecting to see a CCTV image of the black-clad skulker. But no. Tonight was a new figure. Bigger. He sat bold upright, mind going like crazy, thinking *male.*

Why? He had nothing to go on other than that impression just *felt* right. The guy was in the alley scoping out the kitchen from the same spot as the woman had been.

What the hell was going on?

Why case out my place?

SAM?

Naw, that didn't make sense. How would anyone know about him?

Or was *he* the target?

That intuitively made more sense.

"Arnold?"

His attention snapped back to Kara.

"Uh, sorry, just a notification's all..."

He scrambled to remember what the hell they were talking about before the distraction. Then, had it again.

"Yeah, we ran a test. Why? You, ah, still dabbling in computers?" making a thinly disguised reference to her hobby of hanging around the online fringes as a hacker groupie.

She flashed a wry grin.

"Maybe. Why?"

77

He responded with a dismissive sound.

"Just interested is all."

Pitching forward in the chair, fingers clamping the edge of the table, Kara said, "C'mon, man, give it up. I'm *dying* to hear the particulars."

Perfect. The hook was set.

Now all he had to do was reel her in. He shook his head.

"Nope."

"Ah man...why not?"

"That's classified material." Wagging a finger at her, he said, "You should know better."

James Brown started in. A call from Collier.

"Hold on a moment, I have to take this," Arnold said, standing.

Then he passed through the open French doors out into the back yard, far enough from the kitchen so Kara couldn't hear him, but close enough to the alley for whoever was out there to hear every word he said, Chance's questioning eyes following him, wondering if there was anything in it for a pooch.

"Hi, Mr. Collier, what can I do for you?" Arnold checked the time. 7:26.

"Sorry if I interrupted your dinner, but Frank wasn't able to return my call until an hour ago and at the time I wasn't in a position to talk freely. I am now that I'm in the car on my way home, so if I sound distracted, that's why. We want to meet with you and Ms. Patel at seven thirty at the same Starbucks across the street to lock down our next steps. I assume you can make it?"

Arnold had been debating just how to handle a situation like this since walking out of Starbucks this morning. He was counting on the bugs in Mr. Collier's office to do the job, but this was just too perfect.

"That's great" he said enthusiastically without muffling his voice. "We're totally amped to get started. But why not meet in your office instead?"

There! Gambit played.

"Because—" Collier's voice trailed off for a few seconds. "My office..." Another pause. "You sure about this? Absolutely sure?" An added inflection to the question.

Arnold figured Mr. Collier was already piecing his intention together. He glanced at the wall, where his new stalker was probably crouching, ears processing every word.

"Yes sir, I'm certain. After all, we already discussed the most important issue, *right?*"

"Yes, I believe we have. Okay then, tomorrow morning, but Frank and I'll plan on meeting you in the lobby by the elevators to our floors so we can go straight up to thirty-six and bypass the need for you to stop at reception."

And be seen in the process. Perfect.

Crouched behind the security wall, wedged between a green compost bin and a blue recycling bin, Mizrahi heard Gold say, "That's great. We're totally amped to get started. But why not meet in your office instead?"

From the sound of it, he was speaking to the firm's Grand Poobah.

He'd dropped below the edge of the wall the moment that squirrely little shit sprang up from the kitchen table to come barreling through the French doors, phone to ear. Luckily, he wasn't spotted, but who knew. He might've been picked up by Gold's CCTV cameras. Hah! For all the good that'd do, since his head was completely masked with a black balaclava.

Not only that, but he'd only raised his head far enough to peer over the top of the wall to see the house, rendering facial recognition software—should Gold's surveillance system include that—worthless.

Regardless, he was exercising extreme prudence. By now Gold probably knew his place was being surveilled, but so what? He couldn't possibly know why. Or by whom. And truth be told, Mizrahi didn't have a specific objective in mind other than to probe the little fucker for a weakness that could be used to inflict some serious retribution for the humiliation he was forced to endure from the last test.

He glanced at the aching balls of white knuckles that were, under normal circumstances, his hands. Gold's fault. Just thinking about the little shit made him want to crush his neck barehanded. The thoughts were also jacking up his blood pressure to dangerous levels. Normally, Mizrahi considered himself an easygoing, likable person. Not when Gold was concerned.

Then Gold was bidding The Poobah goodnight, followed by silence. He listened for the sounds of footsteps on the back deck, heard them, but didn't move for another minute to guarantee that Gold was completely refocused on that tasty little morsel across the table from him.

Figuring he was now safe, Mizrahi cautiously peered over the wall again. There they were, at the kitchen table drinking beer. Relieved, he scanned the immediate area for some avid Neighborhood Watch asshole watching him from a back porch or an upstairs window. Every neighborhood seemed to have at least one. Couldn't see anyone, but that didn't mean there wasn't some clever bastard out there with eyes on him. You never saw the really good ones.

Ears perked for the sound of approaching footsteps, he considered the information gathered tonight. For the most part, his investigator's report was accurate. The residence was indeed outfitted with security measures to a tier light-years beyond overkill.

However, that didn't mean it couldn't be defeated.

Devote enough thought and effort to the problem and any security system can be beaten. Like every problem, discovering a solution depended on just how much effort you were willing to put into it. If his goal was to inflict maximal emotional and financial damage on Gold, this fortress was the only identifiable target. Extensive internet searches yielded nothing else and there was no evidence of a wife, kids, or family.

But this place…this was the crown jewel. A statement. And

the statement couldn't be less ambiguous. This fucking security wall, for example. No fence. No hedge. No, Gold had built a goddamn cement wall around a house that itself was protected by excessive security measures: CCTV blanketing the property, numeric keypads, retinal scanners.

There had to be something of extreme value inside.

What?

He glanced around again. Still didn't see anyone, so he returned to mulling over the intel gathered tonight. He'd found one major discrepancy from his investigator's reports. Gold wasn't home the nights she had been here. Well, he was here tonight. Perhaps this was because of the little cutie in the kitchen. Perhaps he'd spent those other nights at her place.

The two certainly appeared to be at ease with one another.

Who was she?

And what exactly was she to Gold? Was she important? Important enough to attract further investigation? But that was something to consider later.

The second notable and potentially important point— confirmed a few minutes ago—was the two A/C units of different sizes. She was right about this raising a series of questions. Why two? Why such a size discrepancy? The larger appeared capable of serving the home's HVAC needs, but what was the smaller unit for? It couldn't possibly backup the main unit. It had to serve a completely independent function.

What?

What would be so critical to require a dedicated temperature control unit? A wine cellar? Somehow Gold didn't strike him as the sophisticated-wine-collector type. Hard as he tried, he couldn't think of a reason for it.

The more he puzzled over this, the more this unanswered question gnawed at him. However, it did convince him of one thing: whatever the use, it pointed to something of great value hidden inside the home.

He needed more information before formulating a course of

action. But short of smashing in the door and triggering a tsunami of alarms, how could he determine its function?

The most direct route to find out would be a simple smash-and-enter. But something so crass would be his last resort. There had to be a more elegant method for obtaining the information.

Duck-walking from shadow to shadow along the uneven dirt alley toward 80th, his mind became consumed with that riddle.

Chapter 10

NEXT MORNING, ENSCONCED at his desk savoring the first black coffee of the day, Mizrahi was scrolling through Google News when line two of his desk phone rang. Lorna Glass's name scrolled across the caller ID.

Picking up, he barked, "Yes?" without bothering with a name or salutation.

"And a very good morning to you, Itzhak," she replied with an unmistakable tinge of sarcasm.

Mizrahi remained stony-silent, letting her know her snarky juvenile sense of humor wasn't appreciated.

Five silent seconds ticked past before he finally said, "I assume there's a point to this call?"

"You are correct. But if you don't want me to tell you, hey, no skin off my nose. It's probably easier to just hang up. But tell you what, I'll leave that up to you. Your call."

He rolled his eyes.

Passive-aggressive bitch.

"What is it, Glass?"

"Collier and Frank Smith just met your BFFs in the lobby and are escorting them on an elevator up to thirty-six. I verified the floor via CCTV. Where they go from there is up to you to determine. That is, if you're the least bit interested."

Building security relied extensively on video monitoring. A ceiling-mounted CCTV camera covered the elevator alcove on each floor. Same for each landing on both stairwells. This was how Glass could verify which floor the group exited on.

"Are you referring to Gold and Patel?" he asked, as if this were fresh intel.

"Who else?"

Although it didn't require a tarot card reader to deduce the focus of the meeting, Mizrahi couldn't help but say, "You realize what this means, don't you?"

He didn't bother to mention that this, for him, was old news, having eavesdropped on Gold's conversation with Collier last evening.

"You'd have to be major-league brain-dead to not get it, Itzhak. Why the hell do you think I'm going through the supreme aggravation of trying to give you this information?"

He cast a quick glance at the phone in hand, shook his head, put it back to his ear.

"There's no reason to get snippy about it."

You muff-diving bitch.

He continued. "We just have to be damn certain their team doesn't make it up here this time." Then added a begrudging, "Thanks for the update. I'll let you know if, and when, I learn anything helpful." Which was precisely what he intended to do the moment he hung up. He'd been waiting for the lobby guards to spot Gold and Patel and notify her. Things were working out perfectly. "Have a good day."

Without waiting for a reply, he slammed the handset back in the cradle and switched his monitor to the webcam in Collier's desktop monitor along with the corresponding microphone. Good. He caught up with the group just as they were entering the lawyer's office, so he hadn't missed a word.

For the meeting, Mr. Collier had added two chairs to the two normally facing his desk, then arranged the ensemble so two pairs faced each other across a small coffee table. Arnold and Prisha settled into one side while Mr. Collier and Mr. Smith took the other. Since introductions had been made in the lobby, the four sat in their respective seats after declining Mr. Collier's perfunctory offer of water or coffee.

The lawyer wasted no time jumping straight into the business at hand.

"I believe everyone knows the reason we're here, but to make certain there's no ambiguity, we intend to finalize an agreement for a follow-up penetration test. But before addressing the specifics of our new contract, I wish to reiterate just how impressed we were with your After-Action report. Specifically, it provided us with well-targeted suggestions into how to strengthen security." He paused briefly. "After several subsequent in-depth discussions, we've implemented remedial measures that we believe rectify those shortcomings." Turning to Smith, he asked, "Frank, do you wish to add anything to what I just said?"

With a quick head shake, Smith answered, "No, Webster. That was succinctly well put."

To Arnold, this exchange sounded almost rehearsed.

Returning his attention to Arnold and Prisha, the lawyer continued: "Now that the corrective actions have been implemented, we believe the next logical step is to test their efficacy."

He nodded at Smith to continue.

Smith picked it up with: "North Sound was particularly disturbed by how easily your Tiger Team seemed able to move through the building to your target. After analyzing your report, we instituted appropriate contra-threat enhancements that we believe minimize future exploitation of the identified weaknesses. We intend to test these assumptions."

Translation: *Will they now prevent you from breaking in?*

"Excuse me for interrupting," Arnold said, "care to share any details about these enhancements?"

Flashing a wry smile, Smith pointed an accusing finger at

Arnold: "Nice try, Mr. Gold. But do you really expect me to help you plan your attack?" Then, after a laugh: "Hate to say it, but I'm shocked that you even tried to slip that one by us." Then to Collier: "You're right. He *is* a sneaky little bastard, isn't he."

Arnold shrugged.

"Hey, can't blame a guy for trying, right?"

After another chuckle, Smith added, "Although our staff are obviously aware that our system has been upgraded, they aren't aware of our plan to repeat a test."

"Is Glass aware of this planning?" Prisha asked Smith.

"Not that I know of. But it's a safe assumption that we'd want to conduct a follow-up test for the reason just stated." Smith leaned forward in his chair, hands on knees, looking intently at Arnold, then Prisha, perhaps to emphasize the next point. "How soon is your Tiger Team prepared to move on this? We want to get ahead of any potential bad press should word of the prior test results leak. We have a reputation to maintain."

Per their game plan, Prisha turned to Arnold, clearly defining him as the leader.

Having played enough poker to realize when to appear, well, a bit guarded, Arnold leaned back and glanced up at the ceiling with a thoughtful expression. His attention was suddenly drawn to the ceiling tiles. An idea budded...

"Arnold?" Prisha asked after several seconds.

Refocusing on Mr. Smith, he said, "When we signed on for the first test, we were hoping to get a shot at a follow-up if issues were found, so, yeah, Prisha and I are super amped at the prospect, but as I believe you know, we're a partnership. Which means I can't *officially* accept the job until all the partners vote on a proposal, but there won't be any issue. We'll all be on board with this, and I'll have a formal acceptance and timeline for you within the next few hours. At that point we can put any final touches on your SOW."

Smith continued leaning forward, aggressively, elbows on knees, as if his eagerness would expedite the process.

"As an incentive to put forth your best effort, if you're able to crack our security this time, North Sound's prepared to designate your company as our go-to pen-testers for all our downtown properties."

He sat back, arms crossed, as if this inducement might goose their motivation another notch.

Guess they took the After-Action Report seriously.

Arnold arched his eyebrows at Prisha, but she remained impassive, playing into the stall as planned.

Returning to Smith he said, "That's quite an offer. As I said, I should have a formal answer for you ASAP."

In fact, only he, Prisha, and Brian Ito were partners and Brian had already delegated his vote to Arnold. Vihaan and Lopez couldn't vote yet since they weren't partners. But Arnold suspected that wouldn't stop Vihaan from whining.

Smith nodded.

"Well then, I believe this is all I have for now." Turning to Mr. Collier, he asked, "Webster?"

With a slap of his thighs, Collier stood.

Meeting over.

He said, "Excellent. I expect to hear from you within the next few hours so we can officially sign off on the proposal."

Chapter 11

"WE HAD IT right, Glass. Those assholes were just given the green light to try again," Mizrahi told her.

He stood just inside the threshold to her cramped office, the air a potpourri of orange peel, stale tuna-fish sandwich, and even staler coffee. The specific combination, for some reason, evoked memories of his grade-school cafeteria. Probably the tuna fish, he decided. They'd been so big on tuna-noodle casserole that he got sick of it.

Glass tilted back in her desk chair, eying him, effortlessly interweaving an honest-to-God yellow lead pencil (*who still used those things?*) from finger to finger and back again without looking. A trick she'd undoubtedly mastered decades ago, now running on automatic muscle memory. In spite of going out of her way to portray calm, he could sense nervousness radiating from her like heat waves off sunbaked asphalt. This time, with Smith involved, it wouldn't just be his ass in the line of fire.

After apparently pondering his words, she asked warily, "You know this for fact or is this just more speculation?"

Mizrahi couldn't help but smile.

"It's a fact."

Nodding slowly, she said, "Riiiight." Then, head cocked to the side: "And how did we happen to come by this confidential information?"

Was that a smirk?

Did she know?

With a dismissive scoff, he glanced away, immediately realized his mistake, and looked back at her.

"Glass, by now you should know I don't disclose my sources."

The front legs of her chair hit the linoleum tiles with a solid resonate thump.

"Riiiight," she muttered again with sufficient skepticism to imply that she knew of his unauthorized monitoring system.

How could she know about it unless she was spying on him?

Until now, he'd been operating under the assumption that only the Larkin Standish Board of Governors knew about it. And those governance assholes were so massively uptight about not tarnishing their exalted pristine image to anyone who gave a flying turd that they'd make goddamn sure to not allow the slightest whisper of impropriety to ever ooze past the confines of their closed-door hush-hush discussions.

For—God forbid—if word ever did get out, the reputational blowback would be epically nuclear. He'd made that unambiguously clear to Collier when he threatened to release some of the most damaging material the instant he caught the slightest whiff of peril and so far, his intimidation had worked. Collier had gone silent about firing him.

On the other hand, if Gold was somehow able to infiltrate their network again and find his system, then what?

That was a complete unknown and the conundrum he now faced.

Collier had made it clear that he wanted Mizrahi out of the firm. But where could he get such a sweetheart job, especially at his age? Truth was, he'd lucked into this position during the prior managing partner's tenure. A couple years later that partner retired, and Collier ascended to the throne.

Then Covid hit and much of the firm's work migrated to

virtual meetings which necessitated additional layers of IT security. Then, as the pandemic began to unwind, their law practice slowly began drifting back to more normal on-site activities. Now they were running very much the same as before the pandemic. Except that now Mizrahi had his fingers into every corner of the firm. But this took him right back to the pivotal question that had been bugging him for days now.

Would Collier back off his case if he dismantled the system?

This was, after all, their demand. Huh.

Yes, perhaps Collier would, but he couldn't afford to give up the added protection just yet, so would have to take the risk. Especially with another pen-test now clearly in the works. He needed every advantage that might help keep that little fucker out of their offices. Case in point: today's little eavesdropping session.

Even after running through the pro-and-con arguments once more, he decided that his only chance at surviving this present calamity was to shut down that little fart for good. That way, he could show management how impermeable their updated security system was and put an end to these goddamn tests. Perhaps then, as an olive branch to Collier, he'd be willing to dismantle the network. But he couldn't even think of doing that under the present circumstances.

He and Glass continued to eye-fuck each other straight into a Mexican standoff, both waiting for the other to blink. Yeah, she damn well knew about the system. How she gained that intel was irrelevant because this time she finally realized she had as much skin in the game as did he. And this meant she was as reliant on the edge it gave them as was he.

Yeah, this time she was finally taking the risk to her job seriously.

Together they'd keep that squirrelly little fuckwad out of Larkin Standish. Because, if they didn't...

Arnold and Prisha walked in silence to the elevators, engrossed in their own thoughts about the impending test, rode the elevator down to the parking garage, and then Prisha maneuvered the

Toyota out of the basement parking lot.

Stuck behind a gear-grinding exhaust-coughing garbage truck, waiting for a green light, Prisha finally spoke first by asking, "What're your thoughts?"

Her question jerked him from the issue he'd been mulling over since leaving Mr. Collier's office, and realized he was staring blankly out the side window at passing foot traffic. Took a moment to make sense of her question. Without turning from the window, he answered with a question of his own.

"First, what're your thoughts on getting rid of Rachael?"

He could feel her eyes bore into him briefly as they waited for the traffic to start moving again.

"That wasn't even remotely close to what I asked, but guess it *is* business-related. Interesting question, though. Haven't really thought about it. Whydaya ask?"

A heavily tatted woman with pink and aqua-blue spiked hair caught his attention as she came zooming down the sidewalk on an electric unicycle. He'd toyed with the idea of getting one once but decided that the road rash involved during the skill-acquisition phase wasn't worth it.

At length, he said, "We broke up," and left it at that.

The garbage truck ahead of them belched a puff of dirty gray exhaust and began moving again. Prisha followed.

"No shit? When did that happen?"

Arnold blew a resigned sound. "Oh man...it was, like, when the last pen-test was wrapping up. Just never mentioned it, is all..."

Prisha hesitated before saying, "Okay...so, I gotta ask; why raise the issue now? I mean with this other shit coming down on us."

Good question.

The thought of replacing her had begun nagging him since the night he walked away from the relationship. At the time there was too much other emotional turmoil going on to deal with it then. But now it was front and center.

"As I said, things went sideways about the same time we wrapped up the last test, so I flew straight back. Been mulling it over ever since." He shrugged. "We haven't seen each other, but you know, don't you, that she lives only two blocks from my place, right?"

"Nope. Didn't know that," Prisha replied, tapping her left turn signal in preparation to work their way along to Sixth Avenue.

"Well, she does. And now that I'm in town I worry about bumping into her when I'm out walking Chance or doing the usual shit like shopping at PCC or having dinner at Nell's. That'd be, like, major-league awkward and embarrassing."

Prisha busied herself with the turn, then changing lanes. Arnold waited for her to say something.

When she finally did, she said, "I totally get why that might make you a little twitchy, but I'm not sure that firing her's gonna lessen the possibility of that happening. Know what I'm saying? Like, that's the risk that comes from living so close together. Unless either one of you moves out of the 'hood, nothing will change."

She shot him a quick glance then returned her eyes to the traffic.

"Yeah, yeah, I know. But I'll deal with that if and when it happens." With a sigh, he flashed on the emotional number their breakup had done on him. "Naw, you're right...it's more than that. Truth is, I don't want to deal with her at all right now. Especially not during a business meeting and with this job starting, you know we're going to have a few, right?"

Prisha drove for another block.

"Okay, I get it. And know what? I'm not really shocked you guys disintegrated. I've sorta seen it coming. Don't ask me for specifics because I can't point to any. It's just a vibe I picked up the few times we were together. So yeah, I can see why under the circumstances it'd be a good move to terminate her. *Especially* being our business manager. I mean, if she wanted, she could really do a number on us." She quickly raised her hand. "I'm not even remotely implying she'd ever think of doing that, but there's always the potential. I have no idea what's going through her mind at the moment."

Arnold considered that.

"Naw, I can't see her doing something like that, but you never know about people. Surprises *can* happen."

"But I also gotta say I'd be way more comfortable with this if we had a replacement already in the wings ready to go. After all, business is totally off the hook right now, so yeah, we really do need to address this. Maybe we should start nosing around for someone to do our QuickBooks. I'm sure there're plenty of people out there with those skills."

"No doubt. But it has to be someone we trust. I mean *totally* trust. Meaning, I'm not in favor of picking up someone online. Not only that, but I want someone who's local so we can discuss financials face-to-face when we need to. None of this virtual shit. Agreed?"

"No argument from me on that," Prisha said.

They rode another block in silence before Arnold asked, "What do you think about asking Kara if she knows someone who can take care of us?"

Prisha shot him a serious dose of side-eye.

"Why'd you zero in on her?"

Good point. This idea just seemed logical.

He took a moment to reconstruct his subconscious reasoning. Hmmm...

"Well, she's a paralegal so it seems logical to me she'd be connected to people with those skills..."

Prisha's response: a sarcastic snort.

"Thinking of getting next to her?"

"No, of course not," he shot back, caught himself, thought: *Hmmm, why so defensive?* After all, the thought had floated through his mind. But that was none of her business. Unless, of course, she believed that any involvement with Kara risked creating problems for them. In that case, it *was* her damn business.

"Why do you ask?"

"Oh, come on, dude. You seriously want me to run through all the old axioms? And besides, if I did, you'd just get all insulted and shit."

"I don't know what you're talking about."

He gave an indignant sniff, then immediately realized how idiotic it sounded. He knew exactly what she was getting at. And she was right.

But before he could retract it, she was all over him.

"Look, man, I'm floored you have to even ask." Another quick side-eye. "Okay, let me spell it out for you. She works for *Cain*. And unless I'm totally confused on this point, he's our primary referral source and a rock-solid client. I wouldn't want to do anything that carries the slightest potential of messing up that relationship. But hey, I'm only one person's view. After all, it's your name on our website."

Ouch.

She *was* right, of course. But it wasn't as if he hadn't already considered this.

Because he had.

Regardless, he was looking forward to having dinner with Kara this evening.

Chapter 12

KARA CAME STRAIGHT from work early enough for them
to enjoy a leisurely stroll through the neighborhood on their way
to the restaurant, the air carrying the wonderful fragrance of
freshly mown grass from Green Lake Park, Arnold bringing a
bottle of wine to enjoy before and during dinner.

Because of being a regular at the neighborhood restaurant,
they gave him his favorite table, back in a corner, partially
protected from the hubbub and chatter of other diners, many of
whom came from the retirement home across the street.

They enjoyed a glass of wine while contemplating the menu
and chit-chatting about her work and the ransomware case. Kara
eventually decided on the pork tenderloin. Arnold opted for the
duck breast. They decided to split a mixed greens salad. In the
course of the evening, they did in the bottle.

Sauntering back to his place, the conversation tapered off
into a well-fed, wine-buzzed comfortable silence. That's when,
Kara casually took his hand in hers. A mushroom cloud of unease
detonated in the pit of his gut. Bright neon red letters forming the
word *DANGER* began flashing in his mind's retina.

What's the problem, dude?

She's holding my hand. That's what.

So? It's nothing more than a trivial act of intimacy.

Exactly. That's the problem: intimacy. Exactly what you need to avoid.

Really?

Yeah, really. I need to explain it to you? Well, okay then, try this out: holding hands will lead to a kiss, which will lead to an embrace, which will—

Okay, okay, I get it.

Okay, what to do about it? Couldn't simply let go on account of she had hold of *his* hand. Forcibly extract it? Naw, that'd be, like, extremely awkward. There had to be a better way to weasel out of the situation while salvaging their friendship.

As they reached the bottom of the windy hill up to his house, his mind began jack-rabbiting along, sorting through options for smoothly extricating himself from what would morph into a seriously awkward moment in, oh, about one hundred feet when they arrived at his front walkway.

Tell her how much he enjoyed the evening and let it go at that? Or invite her in for…

See, this was the issue. Invite her in for what, exactly? Another glass of wine? One that would be superfluous. Unless, of course, they were looking for a mutually unstated excuse to sanction what he suspected was foremost on their agenda, which was to screw each other blind.

C'mon, dude, we're down to about only fifty feet now. If you're going to do something to derail this—

Yeah, but we're both adults and—

Bullshit. You're flat-out being stupid if you take another step toward your front door.

Yo, dude, just walk her to her car. Easy enough. Quick. Simple. No hard feelings. That'd be the smart move.

On the other hand…

He felt himself being levitated toward his front door like a spirit-guided planchette on a Ouija board, so stopped and tugged her hand, halting her from turning into his front walk. She turned question-mark eyes to him. Cupping her head gently between his palms, he looked directly into those inquisitive green eyes for a long moment.

"Look, Kara, I like you a lot and find you incredibly attractive. But we have a big problem. What we feel—at least what I *know* I feel—right now puts us at risk of facing some potentially disastrous consequences. I don't think I need to spell it out for you. Thing is, I want us to be able to work together without any, ah, entanglements. Understand what I'm saying?"

She appeared to process the statement for a long moment, then gave a nod of what struck him as disappointed agreement.

Prompting her to say, "Yeah, totally."

Without thinking, he drew her to him and hugged her and whispered, "Thank you."

A moment later, she stepped back, held him at arm's length, appearing to appraise him anew. "When you say you want us to work together, what exactly do you mean?"

An idea that had been marinating subconsciously for the past day or so, finally broke surface.

"I'm searching for a way to involve you in our next pen-test if you're down for it."

Her eyes lit up like bottle rockets.

"For real?"

"Totally," he blurted, having just narrowly escaped one problematic situation by dropping himself smack into the center of another.

Oh well, he and Prisha would hammer out the details once he came up with an actual plan.

A plan he needed to come up with, like, super pronto.

The clock was ticking.

Loudly.

Chapter 13

THE NEXT MORNING, Prisha, Vihaan, and Lopez were at Arnold's kitchen table in their usual chairs downing a box of pastries and a Traveler-size container of Starbucks black coffee that Arnold lugged back from the nearby coffee shop mere moments before their arrival.

Brian Ito had opted out of the online meeting for the very pragmatic reason that his time zone was three hours earlier, so rolling out of bed that early just to hear them plan a test in which he wouldn't participate held little—if any—appeal.

Couldn't really fault the dude.

With the pastries reduced to a few residual crumbs scattered around the bottom of the grease-stained cardboard box, Arnold kick-started the meeting by stating what everyone already knew: "It's official, guys…Larkin Standish wants us to take another run at them. Only difference is this time North Sound Security's a co-signer on the contract."

"I don't get it." Lopez stated with a puzzled expression. "They got a free ride last time. Why obligate themselves to the expense when they know they'll get the report anyway?"

"Reasonable question," Arnold replied. "Our report shocked them enough that they shared it with the property management company. Remember, they market their office space as being one of the most secure in the city. If word leaks that they're not as secure as advertised, they could start losing tenants. That happens, and the property management could start looking to change security services. It's a prime example of shit rolling downhill." He paused for that logic to settle in. "Because of this, they made some significant enhancements"—he bracketed the last two words in finger quotes—"to their system." He raised a finger to stop Vihaan from jumping into his knee-jerk pushback position of not taking on new work. "As an incentive, North Sound said if we can break into the firm again, they'll crown us their go-to pen-testers for all their downtown properties. That should indicate how invested they are this time around."

"Make us their go-to testers? Big deal. We can't possibly take that on. We're at max capacity as-is," Vihaan quickly pointed out.

"Perhaps," Arnold countered. "But it's premature to even worry about that unless it becomes reality. Right now, we need to focus on the test, because we're committed to doing it and don't have a plan yet, much less any idea on our odds of succeeding."

And because Vihaan's constant complaining about their workload was already getting on his nerves, Arnold added, "Besides, we don't know diddly-squat about what our workload will be if we do break in this time. Could be a ton, could be none, or it could be somewhere in between. And just because they offer us a job here or there, doesn't mean we're obligated to take it. On the other hand, don't you think it'd be nice to have the right of first refusal?"

He then immediately felt a pang of regret for his tone. It'd been a little harsh.

"I dunno, man. Seems to me we're setting ourselves up for getting progressively tougher jobs," Lopez said with a heavy note of skepticism and a slow headshake. "There has to be a downside to that. Sorta like being the fastest gun in Tombstone. Every quick draw in the area starts targeting you as the quickest way to make a name for himself. Sooner or later, someone's going to knock you off."

Arnold shrugged.

"No doubt. Face it, we *will* fail at these tests sometimes. That's the game, man. Not every pen-test turns out to be a success from the tester's viewpoint. But from the standpoint of whoever hires you, keeping you out of the cookie jar is a great result, right? And that doesn't necessarily mean the tester did a bad job. Just means your security's buttoned up nice and tight. So, yeah, it's bound to happen now and then." He paused to scan their faces, decided he'd made his point. "For me, it all comes down to do we want to grow our business, or do we want to simply maintain our status quo?"

"Since you put it that way..." Vihaan said, trailing off, politically astute enough to not go up against that argument.

Arnold scanned them again. They seemed to be looking at one another, like no one was particularly anxious to raise their hand and say they were eager to maintain the status quo. All except Vihaan. Arnold knew it was only peer pressure keeping him from manning up as the sole dissenter.

After a few more seconds of dead silence, Prisha said, "Okay kids, recess is over. Let's get back on point. We should be knee-deep in some serious planning. I mean, c'mon guys we have a ton of work to do. We're way behind and the clock is ticking."

That Prisha! Always on top of it.

Just another reason Arnold loved having her as second-in-command and another lightning rod for some of the responsibility of moving the crew along.

Silence.

Lopez hand-signaled for a timeout.

"Problem with trying to plan anything is we have no idea what their security *enhancements* are. We need to know that before we can make any serious plan of attack." Then, to Arnold: "I assume you asked."

"Twice. Once with Mr. Collier, then again with Mr. Smith." Arnold coughed a sarcastic laugh. "Dudes had that one covered like freaking Saran Wrap. Claimed it's officially classified material and by keeping us in the dark, they'll get a better real-life indication of its effectiveness. Hey"—he shrugged—"can't fault their logic. Makes life a little more difficult for us but more realistic for them. But I think we can still come up with a foundational plan today, then fine tune it as we learn more. And you better believe we're going to dig up some facts one way or another." He paused. "Okay, so let's start by outlining what things we *do* know, like, what did we purposely omit from the After-Action report in case we got this redo."

Prisha said, "First thing comes to mind is their comms sys. We didn't mention being able to monitor their radio traffic. But if they took a serious look at their comms, that part is, like, glaring. The good news is that's one thing we can find out right away."

"Be bad news for us if they changed anything," Lopez said offhandedly.

"I don't think they would," Vihaan offered.

Prisha: "Why not?"

"First off, I don't think they realize how much we relied on it. And since we didn't mention it, it probably didn't blip their radar. Secondly, considering the junk gear they're using, switching would mean replacing every single radio they have. That'd be money they could sink into other more productive things. But hey, that's an easy enough question to resolve."

With an enthusiastic nod, Prisha said, "I'll run down there in the morning to take a listen." She laughed, said, "I can check it out without getting out of the car."

"Cool," Arnold said. "That's one item taken care of. Can anyone think of some other shots?"

After a moment of silence, Lopez said, "We haven't heard a progress report on your assignment, yet. Have anything for us?"

His task was to figure out the tactic for breaking into the firm.

Arnold cringed.

"Not yet, but I'm on it."

Silently, they continued to eye him, like, get busy, dude, clock's ticking.

"No, seriously," he added. "I'm working on it. Just haven't come up with a plan is all."

Which pretty much killed the agenda. So, with pastries and coffee gone, the team drifted out to Prisha's Toyota while Arnold left a message for Mr. Collier to call. After straightening up the kitchen, Arnold shrugged on his black rucksack, slipped the reflective halter over Chance and started off toward PCC Market to pick up lunch and dinner while wracking his brain for a way to break into the firm. Where was his creativity when he needed it? So far, he had nothing, not even a nidus of a plan.

As they were leisurely meandering back, Arnold's phone rang.

Mr. Collier.

"Okay, we officially accept the job," Arnold told him. "I'll send you and Mr. Smith the updated copy of the SOW within the next twenty minutes so we can sign off on it whenever you'd like."

"Excellent." Collier replied. "I'll set that up for later today. The sooner this issue's resolved the better."

Yeah, I bet.

Whereas Mr. Smith's priority was to test the effectiveness of their whiz-bang security enhancements, Mr. Collier's priority was to neutralize a vindictive Mizrahi before he could inflict serious reputational damage on the firm. Now all Arnold needed to do was figure out how to steal their network and then sneak into Mr. Collier's thirty-sixth floor office to take the money shots without getting caught.

Jesus.

Moving Chance along now, heading home, he dialed Prisha.

Perhaps by bouncing ideas off each other they could jointly hammer out something. She might just give him the much-needed creative spark.

Chapter 14

AT 7:55 THE next morning, Prisha and Arnold strode briskly over the polished granite floor of the plate-glass and steel lobby to the shaft of elevators that served the Larkin Standish floors. As they approached the area, a woman in a well-tailored business suit pressed the UP button. A moment later the doors to an empty cage parted and they all piled in.

As planned, Arnold had a copy of the keycard he'd surreptitiously cloned from Mr. Collier during the prior pen-test. As the woman entered, she swiped her card across the reader, thumbed the button for floor fifty repeatedly as if to speed things along, then stepped away from the panel.

Prisha leaned in and pushed thirty-four: one of the few floors not requiring a fob. Arnold's turn. Holding his breath, he swiped his card across the reader. Bingo. The LED turned from red to green. Cool. One more item they could scratch from their checklist. Not only were the old cards still useable, but they could delete a complete keycard overhaul from the list of possible security enhancements.

A critical piece of information to have.

He could feel the woman watching him impatiently, as if the elevator wouldn't move unless he thumbed a button. Like it somehow knew how many people had entered and was waiting for each one to press a floor button. Arnold just stood by the panel, blocking her view of it. The doors slid shut and the elevator began to rise. In another few seconds the light would time out. Would she notice? Would it look seriously suspicious? Press a Larkin Standish floor?

Okay but then what? Her floor was 50 while his and Prisha's was 34. How would it look if he pressed, say, 36 yet walked off with Prisha? Did she even give a rat's ass?

Arnold decided to simply continue blocking her view of the panel. And if she noticed that he got off with Prisha, so what? What was she going to do about it? He smiled at her. She turned away.

Collier and Smith were standing near the elevator alcove as Arnold and Prisha stepped out of the cage, Arnold asking, "I'm sorry, are we late?" with a glance at his watch.

"No, no, punctual as ever. A minute early, in fact. This way," Collier said, with a sweep of a hand toward the familiar hall to the left of the reception desk. "We're in the same conference room as last time."

Collier led them to the small room, stood by the door until they all filed in and were seated, then shut the door and settled into the remaining chair, with Arnold and Prisha on one side of the rectangular conference table, Collier and Smith on the other.

"I assume you have the contracts," he said to Arnold.

"I do."

Arnold plunked his attaché case on the table, hinges toward Collier and Smith, popped the locks, raised the lid.

"I have two copies for each of you to look over." He handed both men a manila folder containing the detailed SOW, or Scope of Work. "Since you apparently had no issues with the draft I sent yesterday, nothing's been altered. Unless there's an issue, please sign both copies and keep one. I've already signed them. Take as much time as you need to look them over. We're in no hurry."

As the two men busied themselves reading the document, Arnold—using the opened attaché top to shield his hand—aimed his Flipper Zero directly at the keycard dangling from a blue lanyard around Smith's neck and squeezed the trigger. It beeped softly. In spite of muffling the sound with his free hand, he cringed.

Did they hear it?

Then again, he was listening for it, and they weren't. He stole a quick glance at Prisha. She returned a barely perceptible headshake. Good. It might just squeak past unnoticed.

A couple of minutes later, Smith slapped his copy of the contract on the table, looked from Prisha to Arnolda and said, "It's acceptable to me." Then to Collier: "Webster?"

Collier raised his eyes from the document and nodded, then took another moment to tap the sheets into perfect alignment before confirming.

"It's no different from our prior agreement, so is acceptable."

"In that case," said Arnold, "please sign both your copies and keep one."

As the two men were scribbling out signatures, Arnold asked offhandedly, "Which of your new enhancements do you think will keep us out of the firm?"

Smith abruptly stopped writing to glance disapprovingly over the tops of his readers.

"What did I tell you last time?"

Oh well, worth a shot.

"That that's classified information," Arnold offered with a shrug.

Shaking his head, Smith said, "Rest assured, nothing about that policy has changed."

He handed over the paperwork.

"Hey, it was worth a try, right?" Arnold muttered.

Without even looking up, Smith made a *tsk-tsk-tsk* sound and shook his head.

On the ride back down to the lobby, Prisha asked Arnold, "Why'd you take the risk of cloning Smith's key? We already have Collier's."

"Couple reasons," he replied, adjusting his grip on the attaché case handle. "First, why not? I mean, we're right there with the perfect opportunity staring us in the face. Totally easy pickings, girl. And besides, you never know when something like that might come in handy. And what're the odds they'd even know what I'm doing unless they specifically know that sound, which is, like, outrageously unlikely, right?"

She seemed to roll that one around for a moment.

"Okay, you do have a point, but do we intend to use it?"

Arnold shrugged.

"Don't have a clue. Maybe. Maybe not. But far as I'm concerned, it was too good an opportunity to pass up, so"— another shrug—"I took it. More importantly, we got away with it."

Seeing a flicker of doubt cross her face, he quickly added, "Okay, let's say one of them heard the beep. What're they going to do about it? Demand to see what's in the attaché case? And say they look. You seriously think either one of them knows what a Flipper Zero's used for?"

"Probably not Mr. Collier, but Smith? I dunno, man, dude's a totally different issue. After all, he heads a security company..."

"So?"

After a moment she said, "Since you got away with it, you may just have a point. But barely."

"That's exactly what I'm telling you," Mizrahi said to the platinum-blond investigator.

"Explain to me why you've developed such an all-consuming interest in his house?" she shot back, still standing straight, not at attention, just straight, arms at her sides, hanging loose.

Mizrahi squelched the urge to say it was none of her fucking business, that she should follow orders and collect her paycheck because that's all she was getting paid to do, but she was inquisitive. That could be good or bad, depending on how he channeled it. Perhaps by explaining his reasoning, she might develop an interest in the project and put a bit more effort into it, perhaps even think of something he'd missed, remote as that might be.

"Come over here," he said, motioning to the side of his desk.

She did as asked while he unrolled the architectural plans for Gold's house and turned to the overview page of the basement. The paper had been rolled into a thin tube for so long that it was impossible to get the pages to lay flat, forcing him to anchor the right side with his phone, smooth out the pages, then secure the left side with his coffee cup, but even then, the corners curled.

She stood to his left, peering down at the plans.

He started with: "This is our target's basement. Notice anything unusual about it?"

He used the inclusive *our* as a clever device to catch her interest.

She frowned for several seconds.

"It's a basement. So what? What exactly are you asking about?"

"This room here," he said, tapping the rectangle with his index fingertip, "fascinates me. Why? Because that small air conditioning unit we've discussed is directly outside. There has to be a reason for that system and the only possible explanation is to control the temperature of this one room." *Tap-tap-tap.* "Aren't you the least curious to know what's in there?" He glanced up at her and waited.

She stared back, poker faced, as if deciding whether it was a trick question or a joke.

Then: "No."

Emphatic, leaving no doubt.

"No?" he repeated, rearing back in shock.

She furrowed her brow at him. "You seem so...shocked. Why? What possible reason would I have to even wonder what's in that room?"

When he didn't answer immediately, she added, "You just don't get it, do you." Not being an actual question, she continued with: "A critical point you seem incapable of grasping, Mr. Mizrahi, is the firm pays me, not you. Your apparent fascination with Mr. Gold strikes me as part of some personal vendetta instead of legitimate firm business." Pause. "Of course, if you believe I'm way off base about this, I'm more than happy to have Mr. Collier clarify this point for us. Yes?"

She raised her eyebrows while drilling him with those sapphire eyes.

Dead silence.

She nodded knowingly.

"Listen carefully to what I'm about to tell you because I don't want to repeat it. If you're so intent on finding out what's in that room, be my guest. But don't try to involve me in your personal business."

She turned and marched from the room without bothering to close the door.

Mizrahi sat in his chair, motionless, eyes on the opened door, a slow burn eating at him like a measured drip of nitric acid on metal. That self-righteous little cunt couldn't possibly appreciate the anger gnawing his insides: indignation fueled by the devastating humiliation that little shit had dealt him by breaking into Collier's office.

Years of hard work establishing his image within the firm was flushed straight into the sewer in one night. His only satisfaction now would be to inflict equal or greater injury on him, perhaps by robbing him of something of extreme value. An eye for an eye. Although a tangible asset could never compensate for reputational damage.

He had no idea what Gold might be hiding in that basement, but whatever it was, it must be extremely valuable if it required such over-the-top security plus a thermostatically regulated room served by a dedicated HVAC unit. Yes, something of significant value was in there and he would find out what. One way or another.

Maybe her suggestion had merit. Maybe he *should* just bogart in and find out for himself. Who cared if breaking a pane of glass triggered an alarm? With the present SPD manpower shortages, the question wasn't how quickly could they respond, the question was, *would* they respond?

Yes, he could bust in and be inside that room in seconds. Just had to make goddamn sure Gold and that fucking attack dog weren't home.

The more he thought about it, the more the idea resonated.

Chapter 15

THE CREW WAS ensconced in their usual spots around Arnold's kitchen table, scarfing their favorites: a fennel sausage with roasted peppers and provolone, and a mozzarella with tomato sauce and basil.

The sink was fully stocked with bottles of Anchor Steam packed amongst three bags of chipped ice that Arnold had picked up at a nearby 7-Eleven. Chance lay stretched out on his belly on the porch, eyes closed, paws to either side of his black snout, perhaps snoozing, perhaps just enjoying the ever-changing odors wafting through the neighborhood, including some mouth-watering smoke from a nearby charcoal BBQ.

Once the intensity of the feeding frenzy began to ebb, Arnold kicked off the working part of the dinner.

"Okay, guys, there's no such thing as a free lunch. Or dinner, for that matter, so this is intended to be a working dinner."

He paused to make sure everyone was paying attention. They were.

"So, the first order of business is, anyone have any new developments to share?"

"I'll start," Prisha said, waving a partially chomped on slice of pizza as she spoke. "Picked up some excellent news today." She paused for a sip of beer. "Their radios? Same ones as last time. All I had to do was drive into the garage and I was listening to their chatter."

Vihaan clapped briefly before taking another bite out of the piece he was working on.

Arnold's turn.

"More good news. When I went up to their offices to collect the paperwork, I tried one of the clones from last time and it worked. So, we can scratch new keycards from the list of possible enhancements. That narrows the options."

"Yes, but that still leaves a ton of possibilities," Vihaan said with a borderline whine.

"Not really," Arnold said, leaning back in his chair, beer in hand, trying to appear casual when he was anything but on account of still not having a plan of attack, not even a bud of one. "Not if you break their system down into components." Arnold paused to make sure everyone was paying attention. "Their security is built solely around access control, right? Sure, they have a guard or two keeping an eye on the lobby and perhaps one patrolling the garage and random floors, but the lion's share of the work their employees do is monitor CCTV, right?"

"Right," Prisha echoed. "Okay, I see where you're headed with this. Their biggest bang for the buck is to upgrade their CCTV and keycard systems. Sure, they could increase the number of guards per shift, but this won't necessarily do anything to improve *effectiveness*. If they intend to throw money at the problem, they'd focus on their computerized systems."

"Shit, she's right," Lopez said, suddenly sitting up, eyes sparkling with interest now as if someone just cattle-prodded his brain. "If they didn't already have some AI in their system, I bet they have it now. And if they did have some, it'd be uber-easy to upgrade it significantly."

"Exactly," Arnold said with an enthusiastic nod. "Our After-Action report pointed out how much we relied on the stairwells to access the target. I've always suspected we got away with it because no one was paying any attention to those feeds."

Lopez raised a just-a-minute-finger and leaned forward, eyes gleaming with excitement.

"Exactly! And that's the reason I think their video feeds didn't have any facial recognition running. Or am I just crazy?"

"No, that makes a ton of sense," Prisha said, also getting into the exercise.

"So, if I'm Smith," Arnold added, "the first thing I'd enhance is the stairwell CCTV monitoring. Hey, easy enough to do. Just patch in facial recognition software to the video feeds, especially for the lesser used out-of-the-way-areas the guards ignore. Tighten all their weak spots."

Lopez jumped in.

"Know what else would be an easy upgrade? Adding some serious workflow analytics to the keycard monitoring system. After all, they've got everyone with a keycard in their database already along with what floors they have permission to access. It'd be trivial to layer on some complementary analytical parameters like what time Suzie Q. Lawyer routinely comes and goes each day and when or if she moves through the building. More you think about it, there are several cool spins to add to this without much problem. All of which would tighten security like crazy."

"For example?" Prisha asked.

"I suspect," Vihaan said, "some people in the building have irregular hours. Some Larkin Standish lawyers, for example. I'm sure a receptionist has pretty regular hours in comparison to Mr. Collier. For people like him with irregular hours, you could link their keycard with the facial recognition software for verification. Say, for example, his fob is used to access floor forty-three at two thirty in the morning, that's not normal and should trigger the algorithm to verify his identity. See? Yep," he said, nodding in self-agreement, really getting into it, "this is beginning to make a ton of sense. In fact, I bet we just nailed their mysterious enhancements."

He put the last word in finger quotes.

Wow, quite a statement for pessimist Vihaan.

"Okay," Arnold said, reaching for the small notepad he kept on the counter, to take a few notes for himself. "So our next step is to figure out a way to validate these assumptions, even though I'm betting we pretty much nailed them. Any suggestions?"

Lopez offered, "How about having Prisha chat up a guard like last time, see what she can find out? Maybe she can pick up some clues by scoping out a CCTV screen or two."

"Naw," Arnold said, again, Mr. Negativity. "Every one of them is looking for us now. And besides, Mizrahi and Glass damn well already know this is in the works. Every guard in the place is now on hyper-alert for us."

"Unless we figure out a way to bypass all that," Prisha said.

"Such as?"

Prisha raised up a silencing hand, paused to think something through. "What if we take a two-pronged approach? We work on verifying exactly what their enhancements are while at the same time work on a plan for getting you on thirty-six for a legitimate reason during normal business hours, then find a way to hide you there until it's safe enough to do your thing. Whatdaya think about that approach? Can we work with that?"

Her comment suddenly coalesced two seemingly disparate earlier thoughts into a possible plan of attack. He muttered, "Holy shit! You may have just nailed it."

All eyes were on him now, waiting for him to explain.

Thumbnailing swaths of label from the sweating Anchor Steam bottle, Arnold continued working up the idea.

"For some reason during the last test I seem to remember a utility closet tucked away in the back of the central core. It's crazy, but that stuck in my mind. There must be one on every floor, right?" He paused. "Wonder how you access it? I want to say it requires a keycard but can't be sure. And if it does, who can access it? All maintenance staff probably have access, right?" he asked Prisha, then added, "That makes the most sense."

Prisha appeared to consider the question a beat.

Allen Wyler

"Maybe. But you've got Smith's key now. Why not try it? I mean, shouldn't he have, like, a Supreme Master-level clearance or some shit like that?"

"Sounds about right," Arnold answered, already thinking ahead to related obstacles. "But the only way to know for sure is to try it out. And do it without Mizrahi finding out or we blow our plan."

As if they had a plan. Which they didn't, but he now had a handle on an embryonic one. And he was pretty sure he could forge it into a solid one. Everyone's eyes were glued to him.

"Before I take the risk," he added, "I want to clone one from someone in maintenance and, if possible, one of the guards. I'm probably only going to get one shot at this, so want all possibilities covered."

Lopez said to Prisha, "Man has a solid point."

"True, but all of this takes time," Prisha said. "Time we're running out of."

Just then the security app on Arnold's phone buzzed. His video cams were locked onto the heat signature of someone in the alley: either a neighbor taking a shortcut, or his stalker back for an encore. Weighing his options, Arnold decided to simply wait and see what played out. He dumped the phone back on the table beside his paper plate to keep an eye on the video.

"It'd really help to have someone on the inside," Arnold finally suggested. "A spy."

"Inside North Sound or Larkin Standish?" Lopez asked.

Arnold shrugged.

"Either one would work." Another thought hit. "What if we try to get one of you"—pointing from Lopez to Vihaan—"hired at North Sound. That'd make it a slam-dunk."

Shaking his head, Lopez said, "I dunno, man...too many things to go wrong. And besides, that'd take way too long. We're too seriously behind as it is. We can't afford the delay."

"Naw, you're right," Arnold said, reaching for his last slice of pizza of the evening. But another idea struck. He turned to

114

Prisha, who was taking a pull on her beer. "How about seeing if Kara can sniff out some information on the enhancements?"

With a suspicious look, she asked, "Yeah? How's that supposed to work?"

Once again, he'd shot off an intuitively logical thought before working it out, so had to pause, back up and try to piece together his reasoning.

"Gossip through the lawyer pipeline. Odds are pretty good that she knows someone from the firm that she could ask." He spread his hands. Mr. Innocent. "Hey, I'm just saying..."

Prisha flashed him an admonishing look.

"Involve her in any way, any way at all, she'll start asking questions I don't think we wanta answer. My opinion? It's best to keep our activities strictly in-house. Plus, I think it's super likely that most of that firm's employees don't know diddly about what went down last time. I simply don't see any upside to that being a hot topic over there."

"Valid point," Arnold said, unwilling to admit that Kara already told him that the word was out. But then in a flash of creativity, blurted, "Okay then, how about we go straight to the source?"

"Source? What're you talking about?" Prisha asked.

"We simply hack Mizrahi's computer. He should have a ton of emails in there about the mods..."

Whistling and clapping enthusiastically, Vihaan said, "Now *that*, lady and gentlemen, is a goddamn excellent suggestion. We can make it even better by using his account to leverage a way into Glass's account. I mean, we're breaking into the firm's network anyway, why not pick up Glass in the process?"

After a moment of stunned silence, everyone began exchanging high-fives. They now had an operable target.

"It always amazes me," Arnold said as the jubilation began to die, "that an obvious path can be so hard to see. Man!" shaking his head. Then, after a moment: "Okay then, plan is to start with Mizrahi and work our way into Glass's accounts, right?" He added, "Anyone thought to try the back doors we embedded last time?"

Speaking of blatantly obvious things to do. Should've thought of doing this before now.

"I'd be totally shocked if they were," Prisha said, as if this excused the oversight.

"Easy enough to check," Arnold countered, reaching for his laptop on the kitchen counter. With the others huddled around, eyes on the screen, he systematically tried to access the Larkin Standish network via trap doors embedded during the last attack. To no one's surprise, all three were gone.

Soon as the last attempt failed, Arnold said, "Guess this gives us some indication of just how seriously Mizrahi took the joke."

"Hey guys, cheer up," Prisha said as they settled back into their seats. "There's a bright side to this: we now have a plan we can start working with and the first step is to figure a way to hack Mizrahi's email since that gets us back into their network." Looking at Arnold, she added, "I seriously doubt we'll be able to sneak a phishing attack past anyone."

Arnold shook his head.

"Nope."

Prisha to the others, "Suggestions anyone?"

"Not from me," Lopez muttered.

Vihaan looked away.

Prisha asked Arnold, "Whatdaya think about a riff on the USB scam?"

She was referring to how he'd previously tricked a Larkin Standish lawyer into infecting his computer by having a courier service deliver a thumb drive in an envelope disguised to look as if it came from the lawyer he was negotiating with on a patent infringement suit. Within seconds of being plugged into the lawyer's computer, the entire network was infected, and Arnold's team was scrambling to embed as many additional trap doors as possible before Mizrahi's IT techs could realize what was happening and respond.

Arnold shook his head. "Naw. That was in our report. By now Mizrahi's probably made sure every computer in that firm either has their USB ports packed with gum or are superglued shut. You better believe Mizrahi's making damn sure there's zero chance of that trick ever being pulled on them again."

The room drifted into thoughtful silence.

"Okay then," Prisha pushed out of her chair to stretch. "This has been an insanely productive brainstorming session. Think it's time to let our thoughts simmer and see what we come up when we reconvene in the morning. We gotta keep pushing this. Clock's ticking." She looked at Arnold. "You good for now, boss?"

Arnold was also up too, stretching.

"Totally. Let's sleep on it." Then to Prisha, "Have a word with you in private?"

"Sure." She tossed Vihaan a set of keys while saying, "Meet you in the car."

Her husband caught them with a clear expression of mild irritation.

Lopez, who'd driven his own car over, was already slipping on his jacket and called over his shoulder, "G'nite, guys," while starting for the door. Arnold watched him and Vihaan leave.

Arnold turned to her, "We really need to get rid of Rachael and do it ASAP."

After brushing some strands of her black hair from her forehead, she crossed her arms.

"Cool. I get it. But we've been over this. We can't do it until we have her replacement ready to go. Or do you have one lined up and you just haven't gotten around to telling me?"

"Naw, not yet," he admitted, pulling up his glasses to squeeze the bridge of his nose. "But I plan on asking Kara if she's got a bead on someone." He held up his hand to halt the pushback he anticipated, then paused to replace his glasses. "Yeah, yeah, yeah, I already know your thoughts on the subject, and I agree totally. But I also see her as a resource we can and should tap."

She continued to study him before giving a barely

perceptible nod, like, *You sure about this?*

"I know, I know," he replied to the unasked question, having received the message loud and clear.

"But I still believe there's a valid angle there to work.

Chapter 16

MIZRAHI PEERED OVER the security wall again and was surprised to see Gold's group no longer in the kitchen. Neither was that fucking dog. But one of the French doors wasn't completely closed either, so the meeting must be breaking up and they were either in the living room or out front because given the little shit's obsession with security, it was inconceivable that he'd leave the house without locking up, so he waited and watched.

If Gold stuck to his routine, he'd take that mutt out for a walk soon, leaving him the perfect opportunity...

As Arnold watched Prisha's taillights disappear up the windy street, his phone alarm began buzzing again. Another security alert.

Goddamnit.

A quick check showed the same balaclava-clad head just high enough to gaze over the security wall into the kitchen. A moment of pride blew through his heart for having installed infrared sensors sensitive enough to nail the sonofabitch despite his obvious attempt to elude detection. Yeah, installing that equipment was more expensive, but was turning out to be worth every cent.

A mélange of reality-stoked rage and fear doused his high;

although convinced the man wearing the balaclava was Mizrahi, he had no objective evidence to support this. Absolutely nothing but gut impression.

True, but who else could it be?

Well, see, that's the problem. His road through life hadn't exactly been free of the occasional speed bump. There was, for instance, the not-so-minor issue of the debris left in the wake of the terrorist cell incident. Somehow the memories of that chapter of his life conveniently faded from everyday consciousness.

Unfortunately, repressing them wasn't making the lingering threat any less real. Who knew? A few residual cell members could still be out there orbiting his universe. And since the subject of grudge-holders was now glowing brightly, how about some of his other encounters since starting Gold and Associates? Characters such as Ramesh Singh?

He and Ramesh hadn't exactly parted company as back-slapping, beer-stein-clinking buddies.

Regardless, some asshole was staking out his house. Why? What was the point of the surveillance, the objective of this game? Since there was nothing of value inside, whoever was doing this, was either after him or SAM. But no one knew about SAM.

Well, Rachael did, but he couldn't see how she'd be involved in this. Which took him straight back to the terrorists. *They* knew about SAM. How? Because he'd shot off his freaking mouth to Naseem in a sophomoric attempt to impress her. Jesus. He cringed at the memory.

He studied the security image on his phone. Now, more than at any time since this goddamn surveillance started, he needed clarity on that asshole.

Who was he and why the hell was he here?

The question needed to be settled and potentially dealt with.

The problem was finding the answers. Set Chance loose in the back yard to see how he reacts? For sure he'd smell the prowler, but then what? Unleash him to go after the guy? And risk injuring him if he was armed? No, that wouldn't work. And although that might clarify if it really was Mizrahi, it wouldn't answer the more important question of his intentions. Moreover, it would do little to end this stalking bullshit.

Okay, so back to basics. Whoever was out in the alley seemed to be waiting for something. What? Ascertaining his routine? Naw, that didn't make sense. Waiting for an opportunity? Yeah, that made more sense.

An opportunity for what, exactly? To get inside the house?

Thought about that a moment. That seemed more probable.

Easy enough to answer. Just go back inside, halter Chance, take him out for an abbreviated end-of-night potty break and see how things played out? After all, his CCTV would record everything that asshole might do inside the property, which might go a long way to answering a few of the questions. And besides, what did he have to lose? Well, there was always a concern about SAM, but that could be dealt with. Especially since the operable version was in Honolulu.

He worked through the plan more carefully while strolling back into the living room, then on into the kitchen. Settling a few key questions *would* be a massive improvement over being driven batshit-crazy not knowing. And come to think of it, flushing out Mr. Balaclava Head could give him some much-needed ammunition to verify if it really was Mizrahi or not. Yeah, the more he weighed the option, the more the move made sense.

While grabbing the halter from the kitchen counter, he noticed the partially open French door, paused, ran this wrinkle through his game plan. Surely the prowler was aware of it. Would leaving it ajar be too obvious or would it provide just enough motivation to make his move tonight?

With Chance now in his halter, Arnold glanced at the French door again while clipping the leash.

Okay, fucker, let's see what you do now.

Arnold turned and walked Chance back through the living room and out the front door, phone in hand, dialed onto the security camera covering the back yard.

Chapter 17

MIZRAHI WAS PEERING over the wall when he saw Gold stroll into the kitchen, grab the halter and clip it onto his dog, then watched the two of them disappear into the front of the house.

Excellent, the little shit was taking out the mutt for his evening walk.

Not only that, but he couldn't believe his luck: the fool left the French door ajar, which mitigated any risk of triggering an alarm. Those video cameras would undoubtedly record him crossing the small back yard, but with the balaclava and black clothing on, what could Gold learn? Not a damn thing. Furthermore, what could he do about it? Nothing. Besides, he would be in and out before anyone could even contemplate responding.

He grabbed the handle to the back gate and pulled. Locked. No surprise there, but it never hurt to try. Took another look at the wall, decided not a problem, pulled himself up and over, then dropped feet first onto the ground, then was streaking for the back deck, on through the door, and into the kitchen.

He stopped and yelled, "Hello. Anyone home?" and listened for the skittering of paws on the polished concrete.

Instead, heard only dead silence.

Deadly Odds 7.0

Relieved, he opened the door to the basement stairs and scrambled down to the unpolished cement of an area known only from poring over the blueprints. Then he was facing the door of the mystery room. Opening it, he reached in to where a light switch intuitively should be, felt it, flicked on a set of overhead LEDs. In the center of the room stood a three-shelf battleship-gray metal rack crammed with Dell computers. He heard the soft, white-noise hum of power supplies and smelled the faint resin of electronics.

WTF?

Mizrahi rubbed his right cheek in disbelief. Of all the things...then again, why such surprise? Gold was, after all, into computers. But this...standing motionless, his mind brimming with confusion, elation, and excitement all blended into an uninterpretable emotional soup. He now knew what was in the room, but what the fuck was it?

Warning bells clanging in the depth of consciousness, began growing louder. Time for a strategic retreat before the little rat-fucker returned. After all, the mission was a success. Actually, more successful than anticipated. Get out now before being confronted. He shot up the stairs, on through the kitchen without bothering to shut the basement room door. After all, entering the house had probably been documented somewhere in Gold's elaborate security system. Trying to cover his tracks would be senseless and a waste of effort.

Arnold watched Mizrahi come up over the back wall and drop into the grass, streak toward his French doors and out of range of the camera's field of view. True, the person was disguised, but his build and gait left little doubt it was Mizrahi. And knowing this triggered a weird combination of anger and relief. Relief that it wasn't one of the terrorists. Anger at Mizrahi for violating his space.

"C'mon boy," he told Chance, cutting their usual evening stroll short.

Chance initially resisted, sensed something, and relented. As they approached the front door, Arnold deliberated what to do next. Mizrahi probably wasn't armed, but you never knew. Especially since knowing that his job was on the line and that Arnold's finger was poised over the guillotine switch.

He glanced at his phone again, the screen still displaying the view from the backyard camera. Just then, Mizrahi reappeared, moving fast toward the back gate. Giving a long sigh of relief, Arnold slowed and thought...

Wow, that was quick. What the hell was that all about?

SAM!

Then he was in the basement, standing at the threshold to his computer room, doing a quick visual inspection of the contents. A cursory glance seemed to show nothing disturbed, but he wouldn't feel safe until a full system scan cleared the system. All it took was an infected flash drive inserted into a USB port for two seconds to destroy SAM. He ran upstairs, awoke his laptop from Sleep Mode and quickly severed the encrypted connection between the Seattle and Honolulu SAMs. This sent a rush of relief through him.

For a moment he stood still, taking deep measured breaths while allowing the acute panic to subside so his mind could begin assessing the potential situation. He was, in fact, in good shape. Worst case scenario was that Seattle SAM was infected with malware that had already spread to Honolulu SAM.

Using his laptop, he logged into Honolulu SAM and initiated a full system scan. With that now running, he did the same for this SAM. Next, he halted the routine system backups until he manually restarted them. Next, he took a moment to review his actions, decided they were appropriate and that for the moment, there was nothing more he needed to do but wait and assess what may have happened.

More at ease now, able to think more rationally, he reviewed what had just taken place. Well, one thing for sure: Mizrahi just upped the ante on what was already a high-stakes game.

He checked the progress of his ongoing scans. So far, so good. No malware detected, but a real full-system scan of all the computers would take much longer.

Arnold poured a glass of wine and settled in at his laptop to review the details of the camera footage and came away even more convinced that the balaclava-clad intruder was Mizrahi. However, proving it—especially to Mr. Collier, a lawyer—would be close to impossible. Which was seriously pissing him off.

Reviewing the footage also gave him an accurate accounting of the actual elapsed time Mizrahi had been in the house. Although he could've made an attempt to infect SAM, it would be cutting it close. He checked the time he cut to network and factored that into his estimate. That too, gave him more confidence of being unscathed.

Jesus.

After rummaging through the kitchen junk drawer, he found his red stress ball, propped the small of his back against the counter edge, and began aggressively squashing it, his mind now consumed with how to take revenge on that sonofabitch.

Chapter 18

TILTED BACK IN his stain-repellent La-Z-Boy, Mizrahi stared blankly at his off-white popcorn ceiling, mulling over what the hell Gold could possibly be up to in that basement room.

Made perfect sense for an IT technician to have a computer or two scattered throughout the house, but a dedicated room with a neatly engineered rack of servers was a galaxy removed from that. Was he hosting a chat room? Running a kinky dark-web porn site? Trading crypto? Huh. And short of inspecting the software, there was no way to know. Regardless, it was now the obvious target for retribution.

The ultimate vengeance would be to destroy it completely. That would include any copies because surely Gold would back up the network at least daily with copies stored across multiple external sites. Thus, unless all the copies were rendered useless, making the system whole again would be an easy restore.

Fine. Settled. How?

Couldn't be physical and brutish like smashing the equipment with a sledgehammer. No, the solution had to have an elegant flair in addition to being fail-safe and one-hundred percent effective. Malware, obviously. Ideally, malware that could be programmed to lay dormant until it'd been written into all backup copies. Then, and only then, unleashed.

Good. Now he had a plan. The question now was how to execute it?

Eyes closed, he recalled the image of a three-shelf steel rack with the rows of machines side by side, all neatly cabled together with zip-ties.

Yeah, it was a network, alright.

Meaning that to render it functionless, all he needed to do was infect one machine with a rapidly spreading, highly destructive virus. And this could be done by simply slipping an infected flash drive into the first available USB port, and *hasta la vista,* motherfucker. The entire network could be destroyed in less than a minute.

He nodded with glowing satisfaction at finally coming up with a way to inflict staggering retribution on that little fuckwad.

The problem now, of course, was to do the preemptory strike before Gold could coordinate the pen-test. And he had no idea where in the planning stage Gold and his clowns were. Especially with that asshole Collier on a tear to terminate him from Larkin Standish. His plan was making more sense now: Gold was Collier's only weapon to pry him from the firm. And the only way he might convince Gold to either back off or purposely fail the test was to send him an unmistakably clear wakeup call that said: "Fuck with me and I'll destroy you."

The most expedient route to get the job done would be to hire hackers who specialize in this line of work. But he lacked the connections. Sure, he could ask around, maybe get a line on a group, but that would take time and leave a trail. He didn't want to assume the slightest risk of this ever blowing back on him. Bottom line: he needed to do this job himself and do it ASAP.

Since he didn't have the skills to make a serious attempt at penetrating Gold's firewall, his only option was to break into the bastard's house again to physically infect the network. He smiled. Having been there once before would mean he could be in and out in a under a minute. The major problem would be gaining access. There was no way he could possibly hope for a repeat of the serendipitous situation he'd stumbled onto.

No, this time he would need to smash a pane in the French doors, but so what? He could be in, out, and long gone before anyone had a chance to react. Stupid Gold would never suspect that the goal was nothing more than to plug a flash drive into a USB port for a few seconds.

Smiling, he nodded again in satisfaction, his confidence in the plan growing with each detail hammered out. Now, all he needed was to get his hands on an appropriate USB drive and virus.

Ah yes...ironically, Gold had provided that information in their After-Action report. In particular, there was a description of the device used to infect their network. Mizrahi had a copy of the report on the table just to the side of the chair. He swiveled the La-Z-Boy around, leaned over, sorted through the stack of material, found his copy of the report and began thumbing through pages until he came to the appropriate section.

Ah yes, here it was, a Hak-5 USB Rubber Ducky.

Not just any USB drive. No, this one would automatically inject the malware of choice into the recipient computer.

At the dining room table, he fired up his laptop and did a Google search for it. A moment later he was scrolling through the Hak-5 website's complete line of virus-delivering USBs starting at $69.95. Huh. So many to choose from. After a moment, he chose the one that the site claimed was the bestselling newest version. Obviously, if it was the bestselling one, it must be good. He paid extra for overnight delivery, his excitement snowballing into an avalanche, the sweet satisfaction of revenge its fuel.

Next came a much more problematic step: selecting the appropriate malware for the job. Though the Hak-5 website offered "payloads," he had no idea which one to order.

After pondering the question for a few more seconds, he realized just how little he knew about this end of the game. A game for which he played only defense. He drifted off into a daydream in which he envisioned himself as a fearless linebacker, the one who made the game-saving plays. What he really needed at this point was an ally who routinely played offensive. Ironically, an Arnold Gold.

He sat back, thinking this through. Almost everyone he knew well enough to trust was in the same boat. However, there was one guy...

"You have any idea what you'll be doing, Itzhak?"

What the fuck kind of question was that!

But, when he really thought about it, the question wasn't unreasonable. After all, the guy was a pro at this type of activity. Problem was, he couldn't bring himself to admit that this part of the game would be a challenge for him. Mizrahi decided to sidestep a direct answer with: "Your question sounds as if you have a word of advice for me, so go ahead, I'm listening."

"I just sent you a link. It should pop up on your email momentarily. It'll take you to a Rubber Ducky Payload Repository. Browse through their inventory and choose something that appeals to your need. But look at this as only a starting point because, as I assume you know all too well, the big-gun anti-malware firms make it their job to keep a very sharp eye on these forums. What I'm saying is that if I were you and wanted to increase my odds of making it through your victim's antimalware software, I'd develop my own payload by simply following the development framework those examples lay out for you."

I'm sure you would, but I don't code this shit. And besides, I'll be injecting this straight into his machine.

"I understand" was all Mizrahi could bring himself to say.

"And Itzhak?"

"Yes?"

"At the risk of offending you; be sure the computer you're using when you do this is completely air gapped." Meaning it must be totally isolated from any other device. Especially, the Internet. "Then, as soon as that payload's been loaded into the Rubber

Ducky, remove the hard drive from your machine and then flatten it. Better yet simply swap out the hard drive for a new one and toss it. Oh, and don't forget to have a bootable flash drive ready with a copy of the BIOS on it for installing the new drive. You follow all this?" he asked with an annoying air of superiority, as if he suspected Mizrahi was about to wade into some very deep water that might even be over his head.

"Yes, I follow you."

You sanctimonious asshole.

He struggled to mask his irritation at being talked to like a kindergartener. It wasn't the information Roger was giving him that pissed him off so much (for he was taking copious notes), it was the presumption that he knew less than a sixth-grader about such things. Despite that presumption being fairly accurate when it came to this kind of work.

A few minutes later, sitting back, reviewing Roger's instructions, Mizrahi decided that perhaps the time had come to replace his aged Lenovo laptop. Why not just sacrifice it to the good of the cause and then donate it—infection and all—to Goodwill. Let some asshole thrift-shop buyer think he's getting a screaming steal. He laughed aloud at the idea. Yeah, loved the concept. Loved it a lot.

Whistling Disney's *Heigh-Ho Heigh-Ho It's Off to Work We go*, he logged onto the Rubber Ducky Repository.

Chapter 19

ARNOLD WAS WAITING just steps from the front door to Maximilien, a wonderful little French restaurant tucked in behind the famous Pike Place Market stall where the fishmongers entertain cruise-ship tourists by boisterously lobbing an abused salmon back and forth.

He'd chosen this wonderful little bistro for a business dinner with Kara for three pragmatic reasons: the location was just three blocks from her office; they'd dined here once during the ransomware job he'd successfully pulled off for Mr. Cain, so he knew she enjoyed the chow; and lastly, if he were serious about potentially using her on this job, he wanted to maintain a business-like distance rather than pizza and beer at his kitchen table. At least for the time being.

He checked his watch. She was running late. Typical, given her line of work.

What's Noriko's doing? Showing a house? Does she even think of me now and then?

He realized just how often he caught himself flashing on her during the day. Wow, what a totally foreign freaky situation, being attracted to two women simultaneously. But Kara...well given the circumstances, he'd just have to let his attraction go. Would she seem so freaking appealing if she weren't forbidden fruit? Yeah, for sure. He'd been attracted to her since almost running into her (literally) at Mr. Cain's law firm. That was their first encounter.

Just then she rounded the corner, walking briskly into the hall, heading straight for him, a broad warm smile accentuating her face the moment they made eye contact. Cute as ever in a coy vivacious way.

Lingering thoughts of Noriko vanished.

Extricating a mussel from its shell with a small fork, Arnold casually asked, "You still messing around with your, ah, extracurricular activities?"

He tossed the empty shell into the bowl for that purpose and licked the white wine and butter sauce from his fingertips. A sauce worthy of being sopped up with hunks of French bread once the mussels were consumed. He'd asked her the question before, but she'd been evasive.

During the gig with Mr. Cain's law firm, he'd learned that Kara was a spare-time hobby hacker. Nothing serious or illegal. (That he knew of). Just enough to have a few serious chops at her disposal. It was this side interest of hers that bolstered his suspicion that there might be a way to employ her on this next caper.

His loosely linked logic went something like this: a paralegal with hacking skills with connections to lawyers in other law firms (including Larkin Standish) had to equal...well, *something*. Exactly what that might be remained ill-defined, yet it just seemed logical that there had to be some promise there.

She paused in the middle of forking off a piece of halibut, glanced up, appeared to take a moment to choose her answer.

"This and that," she said, rocking her free hand back and forth. "Why?"

"Nothing in particular, just wondering's all."

She made a dramatic display of slowly setting down her fork, then looking him dead in the eye for a beat before, "Don't give me that shit, dude. You wouldn't ask without a good reason."

He took a shot at the I'm-totally-innocent look, then stalled by dabbing his lips with the white linen napkin, then finally said, "No, seriously, just wondering."

His words sounded about as convincing as an infomercial. He experienced a fleeting pang of guilt for lying to her.

Oh well, it's for a good cause. Right?

Widening her eyes in mock surprise, she primly folded her hands in her lap, sat back in her chair, said, "As long as we're both *wondering* about things, why don't you to cough up some of the juicy details about that pen-test you guys pulled off over at Larkin Standish. You know you've been holding out on me."

See? She does have connections with the firm. I rest my case.

"As I told you last time, that material's classified," he said, a little taken aback. "We make it a policy to not kiss-and-tell."

"Word has a way of getting around, and I want to know what's actually true and what's becoming exaggerated urban legend."

"Shall I devote a moment to explaining what the word *classified* is intended to impart?"

Later that evening Arnold sipped a small glass of wine while trying to brainstorm a clever way of melding Kara into the Larkin Standish creep.

So far, he'd come up with zilch. She was a paralegal and a hobby hacker, but so what? Still, he could feel an idea submerged in the logic stew that had yet to clarify into a coherent plan. Or was this a perfect example of trying to force a play that wasn't there?

Yet part of him knew there was a play here even if he couldn't see it, but the clock was ticking, and he was still spinning his wheels. Meanwhile, Mizrahi's danger to Larkin Standish seemed to be growing larger by the hour. Mizrahi knew exactly what was in the offing and that his job—possibly his career—was on the line.

Allen Wyler

From Mizrahi's perspective, his survival in the firm hinged on making sure their pen-test failed. Of the numerous new tidbits gleaned during dinner was that word of the firm's prior pen-test was now abuzz within the tight-knit legal community, casting unfortunate attention on both the firm and Arnold's team. Being caught in the spotlight seemed to be an unfortunate complication of working for such a high-profile legal firm. Because it was putting more pressure on him and his team.

Then he was up, pacing, convinced there just *had* to be something in his idea, but what?

Well, why not break the skeletal plan into its rudimentary parts and analyze each component?

Cool.

He grabbed his notepad. It was clear that the biggest unresolved issue was how to access the utility room. Did he already have a workable key, or did he need to clone one from a maintenance worker? Was this where he suspected Kara could help? Yeah, matter of fact...but how that might possibly work remained obscure. Especially since she worked for Mr. Cain's firm instead of Larkin Standish. Yet, he continued to be convinced a viable option was there to work with.

On complete whimsy, he Googled Larkin Standish, and got a gazillion matches before he began honing down search parameters and scrolling though to see what might pop up and nudge his creativity. After two iterations, he felt he was making progress. Then on the next one, there it was! An advertisement for a legal secretary or paralegal.

Okay, but so what?

No, something was there. He just couldn't recognize it. Yet. Sat back and nurdled on the ad.

Legal secretary or paralegal...

Then was up, pacing again, frustration mounting over the idea he knew was skulking on the periphery of his consciousness. Back at the counter, he poured another small layer of cabernet into his tumbler wine glass, dropped back into the chair, and continued to churn the suspicion around and around. He reread the notice still up on the screen.

Boom.

There it was, staring him in the face. The Larkin Standish position had one major catch: it was *part-time*.

Was that freaking perfect or what!

Back up again, pacing, rehashing his on-the-fly plan, making sure he wasn't going crazy because it just seemed too good to be true. Perhaps run it past Prisha before going any further? He checked the time. Getting late. Hmmm...

He texted: *Okay to call?*

Thirty seconds later his phone rang.

"What up?"

Five minutes later he muted his cell for the night, downed the last of the cab from the tumbler, washed and inverted it on the drainboard, brought Chance in from the porch and headed upstairs, feeling a tad bit vindicated for his perseverance.

Assuming, of course, everything worked out. What if the position was already taken?

Chapter 20

MIZRAHI WAS SCROLLING back and forth through the Rubber Ducky payloads section on the Github.com website, searching for the perfect malware for trashing Gold's prized network.

So many options to choose from.

All various iterations of what looked like the same basic virus, trojan, or worm…it was confusing. Perhaps he should've ginned up a clever way to ask for a recommendation from his friend without giving the impression of being a complete amateur when it came to such nefarious items.

After all, he had an image to protect. Although the website's touted *raison d'être* was "to provide a repository of malware for people interested in researching the code," he knew that song-and-dance was one hundred percent bullshit.

The site was nothing more than a minimart for asshole hackers not smart enough to build original weapons. He, on the other hand, was using it as a one-time weapon against an enemy intent on robbing him of his livelihood.

After thirty minutes of scrolling, reading, and fretting, he zeroed in on a chunk of malware that he was pretty sure would inflict the destruction he intended.

And if it didn't?

He could pump his friend for more information and try again. He paid with his Bitcoin wallet, then downloaded the virus.

The moment the malware was in his computer, he disabled its wireless connectivity, thereby air gapping it. After rolling up his sleeves, he cut-and-pasted the malware into the Rubber Ducky.

The following morning Arnold waited until Kara should be at her desk before dialing her number. She picked up immediately.

After a casual exchange of greetings, he asked, "You happen to know a legal secretary or paralegal looking for work?"

"What's with you, Gold? You're not going clairvoyant on me, are you? Matter of fact, yes. The kid sister of a good friend just finished training and is looking for work. Why?"

"Because I know that Larkin Standish has a part-time position they're trying to fill."

Kara hesitated.

"I don't know, man...part-time? She's here in the city living in her sister's spare bedroom on a temporary basis until she can afford to rent her own place and her welcome's wearing a little thin. Her sister and husband really don't want her there forever and, truth be told, they're anxious to reclaim the space."

He was getting amped now, seeing a very real possibility materialize.

"Just bear with me a moment. Does your friend know her way around QuickBooks?"

"Wow, that's a pretty specific question. Why do you ask? As in, what's going on, dude?"

Arnold could feel the pieces of the puzzle clicking into place. Here was the connection between Kara and the caper he'd sensed was there but hadn't been able to identify.

Is this how a pig sniffs out a truffle: you know it's there but can't see it until you're right on top of it?

"So, here's the deal," he explained. "Depending on her skill set, it's extremely likely we can pick up enough hours to make the combined compensation equal a full-time job."

"Okay," Kara said hesitantly yet thoughtfully. "That's encouraging, except for one thing: so far I haven't heard a word about benefits."

True.

In his enthusiasm to make the deal come together he'd completely blanked out that component of compensation.

Quickly mentally regrouping, he added, "Let's not jump to any conclusions until we know more what the total compensation might be?"

"...Fair enough. I'll give you that. So, what is it?"

No idea. Yet.

He sidestepped a direct answer with: "Here's a serious inducement: our work's insanely flexible, so it can be done from home without set hours. Our only hard-and-fast requirement is to complete assignments in a timely manner. The lion's share of our work is bookkeeping, so..." He stopped. "What's her name?"

"Maria Sanchez," Kara replied.

"Okay, so why don't you call Maria, explain the situation, and ask her to call me if she's interested in discussing this further. If so, I'll put in a few calls to get the ball rolling, like in the next few minutes. I have no idea how many applicants they're getting so don't even know if they've already hired someone, so..."

Arnold Gold, high-pressure salesman.

Five minutes later Arnold's phone started playing *Three Hearts in a Tangle.* Maria Sanchez.

After introductions were finished, Arnold dove straight into the key question.

"How well do you know your way around QuickBooks?"

"Like the back of my hand," she said with a solid ring of confidence.

Enough to make him a believer.

"Fantastic. Okay, email me your resume the moment we hang up." Flashing on another ripple, he added, "Are you available for a brief interview in, oh, thirty minutes? I'd like another partner to talk with you. We good?"

Arnold Gold, kingmaker in action, working his magic.

"Cool."

Webster Collier wasn't free to return Arnold's call until mid-afternoon, and when he did, Arnold got straight to the point.

"Here's the deal. We're trying to find a legal secretary to help us manage our back office, but only need her part-time. Is there any chance your firm might need some part-time secretarial work?" he asked, as if totally unaware of the want ad. Then, before the lawyer could respond, added, "I'm trying to do is cobble together enough combined hours to generate a living wage for her. The great thing about our work is it can be done remotely without fixed hours. This anything your firm is remotely interested in? If not, I'll start calling around to some other contacts but wanted to give Larkin Standish the right of first refusal."

Collier laughed.

"Your timing couldn't be more impeccable, Arnold. We *are* in the market for either a part-time paralegal or legal secretary, but so far we haven't had any luck filling the position. It seems that nobody's looking for part-time work. What can you tell me about her?"

Arnold explained Sanchez's qualification then texted him her contact information. Mr. Collier thanked him and then ended the call.

Arnold dropped his phone on the charge disk next to his computer, sat back and wondered what else he might do to—if anything—to improve the odds of making this deal weave together. Probably nothing more than what he'd already done. It would either work out or it wouldn't. Time to just sit it out and see how things developed. But he did feel positive about his chances, and that spooked him.

Okay, so now what?

Well, how about going back over the plan for breaking into Collier's office?

He tried, but couldn't concentrate, not with this Maria thing flaming hot in his mind. At the moment, he needed a mindless task to focus on until things settled down. Well, there was always the SAM project downstairs. It still needed work.

After the new house was built, Arnold decided it would be prudent to build a fully functional, geographically remote copy of SAM in this location on the off-chance that Honolulu SAM went down for any reason. Although his island home seemed safe, you never knew what calamity might befall it. The out-of-the-blue wildfire that devastated Lahaina a while back served as a prime example of the unexpected, and he couldn't afford to lose SAM.

The inspiration to build the network spawned from Arnold's fascination with Nate Silver's work. A statistician, writer, and poker player, Silver developed a system capable of predicting the outcome of sports events and elections with uncanny accuracy.

In 2009 Silver was named one of The World's 100 Most Influential People by *Time* magazine after correctly forecasting the outcomes in forty-nine of the fifty states in the 2008 U.S. presidential election. In later years, some election predictions weren't as accurate, but by then Arnold was already a devoted disciple of his work.

SAM officially became a long-term project the day Arnold linked two computers together to form an elementary neural network: a form of machine learning that simulates the interconnectivity of neurons within the human brain.

Didn't take too many months of dedicated work before those two computers grew into a smoothly functioning network of twenty machines. Unfortunately, that original network became a smoldering heap of melted plastic and metallic debris when Arnold detonated an improvised explosive device in the basement of the family home, in a last-ditch scorched-earth effort at self-preservation.

Last-ditch because he was about to be executed by a group of radical terrorists after refusing to employ SAM to help them plan large-scale urban bombings. Within hours of that fiery blast, Hans Weiser (aka Arnold Gold) was tossing back miniature bottles of Johnnie Walker on a Seattle-to-Honolulu flight while the few remaining cell members were scouring Seattle, hell-bent on using his head as a hood ornament.

A few hours after Noriko handed Arnold the keys to his new Honolulu home, he was in Best Buy, picking up enough hardware to start rebuilding SAM as quickly as possible. Once the new computers were networked, all Arnold needed to do to resurrect SAM was download the last backup of Green Lake SAM from a cloud storage site and *voilà*, his neural network was up and running.

Arnold christened it SAM 2.0.

What exactly is SAM?

Well, think of it as an artificial intelligence package similar to Siri or Alexa, but with exponentially more power. As SAM's capabilities grew, so did Arnold's reliance on it for managing critical day-to-day chores, including actively trading his growing stock portfolio as well as monitoring the security systems for both homes.

Early on, as Arnold's reliance on the network began to increase, he realized just how critical it was for the system to never go down for any appreciable period. Consequently, he made sure that the spare room housing SAM had a backup power source as well as an independent temperature control. Automated routines ensured that the software was backed up to multiple cloud storage sites at midnight every day.

For any system as critical as SAM, it's always a good practice to have a clone system in a geographically separate location, ready to seamlessly continue working should the primary system fail. Soon as the Green Lake house was rebuilt, Arnold began assembling a clone, but because the bulk of his time was spent in

Honolulu, this project was taking a long time. But now he expected it would be up and running in a few days.

He was working on the project when Maria Sanchez called, all excitement and ebullience.

"I can't believe it," she effervesced. "Mr. Collier and the HR person hired me *on the spot* and wanted to know if I could come in for orientation first thing in the morning. I told them absolutely." After an audible inhale, she gushed, "I'm thrilled beyond belief! Oh, Arnold, thank you thank you thank you! You don't know how much this means to me."

And vice versa.

Talk about killing two birds with one stone...

"Cool," he said with heartfelt enthusiasm for her. But also, with glowing satisfaction for Gold and Associates. Both companies could now move forward. "Let me know soon as you're free enough for an online meeting to get you started. In the meantime, I'll send the link to our shared Dropbox account, and you can begin familiarizing yourself with our system. Welcome aboard."

After disconnecting, he glanced at his watch. Later than he thought. Better start getting things ready. Prisha and Vihaan were due to arrive soon for a working dinner.

Prisha, Vihaan, and Arnold were ensconced at their usual spots around the kitchen table scarfing pizza and Manny's Pale Ale when Arnold casually tossed out, "Remember I mentioned Maria Sanchez?"

Prisha squinted at him with a you-for-real? expression, then said, "Be kinda hard to forget since that was earlier today. Why, what's going on?" she said, setting down the pizza slice she was about to bite into, eyeing him suspiciously.

"Well, after interviewing her, I decided she'd be an excellent replacement for Rachael."

When Prisha didn't respond, he added, rather lamely, "She knows QuickBooks."

Prisha picked up the tranche of pizza again and began inspecting it, clearly borderline pissed.

Arnold swallowed. And waited for the explosion.

Registering that something was going on, Vihaan's eyes began oscillating from one to the other, not sure of the unfolding dynamic but acutely aware of something amiss.

A moment later she nodded, said, "Okay...so when do you want me to interview her?"

She skewered Arnold with an accusingly knowing glance.

Uh-oh.

"...Well, so, here's the thing. I made an executive decision to hire her."

Still eyeing the piece of pizza intently, head cocked slightly to the side, she said, "*Really.*"

One word. Neither question nor statement but delivered with sufficient *edge* to send an unambiguous message: he'd messed up. Should've run it by her. He knew this at the time, but just couldn't risk losing the made-in-heaven situation.

What was there to say other than, "Well, things just started steamrolling and..."

His sentence slowly petered out into the hollow oblivion of culpability.

After letting him marinate in his guilt a bit longer, she said, "I guess that's why we're named *Gold* and Associates" before finally taking a bite of the pizza.

"Ouch." He slumped in his chair, hoping to demonstrate regret. But his gesture came across as superficial and hollow because instead of feeling remorse, he was actually hugely relieved at having resolved a colossal problem. "Sorry. I know should've run it by you, but I saw a unique opportunity and didn't want to risk losing it."

"Oh, don't give me that bullshit, dude. Maybe you're a *little* sorry," she said, holding her index finger close to her thumb as a measure. "But I bet that remorse is completely swamped by the delight at finding a solution to a knotty problem." She locked eyes with him. "Am I right or am I right?"

Why even bother to answer?

Prisha paused to sip beer.

"She know it's only part-time?"

Ah, good. This meant she actually appreciated the pragmatism of his decision.

"See, that's the totally chill thing. Larkin Standish was looking for some *part-time* legal assistance, so I was able to swing a deal where her combined earnings come out to a living wage."

Prisha carefully placed the half-eaten slice of pizza on her paper plate, sat back in the chair, and slowly began wiping her fingers with a paper towel, a slight grin playing across her mouth.

"Ah, I get it now, you sly dog, you."

Eyes twinkling.

"Well, it might just work. We'll just have to be, like, super discreet is all."

Glancing questioningly at his wife, Vihaan asked, "What're you guys talking about?"

"Never mind. I'll tell you when you need to know."

Arnold picked up his phone.

"I'll call Brian so we can vote on it. Okay?"

Prisha paused, the half-eaten slice of pizza held up to her mouth again.

"Don't see why we need to vote on something that's already a done deal, but if it soothes your conscience, feel free."

She took a large bite.

Arnold told Brian Ito, "So we propose to replace Rachael with Maria Sanchez. You okay with this?"

After blowing a *pffffft* out the side of his mouth, Brian said, "Hey, if you guys think that's what we need, I'm totally down with it."

The phone was on speaker so everyone could hear the exchange.

Prisha added, "Cool. Soon as we're off this call I'll change the password to the Dropbox account," giving Arnold the eye, just to make sure he didn't forget this step. "We'll send you the new one via encrypted text."

Arnold added, "The only other significant housekeeping item is our Bank of America business account. I'll change that password too."

Prisha asked him, "Rachael can't access to your emails, can she?"

"Naw, we never shared shit like that."

"Before you guys start thinking about ending this call," Brian added, "how about an update on the test?"

"Still in the planning stage, dude," Prisha answered for Arnold. "We'll update you when we have something more definite hammered out."

Call finished, Arnold muttered, "As long as it's front and center in our collective minds, I might as well get these passwords taken care of."

He grabbed his laptop off the nearby counter.

With that job finished, they called Lopez to update him and give him the new Dropbox password.

Details taken care of, Prisha asked, "So this brings us to The Big Question." She paused dramatically. "You gonna drop the axe or you want me to do it?"

She was referring to firing Rachael.

Chapter 21

"OH, MAN...THAT'S a tough one," Arnold muttered, kneading his tightening neck muscles while remembering a time when a friend suggested that some of Rachael's behavior could be explained as jealousy over the amount of time he spent with Prisha.

He'd blown off the suggestion as absurd. Had that been a mistake? *Had* Rachael seen her as a threat? After all, two people can view the same painting and come away with very different, perhaps opposite emotions and impressions. We interpret our world through the sum of our personal experiences.

Perhaps Rachael saw more than a business relationship between them.

Which wasn't the case.

Did this factor into the disintegration of their relationship?

After thinking it over, he decided no, that he and Rachael lacked too many essential ingredients to maintain a truly sustainable bond. Rachael—the wiser one—had recognized this and moved out. The ironic twist to it all was that, in truth, she'd done him a favor. One he didn't fully appreciate until his dinner date with Noriko. Or even his brief socializing with Kara. Time and distance can certainly alter a perspective.

So, how would it play if Prisha delivered the news instead of him?

Did it even matter?

Well yeah, in a way it did.

Why, exactly?

Was it arrogance on his part to think that the messenger would make a difference to her? Maybe. Maybe not.

Who's to say she doesn't want out of the situation but isn't sure how to swing it.

And besides, wouldn't it be easier to delegate the task?

"Look, it's clear you're having a problem with this," Prisha finally said. "And I know it'll be super noxious for you. Hey, we all want and need it done, like, now. Face it: it's a distraction. And it's one we can't afford right now. Bottom line is, it's best for everyone if I just get it over with so we can focus on work. Lemme take care of it so we can move on. Agreed?"

Put like that...

"Perfect. Thank you."

A combination of relief and remorse flooded him. Relief that the issue would finally be settled. Remorse over cutting the very last tenuous connection with her.

No one spoke for several seconds until Prisha asked, "This mean we're done for the evening?"

She pushed up from the table.

Arnold raised his hand to stop her.

"Not quite yet. One more thing. We have a problem."

When she sat back down, he went on to describe stalker number two and the intrusion last night. She listened intently.

When he finished, she asked, "Whatdaya think's going on?"

"I think it's Mizrahi and I have a strong suspicion the female is one of the firm's investigators."

He brought Vihaan up to speed about asking Mr. Collier about her and his evasive answer that did nothing but increase his suspicions.

Seemingly puzzled at the story, Vihaan asked, "Why would he do something like that?"

Arnold was up pacing now. He'd been asking himself the

same thing since the first alarm.

"You referring to Mizrahi or Collier?" Arnold asked, then waved away an answer before Vihaan could clarify. "Mr. Collier's no mystery. He's trying to protect the firm. His evasiveness confirmed that for me." He paced off a few steps before: "As for Mizrahi? I have no idea…maybe he thinks that by getting inside my house he'll find our plans for the next test or he's looking to get back at me for getting aced last time. After all, you know how thin-skinned he is." He faced them: "Or am I sounding totally insane?"

Prisha shook her head.

"No, not really. Not given what we know about him. But this brings up the obvious question, if he's setting up some sort of reprisal thing, what's it gonna be? Any ideas?"

Massaging his neck again, Arnold resumed pacing.

"The other night, he was in and out in a blink. Like he knew exactly where to go." *Careful now, they don't know about SAM.* "Didn't touch a thing, at least not that I could see. It felt like he was there to check on something and I have every reason to believe it was my computer room."

"Computer room?" Vihaan asked.

The only other person who knew about SAM was Palmer Davidson, his lawyer. Even Rachael didn't really know what SAM did despite knowing he relied on it for a variety of things. He decided to not tell them. The fewer people who knew, the better. Even Prisha.

He simply said, "I have an office in the basement."

"In your basement?" she asked with a marked edge of skepticism.

Arnold shrugged.

"What can I say? It's quiet."

Vihaan: "Anything of value in it?"

"Couple computers is all," he quickly answered in an over-trivializing tone.

One he knew Prisha would pick up on.

She shot him a healthy dose of side-eye, like, *C'mon dude*, but said nothing.

After an awkward pause, she said, "We all know you're shining us on, but I assume you got your reasons. In which case I gotta ask, what exactly is it you want from me on this?"

He wanted her advice, but not at the price of telling them about SAM, which put him in zugzwang.

He cut a middle ground by saying, "I'm debating whether to show Mr. Collier the security videos and ask if he agrees that in spite of the balaclava, everything about him screams Mizrahi. What're your thoughts about that?"

Prisha looked at her husband, who shrugged. To Arnold: "I think we need to see the videos before we can even consider an answer."

He brought up the file containing the edited relevant footage of the two times he'd captured the male creeper, gave her the chair in front of the laptop, hit Play.

After watching the video three times, she sat back with a vague nod, said, "Gotta agree. Makes me wanta say it's Mizrahi, but that disguise makes a positive identification impossible. Which makes me think that Collier will refuse to buy it. After all, Mizrahi works for the firm, and Collier's priority is to protect their image."

She raised a hold-on-a-minute-I'm-thinking finger.

Arnold waited, mind going like crazy.

Prisha again: "If you're right about this being a vendetta thing, then you know that dude'll be back..."

She let the sentence trail off, a diabolical grin creeping over her face.

Arnold suspected he knew exactly what was coming next because he'd been toying with the same thought.

She finally added, "So instead of trying to rat him out—which I think will get us nowhere—how about we figure out an egregiously devious way to screw him over when he does?"

Next morning while putting the final touches on his attack, Prisha called.

Arnold answered the phone with: "What up, girl?"

"It's all taken care of."

Took a moment to sink in.

Then: "It's done? She's terminated?"

Terminated. Sounded so...harsh, cold, electric-chairish.

"Roger that."

A pang of seller's remorse struck, dropping the bottom from his gut as he grasped that Rachael was completely out of his life, that any thread of a relationship no longer existed. There was, however, an upside: Rachael was no longer their business manager. Paradoxically this realization brought huge relief, bookending a major disappointment in life, and finally freeing him to move on.

With a clear note of compassion, Prisha added, "Dude, if it's any consolation, when I finally talked with her, she was in Honolulu closing down the apartment, getting stuff ready to ship back here."

Yeah, that sounded about right.

Efficient Rachael wouldn't waste any time getting that chore off her checklist. Nurses have been in high demand since the pandemic burned out so many, so she undoubtedly had a good job lined up in here.

Although, he knew better, he couldn't help but ask, "How'd she take it?"

What exactly do I expect to hear?

Prisha hesitated, sighed reluctantly, then: "She asked why it took so long?"

Well, not that exactly.

"...Oh..." was all that came out before his voice trailed off into a morass of confusing disappointment.

What did I expect?

Didn't have an answer for that either.

Chapter 22

WITH THE MALWARE-LOADED Rubber Ducky securely in his front pocket, Mizrahi raised up enough to peer over the edge of the security wall and into Gold's kitchen. For forty-five minutes, he'd been watching the front of the house from the same shadowy patch of ivy the investigator had used.

Five minutes ago, having seen no activity in the living room area, he'd crept down the rutted compacted dirt alley at the back of the property.

From this vantage point, Gold wasn't in the kitchen either. However, his goddamn guard dog was stretched out on his side on the back deck, apparently sound asleep. Given the time of evening, Mizrahi suspected the little shit was out for dinner. Damn shame too, because if it weren't for that vicious attack dog, this would be the perfect opportunity to break in to install the malware.

Glanced around, self-conscious at being out here in spite of his excellent disguise and hiding place. He tried to dampen his anxiety by assuring himself he was completely hidden from prying eyes.

Mizrahi glanced at his watch. Still early. Probably just out for dinner. Maybe with his team. Because the pen-test had yet to happen, it was fair to assume they were still in the planning phase. And knowing Collier, Gold was probably under massive pressure to complete the job. Meaning he should return soon to walk his mutt around the neighborhood and get back to work.

Regardless of how long he needed to cool his heels back here in this fucking alley, he needed to strike first and do it tonight if he stood any chance of getting that little shit off his back. Resigned to waiting for however long it took, he lowered himself back onto his haunches.

Out of nervousness, he patted his pocket. No, his prized USB drive hadn't inadvertently slipped out of the pocket during the move from the ivy patch. Yes, it would be put to good use tonight.

Arnold had invited Prisha, Maria Sanchez, and Kara to join him at Uptown China as a way to get to know each other personally rather than just another disembodied phone voice or a two-dimensional face on a computer monitor.

After all, Arnold wanted Maria to meld into their smoothly functioning team. But he also wanted to continue defining a professional boundary between himself and Kara. (Having taken Prisha's well-directed advice to not muddy the referral waters.) And besides, he and Noriko were now texting multiple times a day, making him feel a bit, well, slimy about still being so attracted to Kara. On the other hand, she sure was tempting…

So far, the dinner seemed to be going as he hoped, with most of the chitchat ricocheting between the three women. Fine with him. Particularly, since such vacuous conversation (as he considered it) wasn't one of his fortes. He was especially pleased to see Prisha and Maria getting along warmly and hoped it soothed some of the sting of being excluded in the hiring decision.

Maria glanced from Kara to Prisha to Arnold while saying, "I can't stop telling you guys just how grateful I am for putting this job together for me. I mean, it's so insanely *perfect*. I was getting so bent out of shape, worrying that I was going to have to move back home…" During a pause, she seemed to rein in her emotions. "I mean, you all know how expensive rents are…" Then she shook her head. "The thought of having to move back to Wenatchee after all the effort I put into getting good grades. Oh, man, it's a huge relief to know I'll be able to get my own place soon. I know it'll be small and all, but at least it'll be mine. Thanks again."

She came across as an emotional Mount Vesuvius, spewing enthusiasm steeped in gratitude.

"When do they want you to start at Larkin Standish?" Arnold asked offhandedly, although he already knew the answer.

Maria's entire face exploded in a wide smile, crinkling the corners of her eyes.

"First thing in the morning. They want me to go straight to security for a photo ID keycard. Once I've been issued that, I'm supposed to go straight up to reception where someone from HR will give me the grand tour, but I know I won't be able to keep it all straight, there being so many floors and all. I'll probably be in a daze for the first week at least."

"Boy, they certainly don't waste time," Prisha remarked, sending Arnold a glance.

Maria gave an adamant headshake.

"Apparently, they've been trying to fill the position for weeks now, but no one seemed to want part-time work, especially without benefits. They hope I'll be able to take some of the pressure off the other paralegals and secretaries. Initially, while I'm getting my bearings, they'll have me just man the reception desk, which the secretaries have been covering. Apparently, they're trying to hire a permanent replacement for that position too. I plan to put the time to good use familiarizing myself with the office layout and who's who." Out came a nervous laugh. "I'm so excited. This is my first real job since junior college."

Arnold said, "I don't want to swamp you, but when you

finish up there tomorrow, Prisha and I'd like to walk you through a few of your responsibilities with us. We conduct all our meetings online. You cool with MS Teams?"

"Oh, totally."

Mizrahi pulled the recently purchased TracFone from his jacket and dialed Gold's cell. He knew the phone would log the incoming number, but so what?

The little shit wouldn't be able to trace it back to him.

Besides, as soon as the call was over, he'd power it down and dump it. Well, maybe use it once more before tossing it. Better yet just drop it out the window onto I-5 to become pulverized debris.

He listened to the connection link up, then ring once, twice, three times before, "Hello?"

Mizrahi just listened intently for telltale background noise, like a TV: anything to hint at where the asshole might be. Ah, there it was: restaurant chatter and clatter. Three more seconds and he was convinced Gold *was* out for dinner.

"Hello?" Gold repeated.

Mizrahi made a snorting sound to keep him on the line a few moments longer while he verified his initial impression.

"What?"

Yes, Mizrahi was certain now that Gold was at a restaurant. Good. Mission accomplished.

He cut the call, slipped the burner into his back pocket, settled down between a garbage container and a recycle bin to wait. If the little shit stuck to his routine—and there was no reason to believe he wouldn't—he'd be back soon to take that vicious watchdog out for his evening walk. Giving him more than enough time. After all, the job required simply plugging the Hak-5 into any USB slot on any of the computers for two seconds and the entire network would be toast.

Dinner over and Jenny off at the front desk with his credit card running the tab, the four of them stood.

As Maria and Kara prepared to leave, Arnold said to Prisha, "Let's stick around for a moment. I have something I'd like to discuss. And besides, I need to get my Visa card."

Kara said to Maria, "C'mon, I'll drive you home. You have a big day tomorrow, girl." Then to Arnold, "Thanks for dinner."

They all hugged, said one more goodbye, and then Kara and Maria headed off, munching their fortune cookies.

Arnold and Prisha settled back into the booth in comfortable silence to polish off the dregs of their Tsingtaos and relax after what had actually been their first business meeting with Maria. Arnold broke apart his cookie and began to pop little chunks into his mouth, one by one, taking his time to savor each taste explosion. No matter how full he felt, his stomach always seemed to have enough room for a fortune cookie.

He finally broke the silence with, "I suspect we'll need to start her off with the bare minimum while she gets up to speed at the firm, right?"

Prisha picked up the last cookie from the round white dish and began to disassemble it using Arnold's technique by first snapping it in half, then pulling apart the sides.

"Yeah, pretty much figured we'll initially go easy on her."

Just then, Jenny appeared with the black vinyl folder containing the slip to sign along with his Visa card. Arnold busied himself replacing the credit card in his wallet before the distraction of computing the tip, having learned the hard way how easy it can be to forget.

Finished the paperwork, Prisha told Arnold, "C'mon, I'll drive you back."

He stood, slipped the wallet into his front pocket.

"Sort of planning on it, since you drove me here."

She punched him lightly in the ribs.

"Asshole."

As they were leaving the restaurant, the alarm on his phone began vibrating.

Shit. Stalker again.

Had to be. Without bothering to look at the screen, he silenced the alarm and slipped the phone back into his pocket, figuring he'd wait to review the footage on his laptop. He much preferred the resolution of a monitor to his phone. Not that it mattered in this case. It was Stalker, and Stalker was Mizrahi. It was that simple.

Once in the flow of traffic, she asked, "Okay, dude, time for the big one: now that you've planted a spy in the firm, how's she's gonna help us hack their network? That is, after all, your reason for breaking your neck getting her placed there. Or did I miss something?"

Elbow up against the side window, right temple cupped in his hand, Arnold was staring blankly ahead, consumed with the plan he'd been refining for the past thirty-six hours.

Prisha glanced at him before returning her eyes to the road, negotiating their way up and over the top of Queen Anne hill and down the other side to eventually merge onto Aurora next to the venerable Canlis restaurant; a route selected to avoid the insane congestion on eastbound Mercer Street this time of evening. The path was longer than cutting down Mercer, but in practice, quicker.

"Still working on it," he finally said. "Sorry. I know I'm way behind on this, but I'm having some serious difficulty getting it smoothed out. Yeah, it's roughed out, but..." Turning to her, he said, "Hey, look at the bright side: Rachael's replacement's now officially on board and that's huge progress, right?"

She appeared to consider this a moment before nodding, then said, "True, but that doesn't change the fact that we're, like, light-years behind on fulfilling our commitment to Mr. Collier. The longer Mizrahi remains on the loose, the more likely he is to use the nuclear option. Do that, we take a gonzo hit. Which neither of us want. What I'm saying is we need to get this job done, like, tomorrow. After all, this is your part of the test, man. Give us something."

Both his hands went up in a "what-can-I-say" motion.

"I know, I know. I'm on it. Having the Rachael thing off my plate has done wonders for my creativity. Trust me, I'm on it."

"Are you *really?*" she shot back with a definite touch of *attitude*, like hey, there's a new sheriff in town. "Because I'm not super convinced, dude. Tomorrow's Friday and far as I know we have exactly diddly-squat."

He blew a long slow breath, frustrated at his lack of progress—frustrated at Mizrahi for skulking around the neighborhood playing Secret Agent with about as much finesse as a prepubescent male fantasizing a ninja-warrior role.

Which, as long as he was on the subject, was probably just another factor derailing his creativity.

He vaguely registered that they were now breezing north along Aurora, approaching Green Lake.

Turning to her, he said, "This Mizrahi thing's part of what's bogging me down."

"What thing? The unidentified stalkers?"

"Exactly."

"Haven't we been over this? He's casing your house. So what? You said there's nothing inside worth stealing. And besides, I thought we had a plan for him if he escalates it to the next level. I mean, what's the big worry? Or is there more to this story and you're holding out?"

She cast him a suspicious glance before returning her eyes to the road.

Once again, he considered giving her a watered-down rendition of his SAM project but nixed it. The fewer people who knew, the better. Period. She was dead on about a couple things; there was more to the story, but he wasn't going to mention SAM.

"Don't worry," he said. "I'm just about there."

"Well, if it's any consolation, I'm not having any luck scooping you on this one, dude."

As the car dropped back into the lull of road noise, Arnold

realized that he couldn't remember if she'd ever turned on the radio.

Several minutes later, as Prisha accelerated from the curb, Arnold opened his front door to be greeted by Chance doing his happy dance.

Arnold spent a moment on his hands and knees, face to face with the pooch, giving him choobers.

Time for his end of day walk.

As he was getting back up off the floor, he realized he owed Noriko a text. Pulling the phone from his pocket, he remembered the alarm that went off as they were leaving the restaurant. Instead of texting Noriko, he opened the security app to view the video.

Sure enough, the back yard CCTV camera had been triggered by the stalker peering over the back wall. Mizrahi. No question in his mind.

Was the asshole still out there?

A definite vibe said yes, and knowing this slithered a chill along his spine.

That asshole.

Leaning his back against the counter, tapping his phone against his palm, Arnold walked through the plan he and Prisha doped out the last time that bastard snuck into the house. So, Mizrahi now knew computers were down there. Did he know their function? Highly unlikely. But that was beside the point. Point was, he intended them harm.

Why else take the risk of entering the house?

To steal them? Nope. To damage them? Most likely.

Why? A reprisal of some sort seemed about right. Or as a warning to back off from doing anything about his unauthorized surveillance system? Some sort of eye-for-an-eye threat? Perhaps, but there was no way to know for sure. The one thing he did know for sure was that he intended to send Mizrahi a clear *Don't fuck with me* message.

Arnold flashed a vertical palm at Chance, said, "Stay," then started preparing his message.

Mizrahi watched Gold stroll into the kitchen, clip the halter over the dog, pull out his phone as if answering an email or text, unclip the leash, and then vanish into the basement. He waited. A moment later, Gold was back, reclipping the leash to the halter, then walking the dog into the front room.

Perfect.

They would be gone for a few minutes. And to his amazement, Gold forgot to close and lock the French door again. Perhaps he intended to not go much further than up the block and back. But that would be more than enough time. What an incredible stroke of good luck. Mizrahi was over the moon with exuberance.

After giving the little shit a sixty-second head start, he was up over the wall, across the backyard and into the kitchen, then down to the special computer room. He flung open the door, flipped on the lights, and was immediately struck by *something...not...quite...right.*

What?

Ahh, total silence.

Total silence? He did a double take at the rack of equipment.

Fuck.

Every piece of equipment was off. It was the hum of the power supply fans he wasn't hearing.

That fucker!

But wait.

Why not simply slip the Rubber Ducky into a USB port so that when he powered them back up...

Yeah, that might just work. Taking a step toward the rack of computers, he noticed a bright yellow Post-it note stuck to the edge of the middle shelf. Leaning in, he read the hand printed note: TOUGH LUCK MIZRAHI. NICE TRY, THOUGH.

"Fuck!"

He wanted to hit someone or something and looked around. The rack? Yeah, push it over. Pressing both palms flush against the middle shelf, he tried to push, but it was heavier than it looked. More importantly, time was evaporating quickly. Too quickly. Gold could be back at any moment and the last thing he wanted to cap such a bad evening with was to dance a tango with his fucking guard dog.

Then he was back in the kitchen heading for the wide-open French door when a laptop on the kitchen counter caught his eye. He stopped, listened, heard no scraping or skittering of paws on the polished concrete floor, so the Hound of The Baskervilles was still out. He would undoubtedly hear the door open, so he could spare a second for a closer look. Huh. A Dell.

Is it password-protected? Because if not…

He poked the power button, and voila, the computer awoke, having been left in sleep mode instead of being powered off. Not only that, but it didn't require a PIN or password.

Man, talk about lucky!

He was about to insert the Rubber Ducky into the USB port when it dawned on him that he'd destroyed his old Lenovo when preparing the malware for the flash drive. Clearly Gold's fault. It only seemed fair that rather than buy a new machine…

The moment Arnold opened his front door and unclipped the halter, Chance rocketed straight to the kitchen, barking, paws skittering against the polished concrete. Calmly, Arnold secured the front door, hung his windbreaker in the coat closet, then drifted on into the kitchen to pour a glass of cabernet.

The first thing he looked for was the laptop. For a long moment, he stood staring at the empty space on the stainless-steel counter where it'd been placed, then walked downstairs to check out SAM.

The moment he saw the computers untouched a wave of relief engulfed him. Next, he checked the circuit-breaker box. The tape covering the switch for the computer room remained intact. Another huge surge of relief. Satisfied, he threw the switch to the room circuits, then powered SAM back up.

Back in the kitchen, he grabbed his wine tumbler from the drainboard and poured a glass of his favorite Rutherford merlot. With his wine on the counter breathing, he ran upstairs to the master closet, retrieved his utility laptop, schlepped it back down to the kitchen, secured the French doors, then settled in at the kitchen table to savor his first sip as he waited for the computer to fully boot.

Once the laptop was ready to go, he scanned *The New York Times* to catch up on the news.

After reading a few articles of interest, Arnold checked his watch. Forty-five minutes since booting the computer. More than enough time for Mizrahi to make it home. Assuming, of course, that was his destination.

Wait a little longer or give it a try?

Stupid question. He'd lose nothing by giving it a shot.

After savoring another sip of wine, he typed the commands to connect him to the Command-and-Control trojan embedded in the stolen laptop, then waited to see if a connection could be made.

Had Mizrahi powered it up yet?

If not, he'd try again in the morning. He watched a link establish, followed by another. Then, voila: he was looking at the wide-angle view from the stolen laptop's webcam, the angle tilted slightly upwards, catching the top of a chair, a bookcase behind that, and at the very top of the image, a wall met a ceiling.

Mizrahi's apartment?

Activating the microphone, he could hear vague background clatter. He watched and listened for several uneventful minutes. Just as he was about to pack it in for the night, Mizrahi's image filled the screen as he tucked into the chair, then leaned forward to use the keyboard.

Arnold smiled.

Gotcha, asshole.

Chapter 23

Saturday Morning

MIZRAHI SET A fresh mug of steaming black coffee next to his new laptop and began to scroll through the installed apps. Interestingly, Gold only had one email account: Hotmail. Hotmail? Couldn't believe a self-respecting techie purportedly as knowledgeable as Gold would use such a security-compromised email account.

He checked the contents of the Inbox folder.

Empty.

Same with the Sent and Deleted folders.

Strange.

Either the little shit had it programed to delete all emails in real time, or this computer was used only for tasks too trivial to move his lazy butt away from the kitchen table to his real computer.

Or—as he began to think it through—was it used only as a terminal to wirelessly control the basement network. Yeah, that made more sense. Regardless, this machine was a perfect replacement for the cheaper one he'd trashed while loading up the Rubber Ducky.

First task on his agenda was to replace Gold's Hotmail

account with both his home and Larkin Standish accounts. With that task finished, he began to rummage through the installed apps looking for ones to remove.

Didn't find any non-essential ones.

Apparently, Gold preferred to run a machine trimmed to bare essentials. Finally, he checked out the security software, discovered that Gold was running Microsoft Defender.

Perfect.

No need to change that either.

Later today, he would toss his infected machine into the donation basket at the Westlake Avenue Goodwill store. That way, they couldn't refuse to accept it, leaving them with the expense and hassle of recycling it, unless, of course, they kept it to sell to some unsuspecting schmuck.

He smiled at his plan.

Yes, things were working out perfectly.

He began humming *Heigh-Ho Heigh-Ho It's Off to Work We Go.*

Saturday Afternoon

Freshly showered and shaved, Arnold took Chance downstairs to the kitchen to let him out into the back yard while he put fresh kibble in his dish.

He started toasting a slice of Ezekiel bread on which to slather extra-crunchy peanut butter mixed with honey. Finally, he poured a cup of freshly brewed coffee and settled in to scan the latest updated stories on *The New York Times.*

Breakfast finished, Arnold washed the plate and knife, replaced them atop the toaster oven for the next morning—Mr. Efficiency—then, poured another cup of black coffee before tucking back into the kitchen table. Chance seemed content to remain stretched out on the back porch sampling the scents of the morning. After all, it was extremely pleasant out.

Took only a few keystrokes for Arnold to be back inside his

stolen laptop. Although the machine appeared to be protected with Microsoft Defender, it wasn't. Instead, it was loaded with access routes.

With that piece of housekeeping taken care of, Arnold turned his attention to the Mail app.

Perfect!

Mizrahi had replaced Arnold's Hotmail account with two of his own: a personal Gmail account and his Larkin Standish account.

Outrageous!

Arnold phoned Prisha and Lopez, explained the evolving situation, and asked them to spend the next hour clearing their decks of projects in progress because if all went well, they would need to devote one hundred percent effort to Phase One of the penetration. They were overjoyed. The project was finally gaining traction.

"Roger that," Prisha answered. "You want Vihaan working this too?'"

"You bet. I'm even putting Brian on it."

Call finished, the pressure was on. This next step was critical for the success of the entire plan. Rubbing his palms together, he blew a long calming breath, then slipped back into the stolen laptop and signed into Mizrahi's Larkin Standish account.

With the email account open on one screen, he used a fake email address on his own computer to send Mizrahi a malware-infected email. In a matter of seconds, the infected email arrived in Mizrahi's Larkin Standish account. Arnold immediately clicked on the attachment, which released a chunk of malware into Mizrahi's office computer that would immediately begin spreading throughout the law firm's email network.

Working quickly but meticulously, Arnold removed all traces of the infected email, then backed out of Mizrahi's computer. Now, unless Mizrahi was watching him in real-time, he would be completely unaware that Arnold now controlled the firm's email network.

Eventually, a routine anti-malware scan would find the initial trojan and remove it, but Arnold was counting on his team embedding some less obvious back doors before the Larkin Standish techs could stop them.

For a luxurious moment, Arnold slumped back in his chair to bask in this delicious respite from stress—although he knew it would only be temporary. After slipping off his glasses, he shut his eyes and massaged the bridge of his nose and inhaled deeply. The first step of his plan was now complete.

He blew a long slow sigh of relief.

A moment later, he signed into their chat room, where the other team members were assembled and shooting the shit, waiting for him.

Soon as he was signed in, Prisha asked, "How'd it go?"

"We're in. I'm texting the relevant info...now."

He clicked on the file he'd put together with step-by-step instructions for getting into Mizrahi's Larkin Standish email account.

"Everyone got their assignments?"

Prisha answered for the team.

"That was the topic of conversation a moment ago. We're primed. Amped in fact, now that we're starting to roll."

"Then I'll leave you to it. Will check back in a bit."

Arnold slipped off his headphones, stood, ran through his stretch routine, then haltered Chance. They'd stroll over to PCC to pick up some eats while Prisha managed the team's choreographed wolf-pack assault on Mizrahi's Larkin Standish emails, searching for ones that dealt with the North Sound security enhancements.

Once back in the kitchen, Arnold logged back into the team's chat room.

Within an hour, they'd uncovered numerous exchanges between Mizrahi and Glass discussing a second pen-test. In itself, this was no big deal, because follow-up tests were common. But what Arnold found seriously concerning was that the guards had fingered them the instant they'd set foot into the lobby. Clearly, they were on hyper-alert, specifically for them.

Well, hell, what did he expect?

Even more fascinating was the apparent united, yet uneasy alliance Glass and Mizrahi had forged from having a mutual adversary: him.

The meat of the search turned out pretty much exactly as they'd anticipated: North Sound had added a package of sophisticated analytics to their two major building-wide monitoring components. A state-of-the-art facial recognition package was added to the CCTV monitoring and an AI algorithm analyzed each employee's work and access patterns in real-time based on their keycard usage.

Now, if an employee fobbed any access port—door or elevator—anywhere in the building, the computer compared the time and location against their database. If, say Employee X accessed a stairwell door or elevator outside of their routine hours, the on-duty guards were to immediately view the video footage and sign off on it as relevant or not.

Along with this human verification, the facial recognition software confirmed if the video image matched the card holder. In essence, humans verified the AI algorithms while the AI software verified the human's performance. Admittedly a tad Big Brotherish, but, hey, it certainly represented a massive improvement over the slipshod monitoring that had been in play during the prior test when Arnold and Prisha were able to move floor to floor because the guards were watching other, more strategic areas.

Incorporating active facial recognition into the system effectively did away with that shortcoming.

Bottom line: there was no way they could use the stairs for this pen-test. This time, all the access routes were monitored tighter than a freaking Supermax one hundred percent of the time. Computers didn't take coffee breaks, pit stops, or play solitaire while on the clock.

Goddamn computers never cut anyone any slack. Ever.

Unless, of course, someone brought them down...

Leaning back in the chair, fingers interlaced behind his head, Arnold pondered this problem for, like, the gazillionth time.

Although their assumptions of what enhancements were added proved to be correct, being forced to face the reality was daunting. A game-changer. A workaround might prove problematic.

"The only good news to all this," Arnold told the group, "is we now know exactly what we're up against. We're just going to have to modify our plan accordingly."

Prisha was the first to state the obvious.

"Sounds to me like we need to find a way to game the algorithm. Anyone have any experience with this?"

When no one spoke, Arnold offered, "I know a guy who can probably give us some advice."

Prisha asked, "Yeah? Who?"

"Goes by the name Radical Dood. I know a few places he hangs, so I'll start looking soon as we're done."

Arnold checked his watch. Getting late. And they'd been at this for several hours now.

And besides, his bladder needed a break, so he said, "Why don't we reconvene first thing in the morning?"

But it wasn't really a question.

Chapter 24

Monday Morning

ARNOLD STEPPED FROM the elevator into the familiar Larkin Standish lobby of neutral-gray industrial nap, floor-to-ceiling plate glass, two uncomfortable small gray couches with six equally uncomfortable matching club chairs, two black coffee tables with perfectly stacked, non-political magazines such as *Architectural Digest* and *National Geographic*.

Maria Sanchez was manning the reception desk, squinting at a monitor, typing. She glanced up at Arnold the moment he stepped off the elevator, a wide smile blossoming across her face in obvious recognition.

Arnold's right hand held a vase of variegated red-and-yellow tulips from the Skagit Valley. His left hand was holding a letter-size manila envelope.

Approaching the desk, he proffered the vase to her with: "Here, these are for you." He dropped the envelope on the desk. "And this contains the signed copies of the papers I promised Mr. Collier."

She accepted the vase of tulips with a beaming, admiring smile.

"Oh, they're beautiful. I just adore the colors. Thank you."

"I brought it from home, so there's no water in there. I was too afraid of spilling it."

"I'll take care of that right now," she said, pushing up from her desk chair. "I'll be right back."

She scurried off toward the ladies' room just to the left of the row of elevator doors.

Soon as she was out of sight, Arnold made a show of glancing down at his feet and saying, "Oh crap, my shoelace."

He knelt behind the corner of the desk as if to tie his laces while quickly slipping a malware-loaded Rubber Ducky into Maria's computer USB port, transferring a malware payload into it, then was back up, strolling innocently toward the elevators as Maria came out of the restroom, water-filled vase in hand.

"Oh? Leaving so soon?"

"Yeah, I need to get back to work. Just came by to drop off your flowers and the paperwork."

"Oh, okay...thanks again, Arnold," she said in passing.

As Arnold punched the Down button, he called to her over his shoulder, "Please make sure that Mr. Collier gets that envelope ASAP," in a voice loud enough to be picked up by Mizrahi's microphones.

With a nod, she said, "I'll take care of it right now," and promptly set the vase on her desk.

While awaiting the elevator, Arnold called Lopez. Carlos picked up.

"It in?"

"Roger that."

"I'm on it, boss."

Plan was for Lopez to use the malware Arnold just implanted to quickly embed another back door into the firm's device network: the one connecting the individual computers to various devices throughout the firm like routers and printers. More importantly, this was the network that Mizrahi's surveillance system used for monitoring conversations.

Getting their hooks into this specific network was the next

critical step for their strategy to succeed. Although they were already into the firm's email server, that network was totally separate from the firm's other two networks.

Arnold was counting on Glass's crew notifying Mizrahi the moment he set foot in the massive, polished granite lobby. If so, it stood to reason that he would be watching him exit the elevator into the firm's reception area. And if—as Arnold believed— Mizrahi's surveillance remained in place, he'd just watched him kneel beside Maria's computer and would recognize the move for exactly what it was: a ploy to infect her machine.

If so, he would take the computer offline, like, ASAP. At this point it was a flat-out race to see if Arnold's team could embed other access points before Mizrahi could shut down the computer.

Arnold's money was on his crew. But you never knew about these things…

Officially, it was game-on.

Itzhak, Gold's on his way up to thirty-six," Lorna Glass said over the phone.

"Thanks, Lorna."

Mizrahi dumped the handset back into its cradle, then swapped the right monitor from the Spider solitaire to the overhead bubble-cam view of the thirty-sixth-floor elevator lobby.

A moment later he watched Gold come breezing off an elevator with a bouquet of flowers in one hand and a manila envelope in the other, heading straight for the reception desk.

Mizrahi quickly toggled from the lobby's overhead CCTV to the built-in webcam on the reception desk monitor, then switched his left monitor to the camera in the picture frame on the wall directly behind the desk. The desk phone was bugged to catch sounds in the immediate area. Ensemble, the devices provided him excellent audio and visual monitoring of all activity in the vicinity of the reception desk.

He watched Gold hand the new hire a bouquet in a glass vase while dropping the twelve-inch clasp manila envelope on the desk and listened to their seemingly innocent exchange.

Innocent, my ass. That little fucker's up to something.

Then, as Maria headed toward the restroom with the vase, Gold knelt down to supposedly tie his shoelaces. Bullshit.

Fucking knew it!

Mizrahi was up and out of his chair and at Serge Valchenka's cubicle in two seconds flat, banging on the wall to catch that incompetent fool's attention. The Russian slipped off his headphones and turned flat eyes to his boss.

"Yes?" he asked in a notably bored tone.

"Gold just implanted malware in the reception-desk computer. I want you on that machine *right now*." Slapping the partition for emphasis. "Get it the fuck out of our network, then find out what malware that little shit just installed in it. I want to know what it is the moment you find it. And you *will* find it. Is this understood?"

The Russian continued to study him with flat eyes. "Or?"

Initially, Mizrahi found himself at a total loss for words. A split-second later he squelched the urge to bitch-slap that smug silly shit-eating grin off the worthless asshole's face. As satisfying as that might be, it would only delay getting that computer off-line. He considered running down to reception to pull the plug himself, but that would only embolden the Russian. No, he needed to stand his ground and exert his dominance. Not only that, but he needed the Russian's help.

"Or," Mizrahi said as calmly as possible, "we'll all be looking for new jobs."

"Oh."

Mizrahi continued locking eyes with the asshole, never wavering, boring down, making his point emphatically clear.

Finally, with a nonchalant nod, the tech returned his attention to the monitors, slipped his headphones back on and poised his fingers above the keyboard.

Mizrahi leaned in, pulled back the left earpiece, yelled, "I want that information *now*."

He let the earpiece snap back into place.

Without a word, Valchenka slowly removed his earphones and casually pushed out of his chair to stroll off toward the stairwell. Mizrahi watched until he saw the heavy fire door securely close behind him before barreling straight for the elevators. Glass needed to be updated.

Chapter 25

BACK HOME, ARNOLD nuked a mug of hot chocolate, carried it to the kitchen table, and checked the time. Still a few minutes before the scheduled team meeting, so he quickly checked on SAM.

Per usual, the network was humming along, keeping on top of his portfolio while taking care of other routine tasks. Rechecked the time.

Still a bit early, but what the hell.

He logged into the chat room and found the team already logged in, shooting the shit.

"Sorry guys, if I knew you'd be on early, I would've joined you."

"No prob, dude," Prisha said. "Just taking a break. It's been pretty frantic, as you can imagine. How'd it go at *The Firm?*"

Arnold said, "Carlos?"

Lopez laughed.

"Smooth as a skating rink. He pinged me on his way out and I was on it, like, *boom.*" He made an exploding-fist motion. He beamed at the webcam. "We now have three additional access ports in place, and I'll work on embedding a few more soon as we're done."

"Anything look different from last time?" Arnold asked,

referring to the network map in general but the unasked motherlode question in particular: was Mizrahi's surveillance network still operating?

"Weeelll, that all depends," Lopez answered, with a playful tone. Messing with them, stoking their anticipation.

"C'mon, dude, out with it," Prisha said.

"First a disclaimer. I haven't been able to check out all three networks. But so far, nothing looks like it's been changed. In other words, our map's still valid."

The law firm's three networks included a small public Wi-Fi access for clients, the email network, and finally the major device network connecting all the firm's workstations, printers, routers, and other equipment.

"They patch the zero-day vulnerability in the printers?" Arnold asked, referring to the known security flaw they'd exploited last time.

Lopez shook his head, saying, "Haven't had time to check that one yet. That's, like, way down in my priorities, man."

Then he was grinning at the webcam, like a freaking Cheshire cat.

After a few silent seconds Prisha said, "Oh for Christsakes, dude, you gonna make us ask?"

Lopez's grin broadened.

"Yep."

"Jesus!" Arnold said, shaking his head. "Fine. Is Mizrahi's system still functional?"

"Totally, man. Totally untouched."

Arnold whistled, shaking his head harder this time.

"Lordy. That dude's in for a world of hurt."

Dead silence for several seconds.

Finally, finger-combing his hair, Arnold said, "Don't know about you guys, but I'm not inclined to rat him out."

"What's that supposed mean?" Lopez asked. "You want to give that asshole a pass? After all, isn't this our primary objective this time?"

"For sure," Arnold answered, "But I just don't want to dime him is all."

"Why not?" Lopez asked.

"Because I want to work it so that dick rats *himself* out."

What started in Prisha as a girlish giggle crescendoed into a full-out gut-wrenching hoot.

Between breaths, she gasped, "Oh, man, if you can pull that off, it'd be, like, totally elegant. Just super karma."

"Just how are we going to pull off something that outrageous?" Vihaan asked.

Arnold explained his plan.

A loud bang echoed off the hollow metal door to Mizrahi's office, abruptly shattering his concentration. He spun around to glare at the intruder. Valchenka was slouching just inside the threshold, wearing his usual silly vacant grin.

Mizrahi glared back at him. Valchenka just stood there, waiting to be asked. That passive-aggressive fuckwad.

"What!" Mizrahi finally conceded, his patience wearing thin.

Besides, he needed to know.

"I found it."

What the hell was that supposed to mean? Mizrahi shook his head. "You're seriously pissing me off, *tovarisch*. And I guarantee you don't want to do that. What exactly did you find?"

"A trojan."

After waiting three seconds for him to explain in greater detail, Mizrahi resigned himself to being dragged into his sophomoric passive-aggressive game if that's what it took to get the information and then get him out of his office.

"Try being more specific, Valchenka. What kind of trojan is it and what did you do with it?"

The tech dug an index finger at something in the vicinity of his upper right molar, inspected his fingernail, seemed satisfied with the result, then, after flicking off his finger to his right, said, "A common, run-of-the-mill Zeus." Pause. "I quarantined and removed it, of course," he said with an implied: *What else would I do with it?*

"You can stop with the fucking *attitude*, Valchenka," Mizrahi muttered while absentmindedly drumming a black Bic against the desk, already deep into his next steps. After a moment, he realized his tech was still there awaiting further orders. Mizrahi asked, "Did you initiate a full system scan?"

"Of course." With even more attitude.

"Well then," he said with a back-of-the-hand shooing motion, "quit standing here and get back to work."

The Russian stared at him an additional silent moment before abruptly turning and disappearing into the hall.

What he'd really wanted the Russian to tell him was whether the malware had been isolated from the network before Gold had a chance to use it against him. But there was no way for the Russian to know. It all depended on whether Gold's crew had been standing by to exploit that advantage before the machine could be removed from the network.

What were the odds.

Fifty-fifty? The good news was that he'd been watching when Gold made his little bush-league untied-shoelace ruse. This incident served as a prime example of how essential his surveillance system was. It boggled his mind that Collier and his pals would want to dismantle their most effective defensive weapon. Didn't make sense. This incident was more than enough reason for him to keep it intact until this threat was resolved.

If he could only prove to Collier just how useful it was...

But what if Gold *did* have his crew standing by? What if they were somehow able to miraculously embed additional access points before Valchenka isolated the computer from the network?

In that case, he had a serious problem on his hands.

The only way to find out would be to run full system scans, but these would only find known malware and the odds were that Gold's team was using their own.

Then again, this whole scenario made no sense because if

Gold knew—or even suspected—that his surveillance system remained intact, why make such a blatantly obvious move?

Huh.

That made no sense at all.

Unless that little shoelace act was a diversion. Because it certainly focused their attention on that machine...

But a diversion for what?

Something didn't add up. He thought through the logic again. Why risk such a blatantly obvious move if you knew you're being observed?

Huh.

Unless, of course, it was some weak attempt at a psych-op to completely throw them off. Thought about *that* for a moment too.

Still couldn't see a way for it to benefit Gold.

Fact was that his bush-league move had been identified for exactly what it was: an attempt to hack the network. An attempt that was subsequently neutralized. Why expose your hand by making a move you knew would fail? Was Gold that naive? Had it failed? What had actually happened during that sequence?

The only way Gold's move would make sense is if he believed he could get away with it because he thought the surveillance *had* been removed.

But knowing Gold's character, he found this difficult to believe.

A quick check of his watch.

How many minutes had the malware actually resided in the computer?

Ten? Couldn't have been more than ten. Taking the machine offline so quickly mitigated the risk of any damage being done. Ten minutes just wasn't enough time to do much at all, if you really thought about it.

And besides, Valchenka probably isolated the infected computer before Gold cleared the lobby. Unless, of course, his crew had been standing by, ready to work on exploiting the malware…still, ten minutes wasn't very long at all.

Huh.

Yet the question lingered: why would Gold do something so blatant if he knew the chances of success were slim at best?

Didn't make sense.

What did Gold know that he didn't?

The Bic was drumming harder and faster now, beating out a staccato tattoo.

Chapter 26

SLOUCHED IN HIS desk chair, Serve Valchenka stared bleakly at the center screen in an arc of three monitors. He faced a huge problem, one fueling a major stream of acid eating into the pit of his gut.

It went like this: a routine anti-virus scan had just uncovered an especially gnarly piece of malware, the Mebroot trojan. What made this particular chunk of code so malignant was that it gave the embedder—in all likelihood, Gold or a team member—complete access to the infected computer.

Total access!

In other words, it was very possible that someone from Gold's crew had been in the network for...? He had no idea how long. Could be minutes to hours. No way to know.

Fuuuuuck!

He'd been notified of the intrusion just minutes ago when his center monitor went apeshit, flashing big red letters across the screen that their security software had just detected malware. He, of course, immediately neutralized and removed the trojan.

That wasn't the issue now doing the funky chicken on Serve's gut. His problem was that Itzhak Mizrahi had received the same automated notice at exactly the same time, so any moment—

Bam!

The slam of the fist on his desk, caused a butt to spasm strong enough to raise him a half inch. Wide-eyed, he spun around, came face to face with Mizrahi glowering lightning bolts.

"I took care of it immediately," Valchenka stammered without prompting.

Mizrahi's glare intensified.

Tick tick tick.

"What?" Valchenka finally asked.

"What do you mean, *what?*"

Again, dead silence.

"Can you try being more specific?" the Russian asked.

Mizrahi crossed his arms, his glare never wavering.

"How long was it in there?"

Bingo.

Without thinking, Valchenka hiked his shoulders in a how-should-I-know motion, a move he regretted instantly because of realizing it would inflame his boss even more.

"It's impossible to pinpoint an exact time, but since those scans run continuously, it couldn't've been more than a few minutes."

A lame attempt to trivialize the exposure because, well, with such a large network it could be up to an hour. But he was in survival mode and doubted Mizrahi knew the time required for a full system scan.

Mizrahi gave an overly dramatic, exasperated sigh.

"Let's try to narrow this down a bit, shall we?" As if addressing a second grader. "How long ago did we discover the trojan?"

Valchenka swallowed and checked the digital clock tucked into the lower right corner of the screen and started drumming his fingers on the desk. "...Let's see...it's twelve twenty-seven now and I removed it ten minutes ago, which would make it twelve seventeen, so I'd estimate somewhere between one and seventeen minutes." He shrugged. "It's impossible to narrow it down any more than that."

"In other words, you have no idea how long we were infected," Mizrahi said without any attempt to disguise his disgust.

Another shrug.

"Guess that's one way to look at it…"

"Which tells us two things, doesn't it?" Being rhetorical, Mizrahi plowed ahead with, "First, you need to scour every fucking byte on every fucking server, printer, and router in this firm to guarantee nothing else's in there. Are we clear?"

With an acknowledging nod, Valchenka asked, "And the other thing?"

Mizrahi froze in mid-pivot, shot a glance over his shoulder, said, "It should be clear that our jobs are on the line. Do *not* let this happen again."

Valchenka rolled his eyes soon as Mizrahi turned away.

Two halls and one elevator ride later, Mizrahi stormed into Lorna Glass's office to deliver the bad news.

At the start of their team meeting the next morning, Arnold said, "Had a very productive meeting with Dood last evening. His reputation remains intact. And I'm embarrassed to not have seen it."

He shook his head, disappointed with himself, it now seemed so obvious, making him feel like an idiot.

"His explanation was, like, forehead-thumping easy when you think about it. Both the facial recognition and workflow AI analytics are nothing but basic machine learning. Which pretty much mirrors the way we learn. Take facial recognition for example. First time we see someone we store that image in memory for future reference and tag some relevant additional information to it, like, hey, that's so and so. Later, when we see them, we search our memory for a match. Newborns very quickly figure out what mom looks like, so when they see her again, their little computer registers a hit. The way computers learn facial recognition is simple. When image of a face is captured, the

Allen Wyler

software takes measurements of numerous distances that remain
constant so the face can't be disguised. Like the distance between
our eyes or the distance from the base of our nose to the upper
lip, etcetera etcetera. The computer stores these measurements
in the facial recognition database for future comparisons. So, for
example, when Maria stopped by building security to have her
keycard issued the other day, they took her picture, right? A
perfect straight-on facial shot and maybe a profile. Providing the
best angles for measuring. Well, the computer then broke the
image down into various measurements that are stored in the
facial recognition database. Same thing for everyone else who's
routinely in the building. Plus, anyone else of interest, like Prisha
and me." He paused. "So now, when a CCTV camera images me
waiting for an elevator, the computer computes as many
measurements as the image allows, then searches the database for
a match. If I'm in there, *voila*, it alerts the guards. The same basic
principle applies to establishing and analyzing work patterns."
Pause. "With me so far?"

He'd be surprised if they weren't.

They all nodded.

With a sly grin, Arnold continued: "So, the best way for us
to get around these enhancements is—"

"To diddle our records in their database. That's where
you're going with this, isn't it," Prisha stated through a wide,
white-tooth grin.

Arnold aimed a finger gun at her.

"Bingo. There's even a name for this: a data-poisoning
attack. The super cool thing is you don't need to make much of a
change for it to work. Small changes can be totally effective.
Those self-driving taxis they're testing in San Francisco? Put a
traffic cone on the hood to block the front camera and it's dead in
the water. There's a ton of other examples. And, far as facial
recognition goes, you only need to change a couple measurements
to totally disable it."

"In other words," Lopez offered, "on top of everything else, we now need to hack North Sound's security network too?"

Arnold grinned.

"Guess you were paying attention after all."

Lopez blew a long whistle before saying, "Oh, man! You know what a bitch that's going to be."

"Seriously," Arnold said. "But just wait till you hear what I have in mind for the rest of the attack."

Chapter 27

PRISHA DROVE HER white Camry up the ramp, into the office building's cavernous first-floor parking garage, circled around a stout concrete pillar painted yellow, and nosed into one of the diagonally angled twenty-minute free parking stalls conveniently located adjacent to the elevators to the lobby, allowing clients sufficient time to run in, drop off or pick up paperwork from a tenant, and escape within the allotted grace period before their astronomical parking fees kicked in. A compensation for the total lack of downtown street parking.

Got to keep the tenants happy, right?

As she jockeyed the car into the stall, Arnold called Vihaan and asked him to stand by, but to keep the connection open so he and Lopez could monitor what was happening and respond accordingly.

Then they were out of the car, ball caps pulled low, brims hiding their faces from the overhead CCTV. They marched through lingering scents of oil, warm tire rubber, and cigarette smoke straight to the stairway to the right of the elevators. Arnold swiped his Frank Smith clone across the wall-mounted card reader beside the door and was greeted by the satisfying metallic snap as the clasp disengaged.

He opened the heavy metal door for Prisha, then followed

her quickly up the stairs to the door into the lobby.

They stopped on the landing and Arnold raised the phone and asked Vihaan, "Ready?"

"Roger that."

Arnold looked at Prisha. She nodded.

They pushed through the fire door on into the cavernous polished-granite lobby of squint-inducing sunlight angling down through three-story windows and marched straight to the centrally located security booth where, in a loud voice, Arnold announced, "Excuse us," while staring straight into the man's glistening gray eyes.

He caught an immediate flicker of recognition, even though the guard tried to mask it.

Having the guard's undivided attention now, Arnold said, "Please tell Ms. Glass and Mr. Mizrahi that we wish them a pleasant and productive day. You *will* be sure to do that, won't you?"

While Arnold was saying this, Prisha was discreetly aiming the Flipper Zero at the guard's keycard. After hearing it beep softly, Arnold turned to her: "Anything you to care to add to that, Prisha?"

Shaking her head, she dropped the small device in her coat pocket.

"Nope, think we're good." She flashed her full-on signature white-tooth smile at the befuddled guard, cocked her head for a pensive beat, and added, "Oh almost forgot. Have a nice day, sir." She flashed the peace sign.

Arnold tossed him a curt salute, did an about-face, marched straight back to the garage elevators with Prisha in lockstep. With the guard now watching their every move, they couldn't afford to use the cloned keycard.

As Prisha cautiously backed the Camry out of the parking space, Arnold switched Vihaan to speakerphone.

He asked, "Did everybody catch the drama?"

185

"We did," Vihaan answered.

Brian Ito and Lopez were logged onto their chat room, stationed at their home computers.

Lopez chimed in.

"Dude seemed at a total loss on how to deal with you. Doubt he has anything in his playbook to address such a bizarre situation, but I'm sure by now Glass and Mizrahi are scratching their heads along with him. They know it's part of our attack but have no idea what the object is. Suspect it's driving them batshit."

"I hope so," Prisha said.

"Where're you now?" Vihaan asked, a note of excitement in his voice.

"We're exiting the parking garage. Speaking of which, how're things going on your end?"

"Me?" Vihaan seemed momentarily surprised. "I'm sitting in their email server watching a shitload of messages fly past. You'll be ecstatic to know that Glass just sent Mizrahi a detailed account of your little drama. The entire encounter was recorded and she's now poring over that. From Mizrahi's last email, it sounds like he's heading down to the monitoring room to view it with her."

"Yeah, for all the good that's going to do him," Arnold mumbled.

"Glass suspects it's a deliberate fact-finding mission of some sort but isn't quite sure what your target was. She asked der Führer his opinion, but he seems just as lost as she is. Guess that's why he's heading down there."

"Did they even guess?" Prisha asked, sounding surprised and perhaps a bit hurt.

She was waiting for the red-and-white striped exit gate arm to arc up.

"Nope, but I attached a trojan to his email, so it's now embedded in her computer. Haven't had time to activate it yet."

"Well hell, get to work then instead of chatting us up, dude," Arnold told him.

The guard arm was up now, so Prisha began slowly nosing

out across the sidewalk, caught a lucky break in traffic, turned left, heading up the steeply inclined one-way street.

Vihaan: "Okay…there it goes."

Lopez said, "I'm on it. Sending out commands now."

The virus that Vihaan had attached to Mizrahi's email was a standard remote access trojan, or RAT. Once embedded in Glass's computer, it would give them total access to it.

As Prisha waited for the traffic light to change, Lopez said, "Okay, we're in."

Ito: "Roger that. I'm all over it."

This being a perfectly synchronized group effort with everyone having an assignment, especially now that they controlled both Larkin Standish's and North Sound's networks.

Vihaan: "Okay, boss, time to get to work. We're out of here."

"Good luck."

The team was now racing to lock down additional access points in various devices like printers, routers, and other servers before North Sound's antimalware protection could detect and neutralize the initial RAT. Each person's role in the complex orchestrated attack had been precision-planned and designated; Lopez was to establish five additional access ports before shifting over to help Ito and Vihaan, search the device network specifically for the facial recognition and keycard workflow databases.

Team members would share and record vital information on the fly via ongoing connection via their chat room, as well as store crucial information on a dynamic database in their shared Dropbox account.

After Arnold and Prisha fist-bumped, he told the group, "We'll join the party soon as we finish an important business meeting," then disconnected the call and plugged his phone into Prisha's charge cord.

She glanced at him.

"What important business meeting you referring to?"

Wedging himself between the door and seat, he tried to

relax as best he could. Until now, he didn't realize just how tense
their little scam was making him. He laughed, more as a tension
reliever rather than from what the question.

"Lunch. What else would I be talking about?"

"Should've guessed. You're so food-oriented." She shook
her head in amusement. "Good call, though. I'm totally starved.
Whatdaya have in mind?"

"There's this great little Thai joint off Green Lake with killer
food. Assuming we can find parking." Parking was a routinely a
monumental thrash in the area. For Arnold, living close by, it was
a chip-shot walk, one he didn't mind, unless it was pouring. "Oh,
and I'm paying. No arguments. You drove, so this'll even things
out."

And once again, he flirted with the idea of getting a set of
wheels for those times he was here. It was a big expense,
though...

After a thoughtful pause, Prisha said, "Well, since you put it
that way..."

Up ahead, a parked car's left turn blinker began flashing.

Arnold sat bolt upright.

"Stop! Grab that spot! Jesus, girl, let's go buy a Lotto ticket.
This is freaking unbelievable."

Seated at an outside table, they ordered Pad Thai and cashew
chicken to split, with only water to drink.

The moment the waiter vanished with their order, Prisha
asked, "Now that we've gone through all the trouble to clone that
dude's key, guess first thing we need to find out is how much—
if any—additional access this gives us. Wanta venture a guess?"

Arnold had spent most of the drive here tossing the question
around.

"No way to know for sure, short of just trying it out. But last
time, we learned that North Sound doesn't have permission to
access any of the Larkin Standish floors, right? I mean they can
physically go there, if need be, but they've agreed to not patrol

those floors, right?"

"Right," Prisha agreed. "But that's not the issue. Question is, do any of our keys open that utility closet? Or am I missing something?"

"Nope. You're right. Cause if none of them do, we need to steal one from maintenance."

Prisha nodded.

"Just making sure we're on the same page."

At which point, they settled into their own thoughts, silently working on the problem. The present iteration of their skeletal plan was for Arnold to hide in the thirty-sixth-floor utility closet until the offices cleared out sufficiently to sneak into Mr. Collier's office, snap the money shots with his phone, then get the hell out of the building without being nailed. The operative word in that last sentence was skeletal. A lot of sinew needed to be packed onto those bones for the plan to have more than a snowball's chance of succeeding.

So far, the major stumbling block was devising a reasonable strategy for getting up to the closet without everyone in the freaking building knowing about it. This dearth of fresh ideas was weighing Arnold down. Being creatively dry was so not him. Usually, his problem was trying to sort through all the dynamite ideas banging around his brain getting in the way of one another. Not this time.

Arnold said, "I think it's super critical to know if their tracking system tracks the guards' keys. Because if it doesn't, we'll have a ton more latitude."

"No shit. But that's totally off-point. There're all sorts of things that'd be *nice* to know but aren't essential. Plus, we don't have time to find out. We're not there yet and we're already out of time, so let's just stay focused on the end game, okay?"

Prisha swiped her fingertip down the side of her water glass, then rotated it to repeat the process, creating stripes though the condensation, forming little puddles at its base.

Silence.

Allen Wyler

"Speaking of the utility closets, where exactly are they? Do we know?" Prisha asked. "I vaguely remember seeing them in the general floor plans…like, in that vicinity behind the central core but am pretty sure I've never actually laid eyes on one."

Eyelids closed, Arnold dredged up an image of the floor plan he'd used in laying out the initial test.

"I want to say you're right," he said. "They're definitely part of the central service core with the elevator shafts and lavatories. I believe they're, like, directly behind the men's room?" Thought a bit more, then nodded. "That makes sense, on account of they probably share some of the same plumbing runs as the toilets. When I get home, I'll pull up the plans to nail that point down."

He used his phone to send himself a reminder.

Prisha cocked her head and studied him a beat.

"I know you want to hide in there, but that could be, like, for hours. What happens if someone needs a mop, and opens the door? You'd be royally screwed."

Just then the waiter brought their orders. Once alone again, Arnold answered her with a sarcastic snort.

"I don't have a freaking clue. But first things first. Right now, we need to find out if any of our present keys—Collier's, Smith's, and the guard's—can open that door, right?"

Prisha was too busy with the serving forks dishing a sizable portion of Pad Thai onto her plate to bother answering. Finished, she offered them to him.

"Want these?"

"Yeah, thanks."

He did likewise, but mostly on autopilot now, his mind working on how to find out if their keys opened the door in question.

Suddenly, Prisha dropped her fork on her plate to stare at him. He raised his eyebrows and waited.

"Would it be totally crazy to ask Collier to try them out for us?" she asked. Then she shrugged, and added: "I mean, seriously, why not?"

"Interesting suggestion…"

His knee-jerk reaction was to reject the suggestion.

But why?

Arnold carefully replaced the serving forks on the plate, his mind now consumed with the question. That would certainly expedite matters. Yet, for some reason, it seemed…well, wrong.

Why?

Well, for starters, that's not how a pen-test was supposed to work. A well-designed test should probe real-life security. Having your employer slip you past security seemed counterproductive.

Okay, but then why go to all the trouble of getting Maria Sanchez planted in their offices?

Well, that was easy: he was primarily trying to find a replacement for Rachael and wasn't really planning on using her unless something became obvious. But on further thought, why not leverage this new relationship to solve their problem? He was pretty sure this idea had been percolating in the back of his mind all along, but for some reason had been floating below the surface of consciousness.

"Hey, Arnold, here," she said, handing him the serving utensils for the cashew chicken.

"Oh, thanks."

Now he had both sets of serving forks, he realized. Oh well…

They fell back into silence, Arnold running the plan one way, then the other, putting on some finishing touches.

Several mouthfuls of Pad Thai later, Arnold glanced up at Prisha, said, "I'm thinking we get Kara's help on this."

Squinting at him, she carefully set down her fork.

"Seriously, dude? How's that supposed to work?"

He held up a just-a-minute finger and said, "Give me a moment. I'm putting on the finishing touches on it."

Worked it a moment longer, decided it might just succeed.

He laid it out for her.

Chapter 28

IT TOOK ARNOLD'S team twenty-four hours of intensely focused all-hands-on-deck effort and some Red Bull, to find exactly what they were looking for.

First, they had to locate the facial recognition database buried within the building's hypercomplex computer-based security system. Once inside it, they faced the challenge of decoding and sorting through a morass of files until they found the data sets for Arnold and Prisha.

Then came the task of decoding the fields to understand them well enough to be able to diddle Arnold's data just enough to disguise him without disrupting the system.

When they finished that portion of their to-do list, Vihaan began pushing for a break. But Arnold and Prisha argued they were already too far behind. Before making a change to North Sound's database, they went back over each step in their methodology to make sure they weren't overlooking something that might trigger suspicion.

In spite of a clean review, Arnold's anxiety cranked up a few notches.

The question they were debating was whether to manipulate the database now or wait until the last minute. Solid, valid arguments could be made to support both approaches, but the group finally decided to leave the database untouched until it was absolutely essential to alter it.

He couldn't know if they might need to use this in the future, so it was best to minimize the risk of being discovered. Then, to diminish mistakenly activating a tripwire or triggering another alert, they carefully backed out of the database and collectively exhaled a mondo sigh of relief.

Which especially delighted Vihaan, the team's taskmaster for the routine work, because now they could focus on whittling down their accumulating backlog. But only after getting some much-needed sleep. It was now 8:12 AM. He got no arguments from the group.

To celebrate this major steppingstone, Arnold invited the crew over for a dinner that evening of pizza and kale salad. And their newly adopted go-to beer, Rainier, now that Anchor Brewery, the brewers of Anchor Steam, had been forced to close shop after one hundred and twenty-five years.

A damn shame, far as the team was concerned.

The now-rested team assembled at Arnold's—well, except for Brian Ito—for dinner. Once the initial feeding frenzy began settling down to the point of contentedly sitting back to enjoy their beer, graze, and generally shoot the shit, Prisha leaned over the table and asked Arnold, "She down for it?"

Meaning Kara.

"Down for it? Hell girl, she jumped all over it."

Shooting him her famous side-eye, she said, "Just as long as that's the only thing she jumps on."

Arnold laughed, almost blowing a mouthful of beer through his nose, swallowed and sniffed.

"Not to worry."

Although they were now officially way behind Mr. Collier's rather aggressive schedule, Arnold was pleased with the progress made and the plan developed.

Mizrahi leaned back in his desk chair with his right foot propped up on the half-open bottom desk drawer, sipping a cup of strong black tea, scanning through the various cameras strategically situated throughout the six floors, keeping a finger on the pulse of the firm when he eyed a perky little redhead stride confidently off an elevator making a beeline toward the reception desk.

Which, considering she didn't work for the firm, was appropriate. The thing that caught his attention was the *vibe* that seemed to be radiating from her, giving him pause. His right foot thudded against the linoleum as he rocked forward to activate the audio feed from the desk phone and caught Maria Sanchez saying "—and punctual as ever."

"Before we do anything, let me make a trip to the ladies' room," the cute little redhead said, glancing around as if searching for it. "Where is it?"

Sanchez pointed an index finger.

"Just to the left of the elevator you came out of. That's one of the very first things I learned." She gave a girlish giggle while pulling out the right bottom desk drawer to extract her purse. "Take your time. I need to call my relief anyway."

Mizrahi watched the cute perky redhead turn and retrace her route to the ladies' room while Sanchez notified her relief that she was ready to leave for lunch.

Why does she look familiar?

Call finished, Maria opened her purse, withdrew a compact, and began to check her makeup. A few minutes later the redhead was back and together they strolled over to the elevator bank and pressed the Down button. Mizrahi looked at the redhead more closely.

I know you...

"Huh," he muttered, unable to place exactly where he'd seen her. She hadn't done anything *overtly* suspicious, yet a cloud of skepticism hovered over her presence; that she had done something while out of view, that she was working with Gold in some way. He had no idea what she might've done, but the more he dwelled on what he'd just seen, the more convinced he became that she was a Gold operative and was here to facilitate the pen-test in some way. Then he realized that she was the tasty morsel he'd seen with Gold in his kitchen.

Now he was convinced she was working for him.

After pushing out of his chair, he steamed down the hall, decided to not wait for an elevator, so hurried down the north stairwell to thirty-four, then stood at the door to the ladies' room asking himself what he expected to find inside. Didn't matter. It was something he needed to do.

He cracked the door just enough to call out, "Security. Anyone in here?" With his ear to the opening, he only heard silence, so pushed open the door wider and yelled louder, "Security. I'm coming in."

The interior of the restroom looked perfectly normal. Checked the two stalls. Nothing suspicious. And again, asked himself what did he expect to find? Again, he got the same negative answer. Yet...

Back in the hall, standing just to the right of the elevators, he replayed events just as he'd watched them play out.

What was it about the interaction that ignited his suspicion?

Ahh, it suddenly came into focus.

It hinged on the little redhead being friends with the new receptionist as well as with Gold. And now it wasn't the redhead he worried about; it was the wetback.

Yes, this was beginning to make more sense.

Gold had shoehorned her into the job to be his agent, his spy. Either with or without Collier's blessing. In fact, the more he mulled over this theory, the more he believed it. He wouldn't even be surprised if Collier was a willing contributor, plotting to overthrow him. His misgivings about the redhead and wetback began to gel into more than mere suspicion.

It now made perfect sense that a half-time position that no one seemed to want was suddenly filled. Especially coming directly on the heels of the decision to move ahead with a follow-up pen-test. The entire scenario was targeted at destroying him. If it weren't for his surveillance system, he would be conducting business as usual without any inkling of the threat barreling straight toward him. Any doubt about keeping the system intact was swept away. For it had just proved itself essential to his survival.

He turned to look at the reception desk again.

Yes, those little bitches were up to something directed against him.

Their entire charade was just too suspicious to be benign.

Arnold opened his front door with: "C'mon in. Thanks for picking them up."

"No problem. It was right on the way," Kara lied.

Flavio's Pizzeria wasn't even close to being right on her way. But Arnold was grateful for her saving him from breaking momentum to run over and pick up the food. She breezed straight past, on into the kitchen, trailing the mouth-watering aroma of salty grease and melty cheese from the two standard-fare pies: a fennel sausage and a mozzarella, tomato sauce, and basil. Both with extra mushrooms.

Per usual, the rest of Team Seattle was clustered around the kitchen table talking shop. Conversation ceased, as if this were a bar scene from a bad spaghetti western, all eyes on Kara now.

After a few silent seconds, Arnold asked, "And?"

With a coquettish smile, she levered the pull tab on a beer can, then indulged in a long leisurely pull.

She held up the can for inspection, and smiling even more wickedly, said, "Great beer."

"C'mon girl, out with it," Prisha said.

The smile morphed into a Cheshire-cat grin as she fished out three keycards from the back pocket of her skin-tight black jeans and handed them to Arnold with: "You're in luck, dude. They all open the thirty-sixth-floor utility closet."

Fist bumps all around.

After the cheers died down, Arnold told the group, "I know

we're all getting sick of this, but let's go ahead and review every detail one more time for anything we may be missing."

The crew groaned in unison.

"Humor me. Tomorrow's D-Day. We can't afford any mistakes."

He raised his beer can in a salute.

Chapter 29

FIRST THING IN the morning, Arnold called Mr. Collier's office. Tony, his assistant, answered with, "Webster Collier's office. May I help you?"

When Arnold asked to speak with Mr. Collier, Tony explained, "I'm afraid he's tied up in a meeting and is not expected to be available until noon at *the earliest*."

Of the many times Arnold had visited the office, he'd met Tony only once. Hard as he tried, he couldn't dredge up a mental image of him.

"Please give him the message that Arnold Gold called with a critical issue to discuss. Ask him to please return the call soon as possible. Again, it's important."

"I'll be sure to give him the message."

"Wait. I'll amend that. Tell him it's *urgent*, okay?"

"An urgent message. I'll be sure to tell him that. But I can't guarantee how soon he'll be able to return your call, Mr. Gold."

Just to be sure, Arnold emailed the lawyer the same message.

Sitting on a patch of grass, back against the gnarly trunk of a Douglas fir, Arnold amused himself by watching an endless procession of joggers, mother-propelled baby carriages, and flaneurs circle the perimeter path of Green Lake Park. He was munching a tuna salad on whole wheat from PCC while Chance's nose explored various patches of grass and shrubs. Just one more lovely day in the park despite the nag of guilt for not working.

On the other hand, he'd read that taking breaks like this periodically was beneficial for long-term well-being and productivity. And besides, Chance needed the exercise, and he needed lunch. So there.

His phone's ringtone started in.

"Arnold, Webster."

His typical succinct greeting.

"Thanks for returning my call, Mr. Collier. I know you're busy, so I'll make this short. I have information you need to hear *in person* in your office, so please let me know what time works for you."

Collier hesitated, Arnold suspected, to check his afternoon schedule.

"Unfortunately, I'm chockablock until late..." A thoughtful pause followed. "Why don't I have Maria meet you in the lobby at five thirty and bring you up to my office straightaway since I'll be on a conference call until then. I'm sorry to make it so late in the day, but that is my only option. Will that work for you?"

Arnold couldn't tell from the lawyer's tone if he suspected what was afoot but hoped so.

"Perfect. See you then, but Mr. Collier?"

"Yes?" Collier replied, drawing out the word.

"So that Maria isn't away from her desk too long, why don't I meet her on thirty-four and she can just fob me up to your floor? That work for you?"

When Collier didn't answer immediately, Arnold swore he could hear the gears turning in the lawyer's brain, reading between the lines.

"How considerate of you, Arnold. Yes, that will work. Thank you."

5:17 PM

Maria was at her desk, looking intently at her monitor when Arnold entered the muted grays of the Larkin Standish reception lobby. She glanced up and beamed at his approach.

"You look busy," Arnold told her.

She pushed out of her chair.

"I prefer it this way, actually," she said, and pulled out a desk drawer to remove her purse.

Arnold motioned for her to stop.

"Tell you what…I know how to find Mr. Collier's office, so why not just fob me up in the elevator, and not waste any more time away from your desk?"

She hesitated in an apparent internal debate, then nodded.

"Oh, okay. I know he's expecting you." She escorted him across the gray industrial nap to the elevators.

"How's the job working out so far?" he asked, partly out of curiosity and partly for Mizrahi's benefit if he was watching, which was very probable.

"Oh, it's great." She beamed. "Thanks again for lining it up for me. Really appreciate it."

Soon as the elevator doors parted on thirty-six. Arnold stepped from the cage to the left of the doors but still within view of the overhead CCTV. He removed his iPhone and pretended to be thumbing a message but was actually recording the width and length of the main hall as well as the distance to Mr. Collier's office door with the Measure app, then stored these values in the Notes app.

Mission accomplished, he returned the phone to his pocket and took off for the lawyer's office.

Mizrahi countered the aggressive pawn advance with a devilishly clever knight move, forking a bishop and a rook. An excellent, very canny move, he admitted in spite of having the game level set low enough for a cognitively impaired third-grader to trounce it. Nevertheless, he loved being able to thrash the machine.

Who wouldn't?

The desk phone rang, shattering his concentration.

"Good afternoon, Glass," he said cheerily, while exchanging his knight for the rook.

An excellent exchange. Just excellent.

He smiled additional approval at his choice.

"Gold just walked through the lobby on his way up to your reception desk."

Mizrahi exercised masterful restraint by not telling her just how cold her "hot" news actually was, having listened in on the earlier phone call between Collier and Gold.

Only moments ago, he'd watched the little shit stroll from the elevator onto floor thirty-four to exchange greetings with his accomplice, Maria Sanchez. If Glass only knew the extent of his capabilities...but she didn't. And he intended to keep it that way. Although he was pretty sure she *suspected.*

With his winning chess position brightening his mood, he decided to humor the treacherous cunt.

"Thanks for the intel, Glass. I'll take it from here."

Mr. In Control, the King of Security for Larkin Standish, at your service.

As Arnold entered the lawyer's office, Mr. Collier was leaning back in his desk chair, phone to ear, apparently listening. Making eye contact, he raised a just-a-moment finger, then pointed to the two guest chairs facing his desk.

After acknowledging the offer, Arnold cast an exaggerated glance around the room before handing him a note along with a nod at the computer monitor.

The lawyer leaned forward in the chair and craftily palmed the note while seeming to study the monitor a beat, before straightening back up and saying into the phone, "Yes, yes, I'll pick it up on the way home and no, I won't forget. Bye."

He gently placed the phone on its cradle.

"Now," Collier said, leaning forward on the desk, addressing Arnold. "What can I do for you?"

"Thanks for working me into your schedule on such short notice, Mr. Collier."

Mr. Collier motioned for him to take a seat.

"Thanks, but this should only take a moment."

Leaning back in the chair again, Mr. Collier crossed his right leg over his left then cupped his knee within knitted fingers.

"What may I do for you? You said you had something important to discuss."

"I do. I wanted to give you the bad news in person." He made a dramatic pause while glancing pointedly at the monitor on the desk. "Because of pressing unforeseen circumstances, we need to delay the pen-test for at least two weeks, maybe longer. I'm really sorry to have to do this, sir, especially knowing how anxious you and Mr. Smith are to wrap up this issue but there's nothing I can do about it."

Collier searched Arnold's eyes briefly before acknowledging the message with a barely perceptible nod.

"I *am* sorry to hear that, Arnold. And yes, you are correct. I—well, we—*do* want this matter seen to as expeditiously as possible, but I do understand how unforeseen issues sometimes have a nasty tendency to crop up when you least expect them and derail planning. I assume you'll let me know the moment you're ready to proceed?"

"Oh, absolutely, Mr. Collier. Bank on it." Pause. "Well, that's all I wanted to say. I felt I had to deliver the bad news in person, is all."

"I appreciate your thoughtfulness," Collier replied, pushing out of his chair.

He strode around the desk, extending his right arm toward the doorway, saying, "Allow me to escort you to the elevator."

While in route, Collier whispered, "Nicely played" from the side of his mouth.

As Arnold pressed the Down call button, Collier said in a normal voice, "Enjoy the rest of your day," then pivoted a one-eighty to return to his office.

Arnold waited until the lawyer was almost twenty feet away before scooting toward the north stairwell and out of view of the overhead CCTV. At the door to the north stairwell, he swiped Mr. Collier's keycard clone across the sensor, heard the metallic clack of the lock disengage but was already moving fast, past the entrance to the men's room, around the corner of the central core, heading toward the back hall.

He halted at the door to the utility closet, quickly replaced Collier's key—banded with neon pink tape for easy identification—with the chartreuse banded one cloned from the unsuspecting guard. Spent a moment to make sure it was the right card before swiping it across sensor.

The lock clacked as the red LED turned green. Opening the metal door, he stepped into the utility room, shut it behind him, flipped on the single overhead fluorescent lighting fixture. Quickly, he slid off his rucksack, dug out his radio, thumbed transmit.

"I'm in."

"Roger that," Prisha replied.

Startled, Mizrahi shot bolt upright, eyes welded to the CCTV feed, an intense queasiness exploding in the depth of his gut. Something felt seismically off-kilter. He knew it. Just fucking *knew* it. Gold and Collier just walked briskly into the elevator lobby, shook hands, and Collier did an about-face to return to his office. But Gold—that squirrelly little shit—went scurrying off toward the men's room like the little rat he was.

Five fucking minutes ago.

His gut sank.

Where the hell did he go?

Grabbing his handheld from the charger, he squeezed the transmit trigger.

"Glass!"

Several seconds later: "That you, Itzhak?"

"Quick, check activity on the north stairwell door on thirty-six."

After a long hesitation, "I'd be happy to if I knew why you're making the demand."

With his free hand, he flipped her the bird.

"Just do it." *Perhaps…* "Please."

"Man, can't believe you're really going to make me ask again? *Why?*"

Mizrahi was up pacing now, back and forth between the front and back wall of his small, cramped office. Three steps, turn, three steps, turn…

"No time to explain, Glass, just tell me if a stairwell door was opened?"

"Okaaayyy…hang on…"

He could hear what sounded like the clacking of a keyboard.

Then, "Yep, the north stairwell door was opened, oh, a little over five minutes ago. Why?"

Mizrahi waved away the question despite being alone in his office.

"Whose key was used?"

"…Your boss, Collier. Why?"

"Because that's impossible. He's in his office."

Another brief pause.

"Perhaps he opened it for Gold?" she said as if grasping for an explanation.

Mizrahi shook his head.

Dumb fucking bitch!

"Give me a break. You're telling me Gold intends to walk down thirty-six floors? That's not happening. Look at the fucking stairwell data and tell me if he's in the stairwell."

He heard more background keyboard noise before, "Nope. Nothing shows up on the monitoring. Look, Itzhak, take a few deep breaths, then tell me exactly what's going on."

Mizrahi opened his mouth to explain but slammed on the brakes before an accidental slip of the tongue divulged even the slightest hint of his monitoring capabilities. He quickly edited his answer into a sanitized version.

"I'm waiting," she reminded him.

His revisionist version began by claiming he was patrolling the south side hall when he noticed Gold and Collier leave the lawyer's office, walk to the elevators and shake hands. But the instant Collier turned to go back to his office, Gold suspiciously darted toward the men's room and out of view. At that point, he said with as much righteous indignation as he could muster, that an unauthorized person—Gold—was clearly roaming a secure floor *unescorted*. And that this was a security violation of the highest level.

She grunted ambiguously, which he took as his cue to continue his narrative.

Curious to see what the little shit was up to, he went on to explain that he'd hung around to watch the men's room door to see if Gold would come out and then take an elevator to the lobby. Five minutes later, when Gold didn't materialize from the men's room, he'd gone in to check but the room was empty. Bottom line: Gold had simply vanished.

Finished with his story, he said, "Check the stairwells again."

He waited impatiently through more keyboarding until Glass finally said, "There's been no activity on either stairwell in the last ten minutes."

"That's impossible."

He heard her sigh, then say, "Look, Itzhak, I'm not sure what more I can tell you other than we have no recorded activity on either stairwell from that floor for the past forty-five minutes. Period. Hey, if you think I'm lying, feel free to trot your ass down here and put eyes on the raw data."

After a blazing mental recap of every step he'd taken, he said, "That doesn't make sense because I just checked that entire area and he's not there."

After a prolonged pause, she asked, "What's to keep you from checking again?"

He glared at the radio in hand.

Bitch.

But what other option did he have?

"I'm in my office at the moment. Stand by and I'll run back up. Feel free to join me if you doubt my word."

"Thanks anyway for the invite, but I'm more than happy to wait in my office for your report."

Radio in hand, Mizrahi stormed up the north stairwell to the thirty-sixth floor and straight into the men's room. Empty. Double checked the two stalls. Nothing different from his last visit. He stepped out of the room into quiet, empty halls. Nothing different here either. He slowly pivoted a full three-sixty. Still nothing. He shook his head, then thumbed the transmit button.

"I checked again. He's. Not. Here. Understood?"

"How about the ladies' room? You check that too?"

He mouthed a silent "fuck," at the radio.

"I checked it last time."

Another noticeable silence, then, "Ask yourself this, Itzhak: if you didn't see him get on an elevator and he's not in either toilet or in the halls, where else could he be? An office?"

"That's very doubtful because of the direction he went."

"Well then, where else is there to go?"

Now that she mentioned it, there was the central core…had that little shit gone around to that side? Maybe to one of the service elevators? But that made no sense. Sure, he *could've*. But why?

To purposely fuck with him? Now, *that* explanation did make sense. That was exactly something Gold might do.

"Stand by while I check the ladies' room again."

Mizrahi pushed open the door to the lavatory, yelled, "Security. Anyone in here?"

Stone silence.

"I'm coming in."

Mizrahi stepped into the white tiled room, glanced around. Just as deserted as the men's room.

He quickly stepped back into the hall and radioed.

"Nope, he's not in there."

"You check the hall behind the central core?"

Mizrahi hesitated to admit that he hadn't because this would be the obvious next step. Especially if he'd been standing in the side hall like he'd claimed.

"Uhhh, no..." he finally said, his resentment toward her growing.

She knew damn well he hadn't done that because he didn't mention it. She was purposely rubbing his nose in it.

"What's keeping you from doing that?"

Glancing at the ceiling, he blew a long breath.

Don't get cute with me, Missy.

It killed him to admit that she could be right.

Through gritted teeth, he radioed, "Stand by, one."

He moved past the elevator doors and the entrance to the men's room, past the rounded concrete wall to a corner where the short hall led to the back hall of service elevators, storage rooms, utility closets, and myriad other quarters of unknown functions. He started moving slowly along the hall until abreast of the maintenance room. For some inexplicable reason he felt compelled to stop and study the door, hands on his hips, thinking...

A plain unobtrusive steel door displaying an eyelevel black rectangular placard with eleven engraved white letters: MAINTENANCE. Drab beige paint. No different from the other nondescript drab beige doors along the hall, all with placards on them. Nothing whatsoever to draw his attention to this particular room other than...a gut feel.

Huh. Could Gold be holed up in there?

He tried the handle. Locked. No big surprise there. Despite his suspicion that his fob wouldn't open the door, he swiped it across the reader. Nothing happened. Massaging his dimpled chin, he continued to stare...did that sneaky little bastard somehow steal a maintenance key? Not likely, yet possible.

After filing that thought away, he radioed Glass.

"The fucker's not here." Then he realized... "You know what this means, don't you?" Being rhetorical, he finished the thought: "We're in the middle of a pen-test. I think you need to get your ass up here ASAP to help search this floor with me, inch by fucking inch. Because he's up here and there are only a limited number of places he can possibly hide."

She radioed, "Everyone copy that?" She and Mizrahi were using the North Sound comms frequency with building-wide coverage. "We now have actionable information that an unauthorized individual is roaming a secure floor. We also know that his last confirmed ten-twenty was thirty-six. I'm referring to Arnold Gold. I want everyone on full alert and locked onto this frequency until this emergency is declared over. I'm going up to thirty-six to assist Mr. Mizrahi."

Five minutes later she was beside Mizrahi a few feet in front of the elevators that Collier had escorted Gold to. They were both staring up at the ceiling-mounted smoked-glass CCTV bubble.

"Is it possible, even remotely possible," Mizrahi asked, rubbing his chin again, now eyeing the elevator door, "that the video we saw is actually from another floor?"

Now he was grasping at any slim way out of this embarrassing predicament, in spite of knowing that any other explanation would be impossible because Gold *did* meet Collier in his office. After all, he'd monitored the meeting in real-time, then watched him walk to this very spot. And Collier's office was on this floor.

"Nope," she answered. "Maybe with the old system that *might've* been an extremely unlikely possibility, but with these new enhancements" —she threw in an emphatic headshake— "no way that's even remotely possible."

Praying for a glimpse of the little shit, Mizrahi continued to pulse laser glares nervously around him like a chipmunk out in the open field of a dog park. No Gold. Each second that bastard remained at large jacked up his stomach acid a notch. The little shit couldn't simply vanish. But that was exactly what he'd done. And in the process, Gold was making him look like a fool.

"Well, he can't just, poof, disappear," he said a bit too sharply and with a hand flourish, his anger beginning to bubble to the surface. "He has to be around here *somewhere*."

"Fine," Glass offered with a note of sympathy, "let's walk the floor together and check every office and possible cubbyhole that a person could conceivably hide. That's what I hear you suggesting, isn't it? That he's holed up somewhere on this floor, hiding."

With a vigorous nod, Mizrahi said, "That's exactly what the little shit would do."

Together they began at the last office in the north hall and systematically searched each office, Mizrahi on one side of the hall, Glass on the other side until they reached the elevator lobby. At which point they moved across the base of the A to repeat the routine along the entire south leg, putting eyes on literally every inch of the thirty-sixth floor including coat closets, and—despite having already checked them—both toilets. As they started past Collier's office, Mizrahi noticed the managing partner still at his desk. He elbowed Glass to catch her attention, then nodded at the doorway. Mizrahi stepped into the office.

Collier glanced up from shoveling some folders into an attaché case.

"Evening, Itzhak. May I help you?"

"You haven't seen Arnold Gold since——"

He slammed on the verbal brakes.

With both palms flat on the desk to either side of the case, Collier's intensely questioning eyes studied Mizrahi as he repeated, "Since?"

Mizrahi realized that the story he'd concocted for Glass contained a few flaws in need of acute patching, so he began

Allen Wyler

scrambling for words.

Glass entered the room and stood next to Itzhak.

"Sir, if I may...our lobby team witnessed Mr. Gold enter the building and take an elevator up to your reception area. After which he was allowed access to this secure floor *without* an escort. Because he's neither an employee nor has authorization to access a secure floor without an escort, our protocols require us to document a supervised exit from this floor. Therefore, his presence here not only is considered highly suspicious but warrants a careful investigation. I'm sure you're in total agreement."

In other words, Collier was responsible for a flagrant security violation.

She paused, allowing Collier an opportunity to comment but he simply eyed them with what struck Mizrahi as bemused silence. Straightening his posture, Mizrahi puffed out his chest and waited. Did the lawyer realize that she'd just incriminated him, should a formal security complaint arise from his error in judgement. She and Mizrahi stood side by side in a demonstration of a united front, a security service symbiosis. But Collier simply returned to organizing his attaché case.

Glass finally broke the strained silence with: "I assume you agree that it's not in anyone's best interests to allow unauthorized people to roam your halls unsupervised?"

With a vague nod of neither agreement nor disagreement, Collier snapped the latches shut and said, "In most circumstances you are, of course, correct, but Arnold Gold is far from an unauthorized person. He has, after all, performed a penetration test for us."

He turned to remove his charcoal gray suit coat from the back of his desk chair, then slid his right arm into the sleeve.

Mizrahi decided it was time to refocus on the problem at hand.

"Did you happen to open the north stairwell for him after he left your office?"

Collier's eyes grew intensely inquisitive, causing Mizrahi to shift weight to the other foot.

Uh-oh.

"How do you know he visited my office?" Collier asked.

Shifting weight to his other foot again, Mizrahi decided to default to the tale he'd spun for Glass, especially with her right there next to him.

"I was conducting a routine patrol of the floor when I noticed him walk *unescorted* into your office."

There! Just in case you missed it the first time.

Collier continued eyeing him with a curiously disturbing expression, as if privy to intel that Mizrahi lacked. Mizrahi clasped his hands together at his waist, decided it made him look guilty, so repositioned them behind his back in a sort of parade rest. Did Collier suspect that his system remained intact? If so, was this entire situation an elaborate ruse to entrap him? Was he already royally fucked? Was Glass in on it too? But Glass continued staring straight ahead, directly at Collier, seemingly unphased. No, he didn't believe she was, but you never knew...

Collier said, "I escorted Mr. Gold to the elevators, shook his hand, then returned to my office." He shrugged adjusted his suit coat before buttoning it. "May I ask why this seems to be such a concern to you?"

The question convinced Mizrahi that the lawyer was well aware that the pen-test was now in play.

Glass piped in with, "Sir, if I may...you shouldn't need to be reminded that this is a secure floor. As part of the team responsible for guarding *your* records, it would be a dereliction of our duty to not investigate his whereabouts. *That's* why."

After removing his attaché case from the desk, Collier paused as if considering the gravity of her statement, then said, "As I just stated, I accompanied Mr. Gold to the elevators, after which I returned here. My assumption is that he vacated the building, but I admit that I didn't personally verify that." His eyes shifted from Glass to Mizrahi. "Now if you'll excuse me, my wife is expecting me."

Mizrahi and Glass trailed Collier silently to the elevators where they stood, nervously surveying the two main halls angling off in opposite directions.

Once the elevator finally swallowed the lawyer, Mizrahi told her, "The only place we haven't checked is the maintenance closet."

Arms folded across her expansive chest, she frowned at the floor, then nodded.

"We've checked every office and accessible room up here. The only rooms we haven't checked are the ones back there." She cast a glance in that general direction and shook her head. "If he didn't leave the floor—which we have every indication to believe is probable—there just isn't any other option."

Making a statement of it. She began a slow walk toward the back side of the central core, to the area housing the service elevators and sundry closets serving various functions.

Then they were in the back hall of the three service elevators and a handful of doors to rooms serving a variety of functions, including the one marked MAINTENANCE.

"He's in there," Mizrahi said, aiming his index finger directly at the maintenance closet.

"What makes you so sure? Why not this electrical room?" Pointing to the next door to the right. Then, with a sweep of her hand, "Or some of these others."

"Because this would be the easiest for him to steal access to."

She furrowed her brow.

"I'm not sure I follow your logic. Why's that?"

"Because..." he trailed off, unable to verbalize a logical answer. He just *knew* this would be the one Gold would hide in.

With a shrug, she brought her radio to her mouth.

"Okay, if you're so sure, I'll call maintenance to come up to open it."

"Hold on. You sure your key can't open it?" he asked with a hint of incredulity. "I'd think that as a security supervisor you should be able to."

After brief consideration and a nod.

"Fine. Point made." Stepping forward, she pulled the lanyard from around her neck. "Let's see what happens."

Mizrahi stood to her right, watching as she swiped her card across the black card reader. The LED immediately turned green. With an I-told-you-so smile, he ordered, "Open it."

She frowned, said, "Gloating doesn't become you, Itzhak," and then, with a dramatic flair, took hold of the handle and flung open the door.

Chapter 30

RELIEVED TO HAVE a rock-solid, voice activated comm link established, Arnold stuffed the radio back into his rucksack and slipped it back on, then turned his attention to the small, cramped room of bare concrete walls seemingly irrevocably suffused with the smells of Clorox, and musty mop water with a tinge of stale vomit.

To his relief, this had the same false ceiling as Collier's office: off-white rectangles of acoustical tile, one with a multilobed rust-colored stain spreading out from the corner nearest a set of pipes.

Next to his right knee was a heavily stained, wall-mounted, porcelain utility sink. Barely enough room to turn a complete three-sixty without banging his shins on a commercial-grade yellow plastic mop bucket complete with mop in the wringer, its handle leaning drunkenly against the wall. Also, a red Shop-Vac and an assortment of brooms and mops.

Bolted to the back cement wall were three shelves crammed with plastic gallon containers with several cleaning agents of various colors and levels. To the left of the shelves was what looked like a gray metal circuit breaker box. Strange, since the door to the next room displayed a placard with the word ELECTRICAL on it.

He studied the porcelain utility sink. Clustered between the right side of the sink and the corner of the room ran three substantial pipes that entered through holes in the cement floor and ran the length of the wall to vanish through the false ceiling, each one bolted securely to the concrete wall with multiple steel bands.

A faint gurgle of water emanated periodically from a large diameter black pipe; the same one that the sink drained into. He glanced from the faucet to the drainage pipe, followed it on up to the ceiling.

Hmmm, strong enough?

Planting both palms on the edge of the sink, he leaned his entire weight on it. Felt as solid as a Jersey barrier. Solid enough?

And if so, what the hell was above the ceiling tiles? Enough room? Hmmm....

"Yo, dude," Prisha's voice popped up in his earbud. "Mizrahi has Glass on full alert now and it's sounding like he's immensely pissed."

Bad news. If they were as smart as he suspected they were, it wouldn't take long before they began to check out the various rooms lining the back hall.

He scanned the interior one last time, burning the location of important items into memory before dousing the lights, sending the claustrophobic room into total blackness. Dug his iPhone from his back pocket, felt the single switch on the right side for orientation, then pressed the spot where he estimated the flashlight app should be. The light came on.

Clamping it between his teeth with the light aimed upward, he grabbed the drainpipe with his left hand and the cold-water valve with his right, placed his left foot on the edge of the sink, inhaled though his nose, and pulled himself up so that he was standing on the edge.

To redistribute his weight to reduce the risk of tearing the bolts from the wall, he began inching one foot then the other along the opposite sink edges toward the concrete wall. Feeling safer now, he listened for the sound of the bolts tearing lose. Amazingly, they seemed to be holding well. Great.

But for how long before they broke loose?

Better not push his luck by wasting time. Time to move.

Gripping the pipe with his left hand, right hand against the wall for stability, he looked straight up at the ceiling. Despite the light shining in his eyes, he could make out the ceiling tiles. Man, it would be a stretch.

Could he make it?

Better hope so.

Left hand still holding the pipe, he pushed up on the tile directly overhead. Heavier than he'd expected. On second thought, this was good, for it meant stronger material. This allowed him his first peek into the space above the tiles. There looked to be some space up there, but with the lousy lighting and weird angle, he couldn't be sure of how much.

After working the tile further aside, he was able to hold the flashlight in his right hand and point it directly into the opening. Perhaps there was three feet of space between the tiles and the clement ceiling.

Okay, I can work with that. Can't I?

Maybe, but now the question was whether the support structure would hold his weight. He inspected the construction: a latticework of interlocked inverted aluminum T-bars secured to the ceiling slab by aluminum rods bolted into the cement.

Okay, it *looked* strong. But was it strong enough to support the false ceiling in addition to his weight?

Good question.

Just then, the doorknob rattled.

Fuck!

Chapter 31

ARNOLD GLANCED FROM the door to the false ceiling to the door again. Get caught or take the risk? Assuming of course he could even muscle his body up there. Assuming of course, the freaking ceiling didn't come crashing down under his weight.

On his toes now, stretching, he grabbed an aluminum suspension rod with his left hand and tugged. Felt solid enough. Tugged again, the act causing his right foot to slip from the edge of the sink. Left foot on the sink, left hand hanging on the rod, his right arm began windmilling in a frantic fight to regain balance. Finally, he was able to slip his right foot back on the edge of the sink to regain his balance.

For a moment he remained still, luxuriating in the comfort of stability. Realized he was wasting time, that the sink probably wouldn't support him like this forever, so he tugged on the suspension rod again. Well, it did feel solid. Solid enough?

Better be.

He grabbed the suspension rod with his right hand just above his left, took a deep breath, and began to pull himself up, feet dangling above the sink. Surprisingly, the strut felt comfortingly solid.

Straining muscles not normally used for anything remotely resembling what he was attempting, he worked himself up hand over hand, until high enough to slip his right knee up over the edge of the opening. And immediately received a thank-you message from his arms and shoulders, which were pleading for a rest.

Under normal conditions he would take a quick break but not with Herr Mizrahi about to come goosestepping through that freaking door with his Panzer division of Storm Troopers. He refused to give him the satisfaction of catching him just because of some muscle discomfort.

He rolled onto his side, now completely hidden in the false ceiling, but cocooned in warm stale air, thick with dust and the off-putting smells of mildew and duct tape.

For a moment, he remained perfectly still, ears searching for the telltale sound of a bolt ripping from the cement slab, but all he heard was his hammering heartbeat and labored breathing. He glanced at the neighboring latticework.

The T-bars weren't bending, and the joints continued to look solid. Amazing. But, he realized, his weight was spread over as much surface area as possible. What the hell would happen when he began to move? Which he better start doing on account of the T-bar that he was laying across was cutting into his ribs like crazy.

Okay, but moving up here was a major thrash. Hardly any headroom. Could he even crawl? Especially with his rucksack on? Better do something. And quickly.

He rolled into a slightly comfortable position, thumbed off his flashlight to preserve power and start dark-adapting his eyes, then stuffed the phone into his rear pocket for easy access.

Next priority: replace the tile. Like, pronto. Before Mizrahi could get a fob to open the door, if he didn't already have one.

Problem was not being able to see what the hell he was doing. Turn the light back on? No, that would only waste power. And besides, he needed his eyes dark-adapted quickly as possible.

Peering into his squid-ink surroundings, he could begin to make out shards of light radiating from seams and tiny openings in the recessed hall ceiling several feet away.

At least these afforded him some faint illumination.

He rolled over onto his stomach, distributing himself over as much surface area as possible, and began to operate by feel in addition to memory of where things were. He felt a rough edge. Ah good, a start. He explored the surface with both hands until convinced it was indeed the displaced tile. Having established that much, he found and then explored the smooth sides of the inverted T-struts.

After a quick mental review of how he'd slid the panel aside, he began to slowly, carefully, work it back into place. When it was almost ready to seat, he wiggled himself into a better angle so he could hold the edge until he was confident it was correctly aligned, then lowered it slowly until his fingertips could no longer hold it, then dropped it into place without much sound at all. Took a little jiggering to seat it as flush as possible, figured it might not be perfect, but good enough.

And besides, it was, like, time to get the hell away from the area.

Tracks now obscured as best he could, he tried to orient himself while resisting an almost overwhelming urge to get the hell away from where Mizrahi's head could pop up at any moment. He couldn't afford to make a mistake by hurrying at this point.

Unless his sense of direction was completely turned around, the building core should be to his left, so he began slowly crabbing on forearms and knees in that direction, navigating by feel rather than sight. The good news was that forms were beginning to take shape in the anemic light. He would use the central core as his primary reference point on which to superimpose his memorized floor plan. Once convinced he was properly oriented, he planned to navigate from his memory of relationships.

By now he was all-in. There was no going back. The test would either succeed or fail. Okay, sure, it was just a pen-test, but Mizrahi had somehow transformed it into something personal: transitioning it from a pragmatic way to expose and patch possible security holes into a titanic clash of personalities. Which placed Arnold in an uncomfortable bind: although he hated to get sucked into Mizrahi's personality pathology, he wasn't about to let that asshole win.

So, though he wanted to get as far away from the storage room as quickly as possible, he also intended to do so without making a stupid unforced error, like crashing through a tile.

One major mess-up and it would be game over.

Each move required positioning his palms and knees as close to the T-struts as possible where the tensile strength of the tiles was greatest. Lopez's periodic updates weren't making things easier. According to him, at this point, nothing short of serving up his head on the point of a spear stood any chance of soothing Mizrahi and Glass.

As seconds jetted past, he began to fall into a rhythm, allowing him to move more quickly. Also, his confidence was increasing as his vision continued adapting to the meager light.

He was halfway through moving from one tile to another when a small dust bunny lodged in the Outer Mongolia of his nasal passage, that ill-defined no-man's-land between nose and throat, a spot unclearable with a simple swallow.

Worse, it was verging on triggering a huge sneeze; a real honker by the feel of it.

Mouth closed, with the crook of his arm pressed over his face as a baffle, he tried for one of those disgusting high-palate, sinus-clearing snorts. Didn't stop the urge to sneeze, but it might've moved the dust bunny a bit.

He tried again. Nope.

That puppy seemed cemented in place. Clamping the opposite nostril shut with his shoulder, he sniffed as hard as possible without making an audible snort. It moved a millimeter further into his throat, yet still out of reach of being dislodged with a sniff or a swallow.

But this only seemed to amp up the urge to sneeze,

skimming dangerously close to kicking off a real doozy. He tried sucking in a few deep open-mouth breaths to sooth it, but only inhaled more dust, triggering a cough. Which he again muffled with the crook of his arm. Then he sniffed hard, sending the disgusting glob slithering into the very back of his throat, triggering a silent gag.

Eyes closed, he swallowed, ending the ordeal.

Jesus!

"Open it," Mizrahi ordered and stepped aside to allow her to access the door.

Glass pulled the lanyard over her head so she could swipe the card across the sensor. The lock responded a smart metallic clack.

With a dramatic flourish, she flung the door open.

The room was totally dark except for the hall light angling in. Glass leaned in, flicked on the overheads, then quickly surveyed the small room. Empty. But she wasn't about to deliver the bad news, so stepped back so Mizrahi could see for himself.

No Arnold Gold.

"No fucking way," Mizrahi said, leaning into the small space, looking right, then left, shaking his head, then glancing at the ceiling.

Nothing appeared out of place.

But then again, how would he know?

The handful of times he'd glanced into one of these closets was in passing an open door. Even then, he'd had no reason to register the contents, delegating the sight to nothing more than visual static in the course of an otherwise hectic day.

Shaking his head in disbelief, he asked, "Does this appear normal to you?"

He couldn't believe Gold wasn't inside, not with all the evidence that suggested otherwise. But almost more than that, he despised being dependent on her for even something as minor as an opinion.

With a shrug, she answered, "The room? How would I know? I've never set foot in one of these before. I suspect you haven't either."

Gold had to be in there.

He stepped into the cramped cluttered closet, looking for places that the squirrelly little bastard could hide. Couldn't help but glance up at the tile ceiling again. Nothing looked different from his prior glance, yet a mental nudge compelled him to look at it more closely. What subliminal message was whispering to him? Every surface in this cramped rectangular room was either reinforced concrete or double sheetrock, with one exception: those tiles. Hmmm…was it even possible? After all, that fucker had to go *somewhere.*

Fine, but why here? And why couldn't he be hiding in one of the other rooms along this hall?

Well, because of all the rooms, this was the most frequently used and therefore had the widest key distribution, making it the easiest access for Gold to steal. All of which was true, but at the moment Gold wasn't in here.

Did that little shit somehow climb into that ceiling? Was that even possible? What the fuck's up there anyway?

He could feel Glass's eyes on him as if telepathically reading his thoughts and simultaneously radiating deep skepticism.

He was just about to open his mouth to defend himself when she cut him off.

"That'd be some serious Spider-Man shit, Itzhak."

Drilling her with angry eyes, he said, "Are you trying to cover for him?"

Taking two steps back, she held up her hands, palms forward.

"Are you serious? What orifice did you pull that from?"

Hands on his hips drilling her with a *look*: "Can you absolutely look me in the eye and state with total confidence that he did *not* climb up there?" he asked with a chin jut towards a water-stained ceiling tile.

She gave a quick headshake.

"I didn't say it was impossible. What I said was, it'd be difficult. They're not the same." She stared at the ceiling, shook her head again. "Anything's possible, I guess."

He returned to the tiles again, thinking it through.

Yes, it would be exactly the type of monkey trick to expect from Gold.

Without moving his eyes from the ceiling, he told her, "Have maintenance bring us a ladder so we can check it out for ourselves."

She did a double take, which he missed.

"Ah, for Christsakes, Itzhak, don't go freaking lunatic on me."

He spun around, eyes blazing thunderbolts.

"Get a fucking ladder up here. *Now.*"

She glanced away, as if balancing the outrageous demand against an exceedingly slim possibility that his hunch might, just might, be correct.

After a brief pause and a resigned sigh, she thumbed her epaulet mic, said, "Hey Washington, could you please find someone to bring a twelve-foot stepladder up to the thirty-sixth-floor utility room?" Then, with another clearly audible sigh, unkeyed the microphone and asked Mizrahi, "Is there any place on this or any of your other floors you can think to check while we wait? I have no idea how long this'll take."

Was she trying to sucker him away from here so Gold could slither back down and escape? Wouldn't put it past her.

In fact, he suspected she would love to do just that.

"No, Glass. Not until we clear this ceiling. By now he must know we're on to him. The moment we leave, even for a few minutes he'll climb back down and vanish before you know it. No, Glass, I want that little fucker's ass. We will not move from this room until we've cleared this false ceiling. Do I make myself clear?"

She shook her head in resignation.

"Since you clearly think I'm being unreasonable, why don't

you have someone in control check what time this room was opened before us?"

She appeared to weigh the request for a moment, then radioed the monitoring room. A minute later she had her response. The room had been accessed by a guard approximately one minute after Collier's card had been used to open the north stairwell. He pointed at the false ceiling.

With a smug expression, Mizrahi said, "See? This is why we're going to look up there."

Arnold heard Mizrahi say, "No, Glass. Not until we clear this ceiling. By now he must know we're on to him..."

Shit!

Slowly, carefully, he began crabbing forward again despite the risk of making noise, especially being so close to them. This was pushing his luck, he knew, but what other choice did he have? He needed as much distance as possible between them before the ladder arrived. He was selecting tiles adjacent to the central concrete core because logic dictated that this would be where the latticework should have the greatest structural strength.

The wall also kept him oriented in this confusing maze of ductwork and conduits. He began looking for something to hide behind before Mizrahi could scan the area with a high-intensity Maglite. Which would happen sooner or later.

Then what?

Didn't have an answer for that.

Enough anemic light was filtering through the thick air to suggest an opening between a sheet-metal duct to the right and the concrete central core to the left. Where the hell it went was anyone's guess.

A dead end? Enough to squeeze into?

Enough space to hide him from Mizrahi's light? His internal stopwatch continued ticking loudly and relentlessly, packing each passing second with anxious urgency. How long before that ladder arrived? Well, that all depended on the priority maintenance assigned to Glass's request and there was no way of knowing whether Glass had suction with that department.

Well, the one thing he did know for sure: no way would he crawl into that narrow black passage blindly. Much as he hated to do it, he pulled his iPhone from his back pocket, thumbed on the flashlight, aimed it into the confined space, saw the galvanized air duct parallel the concrete wall for about six feet, then empty into...? The light was too diffuse and weak to see more than a couple feet, but the space looked large enough to accommodate him. He seriously doubted Mizrahi was about to climb up here to explore.

With the light off, he started inching into the mouth of the narrow passage. Once hidden, he stopped, pressed a hand over his mouth to muffle the sound of his breathing and concentrated on what he could hear. Off to his right a fluorescent light fixture hummed along with the occasional musical tinkling of water tumbling down a pipe.

He grew cognizant of a faint rhythmic *whoosh-whoosh-whoosh*; perhaps from a fan echoing through the nearby ventilation duct. Finally, he became aware of a very faint waxing and waning Doppler effect of what he suspected were elevators transiting the building core.

Satisfied he was adequately shielded from a probing flashlight, he inched on toward the end of the passage where he suspected it fed into a larger space.

Big enough to turn around in?

Carefully, Arnold pretzeled himself through a one-eighty so that he could peer back along the narrow tunnel he'd just weaseled through, the angle in the general direction of his starting point and the spot where he anticipated Mizrahi would pop up.

Now, except for his breathing and jackhammering heart, he lay perfectly still and silent, watching, listening, waiting, knowing that any moment now his concealment would be seriously tested.

Chapter 32

THEY WAITED IMPATIENTLY for the ladder to be brought up from wherever it was stored, Mizrahi's left foot planted firmly inside the closet—as if that would keep Gold stationary—and his right foot in the hall, Glass loitering ten feet down the narrow corridor intensely studying her iPhone, calm as a lobotomized sloth.

In comparison, Mizrahi's intestines were tightly cinched square knots of worry over his surveillance system. Because, if that little fucker somehow was able to hack into the firm's network...he flashed on the new legal secretary and her friend, the cute little redhead...the square knots cinched tighter.

They were in on it too.

Granted, HR *had* been looking for a part-time legal secretary...but there was something about that taco nigger that just didn't pass his sniff test.

And her supposed friend, the cute, perky little redhead. They had to both be co-conspirators in Gold's scheme.

He called to Glass.

"Wait here while I run downstairs," pointing to where she stood. "Be right back."

Then he barreled down the north stairwell, through the fire door, straight to the IT offices and Valchenka's cubicle where the

Russian slouched in his chair staring at the center monitor with a supercilious vacant grin. Mizrahi rapped his knuckles on the glass partition.

In slow motion, Serge's head swiveled toward him, but his eyes seemed to be elsewhere.

"Run another full system scan, *tovarich*."

For a fractional moment, the Russian's eyes flashed annoyance.

"Why?" he asked in a simple straightforward non-challenging tone.

Mizrahi was momentarily dumbstruck. Such blatant insubordination.

He swallowed a cutting reply, cleared his throat, said as calmly as humanly possible, "Because that's an order."

After responding with a vacant-eyed nod, Valchenka turned to face the monitor again, leaving the fate of the order in limbo.

Shocked speechless, Mizrahi glared.

Now wait just a goddamned minute—

"Are you fucking stoned?"

Unbelievable.

Lips pressed tightly together, Valchenka stifled a deep nasal snigger, shook his head, muttered, "Course not."

"Look at me!"

Slowly Valchenka rotated the swivel chair to meet Mizrahi's glare, his expression a clear struggle between smirking and forced seriousness.

He said, "No sweat, boss. I'm all over it," while choking back another snigger.

He slowly rotated back to the screen.

Mizrahi found himself torn between...between...Christ, he wasn't sure what—but he knew that he should be back upstairs before the ladder ended up being sent back to wherever the hell it resided.

He left the Russian looking lovingly at his monitor.

Rounding the corner to the back hall, Mizrahi saw a gray-uniformed maintenance guy grab both legs of a stepladder, test its stability, nod, step back and say to Glass, "Feels solid. Go ahead."

"All set?" Mizrahi asked, approaching.

"Perfect timing. Ready when you are," Glass replied, then to the maintenance man: "Might as well stick around, Darryl. Should only take a few minutes, tops." Then to Mizrahi: "Won't it," in a suspiciously declarative tone.

Mizrahi hesitated before nodding, his eyes drawn to the ceiling again.

"That's right."

"You happy with the placement?" she asked.

Was that thinly veiled sarcasm in her tone? Sounded like it.

He decided to take the high road and ignore the covert slight. *Bitch.*

He started to complain that the back legs were up against the far wall of the closet but realized that if they weren't, he couldn't possibly clear the transom of the door when climbing up. Not only that, but if the ladder orientation were reversed, the width of the front legs would prevent him from slipping into the closet.

Oh well, you make do with what you have even if it's suboptimal.

He glanced at the top of the ladder to the tile directly above it.

Although the ladder appeared well situated, he adjusted it a half-inch just to leave no doubt he was in charge.

Another tentative glance at the ceiling. Both hands firmly gripping the ladder, he tried rocking it again.

Granite solid.

He could feel both sets of eyes boring into his back.

After blowing a breath, he planted his right foot on the first rung, tested the stability again. Then placed his left foot next to his right, glanced at the top of the ladder, then on up to the ceiling again.

What was the lowest possible rung that would allow him a look inside the false ceiling?

No way to know without climbing further. A lot further.

He felt Glass's delight over his anxiety radiating like the sun, but there was no way to mask it. The bitch probably took supreme pleasure observing his nervousness, probably thinking, *What a pussy*.

Although she loves pussy.

He laughed at his little inside joke.

Set his right foot up to the next rung, then his left foot. Again, the ladder felt stable. Took another glance at the target tile, but now the fucker appeared even further away.

Hated ladders.

Hated heights.

But he'd be damned if he would trust Glass with the task. No, had to power through it.

Slowly, step by agonizing step, he inched up to the fourth rung.

"Is there a problem, Itzhak?"

Was that a snigger?

"Go fuck yourself, Glass. This ladder isn't the most stable I've climbed. I'm being careful."

"Well, hell, Itzhak, no way that thing can possibly tip over in that narrow doorway."

"I said can it, Glass!"

High enough now for a peek into the false ceiling, he took a rock-solid grip on the rail with his left hand while pushing up the overhead tile with his right hand.

Surprise: more than enough space for Gold to hide. Assuming, of course, the ceiling was strong enough to support the additional weight. Before Glass could pop off another snarky comment, he took hold of a vertical support rod and climbed one more rung, reassessed his stability, decided it was fine.

Let's see that tub of lard climb up here.

Damn ladder would probably disintegrate under all that fucking blubber.

Now the tricky part.

With his left hand stabilizing his precarious position, he

slipped the Maglite from his back pocket, thumbed it on, then carefully planted his right foot on the next rung up for more height, then using the crown of his head to hold up the tile, peered into a pitch-black void of stale, nasal-clogging air.

Couldn't see a goddamn thing.

With the flashlight at eye level, he slowly swept an arc from left to right, saw only a maze of ventilation ducts, conduits, and lighting fixtures. But that didn't mean the little bastard wasn't up here, for Mizrahi was now convinced he was. Just meant he couldn't see him from this limited vantage point.

"So?" Glass called up to him. "He up there?"

Silence.

"Itzhak?"

Was that a note of gloat in her voice?

He zapped her with a lightning-bolt glare.

Arnold watched the crown of Mizrahi's head push up the ceiling tile, flooding the immediate area with squint-inducing light and casting upward shadows across his face like a 1930s-era black-and-white horror flick.

A moment later a blinding high-intensity beam began sweeping an arc slowly one way, then the other.

Wow, amazing.

He'd only put perhaps twenty feet between the tile and his hiding place. Max. Felt more like fifty. Holding his breath, he reverse-turtled further into the confines of his hidey-hole as Mizrahi began another sweep of the area.

"So?" he heard Glass ask. "He up there?"

Mizrahi didn't answer, just kept sweeping the light in a slow arc to the limits of one side, then back around the opposite direction but never covering more than about a hundred and twenty degrees.

"Itzhak?" Glass, asking more emphatically this time.

"Does it look like I fucking see him?" Mizrahi barked back.

Arnold swore he could hear Glass think, *Told you so*, despite the tactful silence. He smiled at his mental image.

A moment later the flashlight vanished. Shortly after that came the scrape of the tile being manipulated back into place. Then eventually the thud as the utility closet door slammed shut.

Muzzling his mouth with a cupped hand, he whispered, "Sit-rep?"

In his earbud, Lopez said, "Guess it's fair to say they're less than thrilled with the situation."

"Perfect. We couldn't've hoped for more. Now we wait."

Chapter 33

MIZRAHI WATCHED GLASS help Darryl load the stepladder back onto the blue maintenance cart, then bungee-cord it securely in place against the A-frame.

His mental video replay was running an endless loop through memory: the snippet in which Gold beelined toward the men's room.

But the little shit didn't go there.

At least he wasn't there *now*. That being the case, where *did* he go? His options were limited to the two toilets, two stairwells, the elevators, and the storage room. None of which showed evidence of his presence. But that was impossible. Unless...

Wait just one fucking minute.

He turned from the cart to stare at the doors to the three loading elevators. Of course! If Gold had a key for them, he could pretty much travel the entire building. But how could he get his hands on one? There were also the other infrequently used rooms, some of which he knew absolutely nothing about.

Yes, he could be in one of those, but what key would allow him access? And besides, a guard had accessed the maintenance room at approximately the same time. Which made no sense.

He shook his head.

His gaze locked onto Glass, looking all smug and self-satisfied…

"You're in on it, aren't you!"

She glanced up from her phone with a puzzled expression.

"Say what?"

"If he's not up there," he growled, stabbing an index finger at the false ceiling, "and he's not anywhere on this floor, how did he leave? You say he didn't leave by any of the stairwells or elevators. If that's true, it means he either vanished like a little white bunny rabbit in a magic show or you're lying. And I don't believe in magic."

She stared at him with an expression of slack-jawed disbelief.

After several seconds of stunned silence, she replied, "You're full of shit."

"Am I?" He threw that incriminating stare right back at her. "In that case I guess you won't mind taking me down to the control room to personally review *all* the elevator data, including the service elevators, stairwell, and keycards for that period."

Brow furrowed, she paused several seconds before saying, "You're serious," in a calm flat tone filled with disappointment.

"Goddamn right I'm serious, Glass. Do I look like I'm joking?"

Twenty minutes later, they stood side by side in the control room staring at a monitor, the exact sequence of events unambiguously charted out to the second on the time-coded CCTV.

The sequence began with Collier shaking Gold's hand, then pivoting a one-eighty to retrace the path to his office. At which point Gold headed toward the men's room, vanishing from the view of the overhead CCTV feed.

Nor was he picked up by any other camera in the building.

Four seconds after Gold disappeared, a guard's keycard opened the utility closet door. Upon checking the daily records, Glass discovered that this particular guard wasn't scheduled to work that day and, as far as anyone could tell, hadn't set foot in the building.

Arms crossed defiantly over his chest, Mizrahi said to her, "See?"

"I agree with you. He simply vanished and I have no good explanation where."

"You realize don't you, that since one of *your* guard's keys accessed that room, this is going to blow straight back in your lap, and it'll be your boss doing the blowing."

"You think I don't know that?" she replied, finally sounding appropriately concerned.

Mizrahi smiled at that. At least he wouldn't end up being the only fuckee if this invasion ended up badly for them.

"I'm going back upstairs," he finally said. "The bastard has to be up there somewhere."

The only positive spin Arnold could put on his miserable situation was that so far, the ceiling hadn't caved in under the strain of his weight. But he was becoming increasingly twitchy about just how strong the latticework was and how long it would continue to support him.

With Mizrahi and Glass almost directly below him, he felt compelled to either remain motionless or move with hyper-caution for fear that any mistake could produce enough noise to pinpoint his location.

But he was finding it impossible to stay still for more than a few minutes. Just about everything in the gawd-awful space sucked: the thick dusty air, the claustrophobic confinement, the tenuous nature of a latticework engineered and constructed to support the weight of a false ceiling and not much more.

Even if you built it under the philosophy of doubling the calculated load, he was pretty sure his weight was either teetering on or surpassing the limits of tolerance. The best thing he could do was continue to distribute his weight across as many tiles as possible, right?

Right. But given the severe lack of headroom, this meant lying spread-eagle. Both situations—moving or stationary—were fraught with unique difficulties. Supporting himself on elbows and knees for periods longer than, say, five minutes was killing him. Lying flat? Same thing because it meant parts of him rested on edges of T-bars. Although not sharp, the edges really dug in. One workaround was to lie on his side and turn every few minutes like a rotisserie chicken.

Even if the latticework itself continued to hold him, he was concerned about the durability of the supporting rods. Each one was bolted into the concrete ceiling. Four bolts per base. How much load could an individual fixture sustain?

No idea.

And as long as he was tallying up misery factors, how about the freaking sinus-clogging, gritty-eye, dusty air.

Not a damn thing to do but ignore it.

Oh, and pray it was asbestos-free. Which he was pretty sure it was, but only pretty sure. Wished he could be one hundred percent. The good news was that his exposure would only be a few hours. But still…

The other good news? The workday was grinding to a close for the majority of the firm's employees, so very soon most of the Larkin Standish support staff in the offices below would be filtering out. This comforted him. But for the immediate future, his only option was to hang tough, pray that the latticework held, and count the seconds ticking past at the speed of an OD'd slug. Took another glimpse at his watch. Just five goddamned minutes since last check.

Jesus.

Arnold whispered, "Sit-rep?" just loud enough for his throat mic to pick up.

"Not much to report. Radio chatter's at a minimum. Mizrahi's running his usual floor patrols. How you doing, boss?"

Arnold shook his head at the question. How could he possibly answer?

He opted for; "Fine," and realized that it felt good that Lopez asked. Especially since he had no clue just how shitty conditions were.

Maybe it'd help to start moving again.

Besides, what was he waiting for? Mizrahi should be elsewhere by now.

Arnold radioed, "I'm going to start working my way toward the target."

The footprint of the building approximated a stubby, broad-based A with its blunted apex directed toward the harbor. Both legs and the east side of the connecting hall contained offices. The west side of the connecting hall contained the wall of passenger elevator shafts bookended by the stairwells and toilets: men's room to the north, Ladies' room to the south.

The backside of this central service core led to four service elevators, myriad storage rooms, and various utility closets. Webster Collier's office was located midway along the south leg.

Arnold's plan was straightforward: navigate to the tile directly over Mr. Collier's desk using a combination of measurements taken with his phone along with a healthy dose of dead reckoning.

Once situated above the office, he would wait until the coast was clear, slip aside a tile, then hang by a cross-strut and lower himself onto the desktop. Easy concept, right? But the skeptic in him believed that the easy ones were also the ones to land him in boiling water because they were magnets for Murphy's Law.

Anyway, the plan remained straightforward and workable even under the present circumstances. Once the money shots of him in Collier's office were uploaded to the cloud, Lopez would help him sneak out of the building by diddling his data in the CCTV facial recognition software.

At least, that was the plan.

Lopez said, "Roger that, but be careful, you still have bogeys on the floor."

"Copy," Arnold whispered.

By now, Arnold's eyes were so well adapted to the shards of light bleeding through light fixture seams and pinholes that he could easily make out the general shapes of major nearby structures, while darkness swallowed anything further than about twenty feet. For now, the concrete central core remained his one navigational landmark.

Arnold glanced around one final time before heading southward, sticking as close as possible to the central wall. Each move required placing a hand or knee right adjacent to the T-bars to minimize the risk of breaking a tile. By keeping each point of contact on a different tile, his weight would be distributed over the widest possible surface area.

Each move started by grasping a strut with his left hand while sweeping his right hand over the next tile to assure nothing lay hidden in the shadows where he intended to place his right knee. Then repeating the process with his left side, moving silently, step by methodical step. Snail-paced for sure, but he saw no upside to pushing it. After all, Mizrahi was down there somewhere.

He crept toward his intended target tile by tile, keeping the concrete mass on his left. Had to admit, moving felt a bit more comfortable than staying put, probably because the intense concentration required became a distraction from the pain it produced.

After what seemed like for-freaking-ever, he reached the southwest corner of the central core.

Good. A sign of solid progress.

Pausing, he swiped the back of his filthy sweaty wrist across his filthy sweaty brow and wished he was just about anywhere but up here in this awkward, stifling hellhole. But that was, like, impossible. And besides, he'd wanted this job and had worked hard for it. But like so many things in life, the reality of what you wished for can differ markedly from what you imagined.

He paused to relax the tension in his aching shoulders by focusing on a pleasant thought, like the beer and cheeseburger he planned to devour during their post-test celebration. But his shoulders and neck weren't so easily duped, so he gave up and began crawling again. Might as well get to where he was going before resting. Besides, it felt better to be moving than not. Once he reached the target, he would go spread-eagle for a few blessed minutes and hope the discomfort eased.

After another two tiles, he paused to check his navigation. He should now be at the south leg of the A, the point where he had to leave the orientation of the right-angle latticework and central core landmark to wade into a maze of galvanized metal air ducts, runs of electrical conduits, and recessed lighting fixtures; all disorienting obstructions. He suddenly realized that the odds of hitting his target approximated zero.

Best-case scenario?

Might end up close. If he were lucky.

Could he live with that? Did he have a choice?

Sure, but now, thinking about it, faced with the reality of the situation, aiming for Mr. Collier's office was flat-out ridiculous. And besides, Mizrahi knew damn well that was where he was headed.

Why had he ignored this point? Stupidity, that's why.

He needed a Plan B. And to do that, he needed a better look at what he was dealing with. Planning this puppy without benefit of reconnaissance was an open invitation for this type of disconnect. Better pull out the flashlight for a quick peek. Steadying himself by holding onto a suspension strut with his left hand, he reached back to pull the phone out of his back pocket.

Oh, shit!

In perverted slow motion, he could feel it slipping from his sweat-slicked fingers. Reflexively, he made a Hail Mary grab, missed, and for a fractional paralyzed second, waited...

for...

...the impact.

Like a hand grenade exploding.

Arnold went into statue-man mode: ears hyper-alert for sounds from the hallway below.

Chapter 34

MIZRAHI STOOD IN the exact location where Gold shook Collier's hand. He'd been standing here for the past five minutes, gazing at the same offices and halls as he had so many other times since the asshole disappeared.

He was even facing the direction Gold had gone.

Nothing looked different from all those other times except by now he hated the sight of the halls. Yet there had to be something he was missing it.

What?

Once again, he broke the events into logical steps. Only a finite number of square feet existed for that little shithead to possibly go: the men's room, the north stairwell, or the back hall to the service elevators and closets. And if he went into the back hall, his only options were to enter the maintenance room, take one of the service elevators, or continue out the other side of the hall and eventually back into camera range.

There was nowhere else. And then there was the most relevant evidentiary point of all: the maintenance-room lock had been opened seconds after Gold disappeared. He had to have gone into that room.

Yet, the goddamn service elevators kept nagging him like an inflamed hangnail.

Could fobbing the maintenance room have been a diversion and he'd actually taken a service elevator instead?

Could the same keycard access both areas?

Yeah, probably, come to think of it.

But to do that would require gaming the keycard system.

Was that possible?

Probably. Anything was possible.

What if Gold fobbed the maintenance-room door at the same time a service elevator happened to stop at that floor? He could simply step on the goddamn thing and vanish. Poof.

Yeah, that scenario would work perfectly. Shouldn't the elevator stop show up in the computer log?

"Glass," he radioed.

"Yes?"

"Can keycards that open the utility closets also access the service elevators?"

"Dunno." Pause. "Hold one and I'll check. I'm not in my office at the moment. Why?"

Mizrahi took two hesitant steps in the direction of the back hall then stopped. Going there yet again wouldn't answer a damn thing.

He told her, "While you're at it, check the records to see if a service elevator made a stop on thirty-sixth around the time the maintenance room was accessed."

"Okay, but what're you thinking, that Gold used a service elevator to exit the floor?"

"Exactly."

Soon as the words left his mouth, he heard a soft thud directly overhead.

Glancing up at the ceiling, he replayed the sound, then whispered into the radio, "Glass, get your ass and that ladder back up here ASAP, and I mean ASAP. That little fucker *is* up in the ceiling and he's right over my head. I just heard him. Hurry!"

Chapter 35

"Yo, Dude! Got a DEF CON five situation unraveling. Mizrahi thinks he heard you in the ceiling and just called for Glass to get back up there with a ladder."

Shit-shit-shit.

Left hand still clutching a support rod, he groped blindly along the side of his leg where the phone should be. Couldn't see a damn thing down there but dense blackness. His fingertips brushed something, but not enough to know if it was the phone or construction debris.

Just freaking perfect; couldn't reach the damn thing without letting go of the strut.

Do that, and he would lose his balance for sure. Streeeeetching didn't do it either.

He needed to change positions. But carefully.

He took a moment to grapple with how to do this while trying to ignore an ass-puckering urge to crawl away before Mizrahi could get up here with his flashlight. The phone should be in a triangular area between his right foot and the strut.

Carefully, he replaced his right hand with his left, giving him more lateral flexibility to reach down there. When his fingertips touched tile, he began systematically walking them back and forth between his foot and the strut until he found it.

Relieved to have his phone back, he now needed to engineer a way to twist back into position to crawl. But this required freeing his right hand again. Slip the phone into his back pocket again? Probably not, considering...after carefully wedging it between his right knee and the T-strut, he worked himself back into alignment, picked up the phone, thumbed open the Notes app, and checked the distance to Mr. Collier's office.

The office door should be sixty-three feet from the corner of the central core, give or take. He glanced in that direction but could only see dense blackness. Much as he hated to mess with his dark-adapted vision, he thumbed on the flashlight, and aimed it in the general direction of the office. A large, galvanized aluminum ventilation duct blocked him.

Oh, man! What now?

Well, okay, so how far did it extend?

He crawled closer to the duct for a better look. Not enough space to climb over or under it, so he directed his light along the length, but the duct went on and on for freaking ever.

Well, duh!

It was probably the primary air supply for this wing so it would run the entire length of the hall, right down the middle, servicing offices to either side of the hall. Meaning there was no way he could get over to Mr. Collier's office even if he still intended to—which simply underscored his prior need for a Plan B.

He turned the light in the opposite direction.

Although he couldn't see the duct's origin, it made sense for it to originate from the central core near the utility closet. It now made sense that one of those unidentified rooms contained the HVAC system for the floor.

Yeah, thinking about it now, this made perfect sense.

Okay, so what was his Plan B?

Chapter 36

"WHERE DO YOU want it?" asked Darryl, the maintenance man.

His right hand rested on the same utility truck as last time with the same twelve-foot stepladder bungee-corded securely in place. Clearly, he was less than thrilled at being summoned back to chase suspected noises in the false ceiling when other, more pressing work orders continued to pile up.

Well, too fucking bad.

This was more important. Mizrahi glanced up to the approximate spot where the sound came from, then down the hall toward Collier's office. A fist of anxiety began squeezing his gut. That little fucker was already too close. Couldn't allow him to move any closer.

"Right here," he said, stabbing an index finger at an overhead tile, next to a recessed lighting fixture.

With a nod, Darryl began to unleash the bungee cords securing the ladder to the cart.

"Need help with that?" Glass offered when it became apparent Mizrahi wasn't about to lift a finger.

Without bothering to wait for an answer, she stepped up to provide a hand.

Mizrahi caught the quick look she shot him.

243

Hey, you want to wrestle that ladder, bitch? Be my guest, but don't be giving me any attitude in the meantime.

He stepped away, affording them ample room to manhandle the substantial ladder. In the meantime, he contemplated his next move.

"Yo dude, what's going on?" Lopez asked.

Rather than risk so much as a whisper, Arnold double-keyed his transmit switch, then returned to working on an alternative plan. His options were severely limited. He could work his way completely around the central core to see if there was some way to the other side, or simply crawl down this side of the hall to an office in proximity to Mr. Collier's, then figure out a distraction big enough to give him sufficient time to complete the job.

Meanwhile, he could hear them setting up a ladder below. Meaning that he was running out of time before Mizrahi's head would be popping through a nearby tile like a jack-in-the-box. Better think up a plan of action and run with it, like, super pronto or...

He resorted to his typical strategy of breaking the problem into basic components. And it went like this: if this duct was trapping him in the south leg, it stood to reason that the same rule held for the offices in the north hall, trapping him between the two ducts.

Just one more example of unexpected twists you run into when you can't get your hands on detailed architectural drawings. Then again, if he'd had them, did he seriously think he would've thought to check out this particular wrinkle?

Maybe. But probably not.

Okay, since dropping into Mr. Collier's office had been scratched from the list of options, why not just crawl as far from Mizrahi as possible? Before Mizrahi had a chance to pop back up here. He dumped the phone into his rear pocket again and began to crawl in a path he estimated was above the hall that paralleled the bank of elevators, heading toward the north leg of the A.

The more he crawled, the more he considered his options. The flaw he'd overlooked in the planning phase was that Mizrahi knew Mr. Collier's office was the target, so he would probably station someone—if not himself—there. Not only that, but the office was probably bugged worse than the American Embassy in Moscow. No, he needed to find an office remote from there, where he might stand a reasonable chance of dropping in without being nailed immediately.

He continued crabbing toward the north wing, putting as much distance as possible between himself and Mizrahi.

The maintenance guy, Darryl, and Glass backed away from the ladder.

"Have at it, Itzhak," Glass said, with a trace of mockery in her tone.

Mizrahi flashed her a dose of hard-eye, letting her know that her little slights weren't going unnoticed, but that the issue of apprehending Gold before he could slither down from the ceiling and vanish was far more important. He would deal with her pettiness after he'd captured the little shit.

On second thought, he couldn't let that remark pass without some sort of reprimand, so said, "Stow the attitude, Glass. Both our assess are on the line with this."

Once again, she raised her hands in surrender.

"I seriously think you're overly sensitive about things, Itzhak. I'm just saying the ladder's ready to go."

She gestured toward it.

"You don't think I see that?"

Bitch just wouldn't let up.

Instead of dwelling on it, he grabbed the ladder, and tested its stability. Solid. Glanced at the ceiling. Hated ladders. Hated them with a passion. Especially out here in the hall with nothing but empty space around him and a reinforced concrete floor to land on. The utility room was a different matter. At least there, he could reach out to touch a substantial surrounding wall. But here? Nothing but air. Another glance at the ceiling, then back to the concrete wall three feet away.

Shaking his head, he said, "This isn't in the right place. I want it over there."

He pointed to a spot where the ladder would be, maybe a foot and a half from the cement core, putting at least his right side close to a wall.

Darryl raised his eyebrows at Glass. She responded with a go-ahead shrug. He dragged the ladder across the tiles to the spot designated by Mizrahi, leaving little black scuff streaks on the tiles for the night-shift janitors to buff out.

"A little more to the right," Mizrahi ordered before Darryl had a chance to loosen his grip on it.

After this minor adjustment was made, Mizrahi inspected the ladder's position critically, then tested its stability. Still rock-solid. Stepping away from it, he eyed it again, said, "I don't know...is this the same ladder? It seems more rickety to me than the other one."

Glass grabbed the legs and tried rocking it.

"I dunno about that, Itzhak, feels solid to me. Darryl?"

"Oh no you don't," Mizrahi said, shooing Darryl away from the ladder with a hand. "You're both in on this, so of course he'll parrot back anything you say. If you're so fucking satisfied with it, Glass, why don't *you* climb up there and look."

If it doesn't splinter into rubble under all that blubber.

She laughed.

"I can't believe what I just heard. You're afraid of ladders, aren't you."

Mizrahi swept an After-You-Alphonse gesture toward it, then pulled his Maglite from his rear pocket.

"Here you go. I'll even let you borrow my flashlight."

As if this were a magnanimous gesture.

She snorted another curt laugh.

"I'm not the one who's all gung-ho on the idea that he's up there crawling around inhaling asbestos. You are." She glanced at the false ceiling. "Which truthfully I'm not so sure I buy." Then, looking him directly in the eye, said, "In other words, if you're so sure he *is* up there, then get your ass up that ladder and check it out for yourself. But do it now because we've put Darryl way behind today standing around watching you wet your pants like a little sissy."

More than anything, Mizrahi wanted to grab her neck with both hands and squeeze it into the diameter of a spaghetti strand, but assured himself that doing so wasn't particularly prudent. Not with Darryl watching and the overhead CCTV camera recording his every move. Instead, he simply skewered her with a This-Ain't-Over glare for a long moment. Then he adjusted the ladder slightly.

Sissy? He'd show the bitch.

Gripping both sides of the stepladder, he began slowly climbing one rung at a time until high enough to push up a tile and slide it aside as he'd done in the utility room. Holding onto the top step, he was able to grab a support rod with his right hand, then lean his center of gravity forward, with both shins up against the next step for stability.

After a confidence-building moment, he raised his head into the stale, musty darkness to listen for Gold. Heard only the waxing and waning hums of nearby elevators passing and a rhythmic whoosh of a distant ventilation fan but nothing that sounded the least bit suspicious.

Holding a support bar with his left hand, he pulled the Maglite from his rear pocket, thumbed it on and swept an arc to the limits of his position. Through a haze of dust particles, all he could see was a morass of ducts, conduits, and pipes. No one in their right mind would willingly subject themselves to such godawful conditions.

If Gold elected to spend hours up here marinating in this hazardous environment, fine. Let him. But the little shit wasn't coming down anytime soon. He would see to that.

He yelled to no place in particular, "Hope you're enjoying

yourself up here, you little fucker. I know you're there. And guess what? We'll be down here waiting when you try to come down. Game's over, Gold. You lose."

"You see him?" Glass asked enthusiastically from below.

He glanced down. There she was, craning her neck to see something, eyes wide with expectation. Looking serious.

Huh. Maybe she did give a damn this time.

Arnold heard the vague, soft scrape come from somewhere behind him and froze like a forest deer catching a scent, ears tuned for more hints. But picked up only the monotonous droning hum from the ventilation ducts.

After a brief hesitation, he slowly turned his head toward the origin of the noise and saw a high-intensity beam bounce off a galvanized metal ventilation duct.

From this angle, the source had to be close to the corner of the cement core, perhaps close to where he'd dropped his cell. He saw the beam sweep the side of the duct in the direction of the south leg, convincing him that his choice to not go that way was correct.

He resumed crawling.

A moment later, he heard Mizrahi yell, "Hope you're enjoying yourself, you little fucker..." Followed by a voice too muffled to make out. Glass, he assumed. Then Mizrahi said, "Don't see him. But that little shit's up here somewhere. We need to move the ladder."

Oh, just freaking great: now we're going to play Whac-A-Mole.

Pay attention. Keep moving.

Slowly, carefully, Arnold continued inching forward, paralleling the wall of elevators, heading for the north wing.

Chapter 37

WITH ONE FOOT on the floor, the other on the bottom step of the ladder, Mizrahi massaged his dimpled, stubbled chin while reworking his situation yet again, convinced beyond any doubt that Gold somehow had managed to monkey himself up into the false ceiling and was hiding. Probably even watched him sweep the light beam through the area, laughing at him for his fear of ladders and heights.

Well, the little shit better enjoy his dusty new home because he was going to make it his and Glass's mission to make goddamn sure he never came down.

At least not anytime soon. For the moment, Gold could revel in his canniness, but after a day or so trapped up there without food, water, or a place to piss without giving himself away, life might just get a trifle intolerable. Like it must've been for those Hamas assholes when the Gaza Strip was besieged.

That thought brought a smile.

But this begged the question: when, where, and how *would* Gold try to come down?

Huh. Climb back down through the utility room?

That made a great deal of sense, especially since there weren't many other options. The only other possibility would be to lower himself through the ceiling, and then drop to the floor.

Allen Wyler

Or better yet, onto a couch.

Huh. Was that possible?

No, none of the offices contained a couch. A padded chair? Doubtful. For that would require hitting a pretty small target. Gold's best chance would be to aim for the floor and pray he didn't break a leg. Assuming he possessed enough athletic ability to even attempt such an acrobatic stunt.

Even so, it would be one hell of a long drop.

"Talk to me, Itzhak," Glass said, jerking him from his ruminations.

"He's up there," he said, pointing toward the ceiling. "We just didn't look in the right spot." He glanced around as if a sudden revelation would expose his location. At that moment, he hated Gold more than ever for making him look like such a complete fool. If he had a gun, he would begin firing into that goddamn ceiling in random locations. *That* should get the little fucker's attention. Maybe even get him moving quickly enough to give away his location. Maybe even get him to plead for mercy.

He realized he was clenching and unclenching his fists and made an attempt to cover for it by casually reaching for the ladder.

Did Glass notice?

His gut was killing him now. Having Gold inside the perimeter was embarrassing enough, but if he was somehow able to take those pictures…he didn't even want to contemplate that possibility. Fucker had to be stopped.

"If you're right about that," Glass said, "and in no way am I trying to imply that you're not. But if he *is* up there, he has to come down *eventually*."

"True…" he said, realizing an obvious point, then berated himself for not tumbling to this earlier. He started walking toward Collier's office. "I know what his target is."

It didn't matter if or when Gold came down. What did matter was to keep him from taking the evidentiary photos. For without those, the pen-test would be a failure.

250

Glass called after him, "Does this mean you're done with the ladder?"

Mizrahi swatted away the question. At the moment, the issue consuming him was whether or not to phone Collier to say he'd trapped Gold in the false ceiling on the thirty-sixth floor. He slowed to weigh the pros and cons of this strategy. Demonstrating outstanding leadership by enforcing their ironclad internal security should improve his image in Collier's eyes. And that could potentially dampen some of the pushback on his surveillance system.

However, this would only work if Collier could be convinced that the intel generated was essential for protecting the firm.

Yes, he could make a strong case for that.

As for the downside? He couldn't see one. But there must be one, for there always was.

What was he missing?

He stopped in the doorway of Collier's darkened office, the lawyer long gone by now. Seeing the space might unmask something he was forgetting. He flicked on the lights, stepped inside and glanced at the ceiling, and was relieved to see the tiles undisturbed.

On the other hand, what's to say Gold didn't drop into another office then come over here for his fucking selfie? No way to know without...

At the doorway, hand on the jamb, he leaned into the hall and called to Glass, who was still chatting up Darryl.

"Hey Glass."

"What?"

"We need to make certain Gold didn't climb down elsewhere. I want you to search every office along that side" —he gave a sweep of his hand— "while I do the same on this side." And if she was having difficulty understanding, added, "Gold can't replace a tile if he drops through the ceiling. Get it?"

She sent him a look of annoyance.

"Thanks so much for explaining that so clearly, Itzhak. Otherwise, I never would've figured out why you want to do that."

Cunt.

Arnold stopped crawling to reestablish his bearings and give his limbs a much-needed respite, what with every joint and muscle fiber pleading for mercy. He slowly sank into a spread-eagle position, resigned to endure the pain the T-bar inflicted on his ribs.

As uncomfortable as it was, his knees and shoulders really did need a break. Crabbing over such a tenuous surface so awkwardly was emotionally and physically more draining than he could've imagined. Then again, this was such a one-off situation, there was no way to have prepared for it. And then there was the crappy air filling his lungs.

How safe was that?

The stagnant dusty air cocooned him like silkworm. Plus, he was sweating like a sumo wrestler. He wasn't sure how much more of this he could take.

Carefully, silently, he slipped the rucksack off his back, withdrew the water bottle from the side pouch, and uncapped it. To drink, he had to rotate his head to the side and pour what little water remained into his mouth. The few drops tasted deliciously refreshing.

He shook the bottle, hoping for a few more drops, but it was indeed empty; the few drops he did glean making him only thirstier. He glanced around.

Leave it?

No one would ever see it. Unless of course someone happened to pull this specific tile. Which seemed very unlikely. However, littering just felt wrong. And besides, recycling seemed to be an ingrained habit. He dutifully slid the empty back into the side pocket.

Another glance at his immediate surroundings. He was now

just feet from the north hall.

Decision time: drop into an office here or move further down the hall, enlarging the distance from Mizrahi?

He whispered, "Sit-rep?"

Lopez responded.

"Bad news, dude. Mizrahi and Glass just walked the entire floor looking for a displaced tile and came up empty, so they suspect you're still in the ceiling. They decided to camp out in Collier's office to wait for you. He's convinced her that's where you're headed."

Good.

This increased his odds of getting down from this hellhole without being detected.

But then what? How was he going to get the money shots?

"Everyone have a copy?" he radioed.

After confirming the team had a solid copy, he explained his modified plan.

Chapter 38

ARNOLD POSITIONED HIMSELF to the immediate right of a darkened light fixture.

With the light off, he assumed the office was unoccupied. Using the screwdriver blade of his Swiss Army knife, he pried up the edge of a tile enough to grab and lift it far enough to peek inside.

Yep, no one down there.

He lifted it further for a more inclusive scan of the room. Despite the interior lights being off and the door closed, enough city light was reflecting through the windows—especially with his dark-adapted eyes—to make out the interior.

Mr. Collier's office desk was positioned directly below the analogous ceiling light. Not the arrangement here. This desk appeared to be a few feet off to the right, meaning he needed to move to the next tile over.

Carefully, he reseated the tile, then crawled to the next one and repeated the process.

Okay, this would be as good as it got for this office. Not perfect, but doable. Good enough? Well, that remained to be tested.

He doubted that another office would be any better. And besides, any more crawling than absolutely necessary would be intolerable.

This would have to do.

Stealthily, he slid the tile aside, exposing the entire opening. With both hands to either side of the opening, he leaned forward to look straight down at his landing zone.

Oh, man, seriously lucked out.

No keyboard on the desk. That monitor, on the other hand, might be a problem…land slightly off and…. Too bad he hadn't been able to simulate this move, but he hadn't, so here he was having to improvise. Hmmm…perhaps his odds of hitting the target would improve if he moved to the opposite side.

After crawling to the other side of the opening, he realized another humongous problem: being able to contort into the opening without collapsing the entire freaking latticework. The things you never anticipate…

With a resigned breath, he reconsidered his options, but nothing better came to mind. Either give up and surrender to Mizrahi—which wasn't really an option—or give it a shot.

Gripping the suspension struts on either side of the opening, he leaned forward to look straight down again, this time more fully appreciating just how far away the desk really was. But there was no going back now.

Okay, so how the hell could he pretzel himself into the opening?

He tried wiggling his legs in from the side, but the suspension struts were in the way and then there wouldn't be enough headroom to lift his head and get his body over the opening.

He had to figure a way of scrunching over yet still being able to wiggle his legs into the opening. A real bitch in such tight quarters. He backed up again to reevaluate. There had to be a way.

Hmmm…how about instead of approaching the opening from the side of the rectangle, coming at it from the end?

Not only that but lead feet-first. Thought it through once, twice, decided it was worth a shot in spite of it putting more weight on fewer tiles. That was simply the risk he was forced to take.

After crawling into the new position, he wormed his legs out over the hole until the back of his knees were on the edge and both feet dangled into the room. He grabbed a vertical strut and contorted himself sideways and then up into an awkward sitting position bent fully forward, head over the hole with all his weight now on one cross-strut.

Quickly, he worked his hands to the cross-struts directly opposite him and realized that at any moment the single bar supporting his weight could simply collapse.

Then came a cracking sound, like something breaking. Several concrete flakes fluttered down from the ceiling.

Fuck!

He glanced at the struts bolted into the cement slab overhead. The bolts in the base of the two taking the brunt of the weight were looking suspiciously tenuous.

Had no choice now. Hunched over, crown of his head pressed against cold concrete, he sucked a deep breath …

Ah, man…

…and let his butt slide off the back strut, plummeting him feet-first toward the desk, stripping his finger from the cross bar, but enough of a snag to break his acceleration just slightly before his feet slammed onto the desktop, buckling his knees.

Arms windmilling like crazy in a fight to regain balance, his left hand whacked the edge of the monitor, sending it flying off the desk. He watched in horror as its two cables went taut, tethering the monitor to a stop, then arcing it back down to slam the side of the desk like a stick of dynamite exploding.

Balance back, flailing abating, he jumped to the floor, grabbed the monitor, and placed it back on the desk in a position good enough to pass cursory inspection from the hall but not from the office's occupant.

"Yo, dude," Lopez's voice came up in his left ear again. "Glass just heard a noise and thinks it's you. She's got Mizrahi on a tear. They're now searching all the offices on thirty-six again.

Where're you?"

"Can't talk," he whispered, now frantically scanning the room for a hiding place.

No, not the footwell. That would be the first place they'd look.

He pushed the desk chair back into the desk, then glanced around for a hiding place. Nothing. Not even a closet.

Then came Mizrahi's door-muffled voice from the hall.

"Come on out, Gold. Game's over. We know you're here and we're coming for you."

With no alternative, he flattened himself against the wall behind where the door would swing open. Sure, a spot just as much of a cliché as the desk footwell, but—

Just then the door did swing open, sandwiching him against the wall. Through the gap between the door and jamb, he saw a slice of a heavyset female facing the darkened room, hand on the doorknob.

Lorna Glass?

Yeah, probably. The overhead lights remained off. Arnold held his breath.

He heard Mizrahi's voice call, "Anything?"

"Nothing yet," she replied, taking one more step into the room and out of Arnold's limited field of view. Then he heard her turn and watched her pass the crack in the door jamb heading back into the hall, dragging the door shut behind her. A moment later, silence.

For real?

Arnold moved to the spot where she'd stood to scan the room from that perspective. Nothing appeared glaringly out of place and the desk chair sat snugged into the footwell. The office looked undisturbed. Well, except for the missing ceiling tile. But from this angle with the lights off, the ceiling lighting fixture did a nice job of camouflaging the hole. Probably the only reason he noticed it was on account of knowing exactly where to look.

With his hand covering his mouth, he whispered, "Sit-rep?"

"They're still searching."

"Where?"

"Mizrahi's back in Collier's office and Glass's patrolling the floor. They think you may still be up in the ceiling…ah, are you?" Lopez asked.

Arnold elected to not answer in the extremely unlikely chance that Mizrahi had somehow tapped their comms. How that might happen, he wasn't sure, but still, wasn't about to let overconfidence deal him a fatal blow. Especially now that he was this close to their target.

After several seconds of radio silence, Lopez said, "Mizrahi's still convinced you're heading for Collier's office."

Again, Arnold remained mute. After running through their game plan again, Arnold decided that despite this setback, his plan still stood a reasonable chance of succeeding.

He whispered, "Everything set up, ready to go?"

"Hold one." After a thirty-second pause Lopez was back with: "Locked and loaded."

"Roger that. Enable Phase One."

"Copy that," Lopez replied.

Silence. Then: "Phase One enabled."

For Arnold this was it: the supreme test of an intense seventy-two hours of prep work. If all functioned as planned, they would be able to game North Sound's ability to track him through the building. At least, that was the plan. But they all knew and believed wholeheartedly in the sanctity of Murphy's Law.

After wiping his sweaty palms on his thighs, Arnold radioed. "Let's do it."

Chapter 39

MIZRAHI LEANED BACK in Collier's black leather desk chair, staring at the ceiling tiles, willing that little shit to lift an edge for a look at him when Glass yelled, "Itzhak, get your ass out here."

Then he was up out of the chair, striding to the doorway, almost colliding with her as she suddenly filled the opening.

"What?" he asked, registering the concern painting her face.

"Your keycard just opened the south stairwell door on thirty-four," she said, backing up two steps with a don't-kill-the-messenger expression on her face.

"Mine?" he blurted, momentarily confused.

She nodded. "Uh-huh."

He'd been nowhere...then it clicked. "Gold," he said to no one in particular.

"How do you want to play this?" she asked hesitantly while shooting an over-the-shoulder glance toward the stairwell, as if Gold was about to come straight through the door.

He held up a palm while sorting through the melee of questions bouncing through his mind, all fighting for dominance.

How did the little shit manage to get out of the ceiling and then end up down on *that* floor?

Or did this represent a team member playing a game on

them, someone not in the system who could slip right past security?

Regardless, how had Gold cloned his key?

The fucker!

Those questions could wait. The immediate issue was the need to redeploy assets to counter a possible second team member inside the perimeter. Because thinking about it now, there was no agreement that Gold himself needed to be the one to take the evidentiary photos. Why hadn't he seen this loophole before? Regardless, someone from their Tiger Team just used his card. Felt as if the walls were closing in on him. They were encroaching, and he needed to protect the prize…

But what to do about the asshole on thirty-four? Couldn't ignore him, yet he couldn't abandon his post.

Think!

Well, maybe he could leave for a brief period if it meant nailing a team member.

With a chin-jut toward the south stairwell fire door, he ordered, "Get out there on that landing and wait. I'll slip down the north side to thirty-four, cross on over and come back up the south stairs. We should be able to trap that little fucker or whoever's working with him. Advise your people to notify us immediately if the door on thirty-five is fobbed."

Smiling broadly, she gave his off-the-cuff plan an approving thumbs-up.

"Gotcha. Perfect."

She was off, heading for the stairwell door, keycard in hand.

Mizrahi raced toward the north stairwell, card out, ready to trigger the sensor, already picturing the surprised expression on the invader's face when they realized they were trapped.

Try fucking with us, will you…

He pushed on through the heavy steel fire door on thirty-six, then waited for it to lock automatically under its own weight. Ears scanning the stillness for any hint of movement just in case Gold had a third asshole lurking the area. Heard nothing but stone silence.

Waited a few more beats before starting down the flight, moving quickly now, maintaining stealthy silence, blowing past thirty-five to thirty-four, then on through the fire door and across the Larkin Standish lobby, passing the stack of elevators, then into the south stairwell where he paused briefly to listen again.

With the office door cracked, Arnold heard the entire exchange, then watched Mizrahi and Glass scatter to their respective stairwells. Soon as the heavy fire door snapped shut behind Mizrahi, Arnold was on the radio.

"Go to Phase Two," then went flying down the hall for Mr. Collier's office, phone in hand, ready to take the requisite photos.

"Phase Two enabled," Lopez responded.

In the managing partner's office, Arnold snapped the selfie of his victorious face with the silver-framed picture next to it, then the shot of his watch displaying time and date. With the money shots now a wrap, he carefully placed the picture in the agreed-upon position on Mr. Collier's desk.

Job finished, he beelined for the north stairwell, hit the push bar a split second after releasing the lock and was jetting down flights of stairs when he radioed.

"Heading out now, switch everything back to normal."

"Copy that."

Breathing hard, moving fast, he asked Prisha, "Got the photos?"

As they were taken, the money shots automatically uploaded to his iCloud Photos folder, the one she could access using his password.

"We were just admiring your photographic skills. How soon before you're out?"

"Hard to predict. Moving as fast as I can. Will let you know closer to the time," he said between pants.

Mizrahi was just stepping onto the thirty-fifth-floor landing where

Glass was waiting when a guard in the control room radioed.

"Be advised that Mr. Smith's key just accessed the thirty-sixth-floor north stairwell."

Frowning, Glass shot Mizrahi a quizzical expression while putting her handheld her mouth.

"Which Smith we talking about?"

"*Our* Smith. Frank Smith."

After a moment, she asked, "What's the landing cam show?"

After a prolonged pause.

"I hate to tell you this, ma'am, but we're looking at a headshot of Goofy...you know, the Disney character?"

Glass silently mouthed, "Fuck," while sending Mizrahi a we've-been-royally-hosed expression.

Mizrahi shook his head, his rage building faster than a rogue wave. A moment later, he radioed.

"Gold's obviously still in the building. I don't want that little fucker getting out of the lobby without us nailing his ass."

"This is Secure One," radioed a guard in the lobby. "What do you suggest we do if he appears?"

"Detain him," Mizrahi answered as if this were the most stupid question he'd heard in days.

Radio silence for several seconds, then: "What's our basis for detaining him? As far as I know he hasn't broken any law...has he?"

"He's an unauthorized person," Mizrahi barked into his microphone, "who's been roaming through secure office space. We have no idea how much personal information he may have stolen and have in his possession. He needs to be searched. That's your probable cause, shithead."

"Ooookay..." the guard answered hesitantly, "But what evidence do we have of that?"

Mizrahi opened his mouth to speak but realized he couldn't explain without incriminating himself. He nodded at Glass to intervene since she was the boss of the disembodied voice. She responded with a shrug. Which *really* pissed him off.

Why couldn't she manage her troops?

"Just fucking do it, soldier," Mizrahi radioed.

"Soldier?" Glass asked, eyebrows arched questioning. "This isn't the Israeli Defense Force, Itzhak."

It took supreme restraint to not bitch-slap that smug sanctimonious expression off her face.

"Yo, Dude, Mizrahi just ordered the lobby guards to detain you," Lopez radioed.

Arnold was just hitting the twenty-second floor landing when he heard this, so he stopped to catch his breath and process this new wrinkle. He glanced around, realized the floor number, then flashed on the keycard he'd cloned from an unsuspecting elevator passenger during the previous test.

Odds were good that the card wouldn't trigger an alarm, so maybe it would be smart to break rhythm and pause to regroup.

He opened the fire door and entered the hall with his head down to limit exposure to the overhead CCTV despite his facial recognition data being altered, then scurried out of camera range into the men's room. The room was empty, so he entered a stall, and plunked down on the commode to plan his next move. Especially given this latest wrinkle.

"Dude?" Lopez repeated.

Sitting, resting while clearing his brain, he responded.

"Hold on," before wiping sweat off his face.

He needed to zone out for a moment, take a few deep breaths, and methodically work through this new ripple. In a perfect world, a perfect test entailed penetrating the target's security, obtaining the designated material, then slipping away without being detected. But this test had deviated radically from any semblance of normalcy the moment Mizrahi—in complete defiance of the Board of Governors' order—kept his internal surveillance intact, giving him complete access to the confidential planning discussions, right?

Right.

Ergo, didn't this, in turn, give him a carte blanche to also break the rules? Perhaps, by calling Mr. Collier to explain the situation? After all, he'd already penetrated the building's formidable security to score the money shots, right? Couldn't the creep now be declared a victory?

Well, while true, that would somehow feel like whining.

Finger-combing his hair, he asked Lopez, "Any recent radio chatter?"

He tore off a wad of toilet paper to mop off some sweat from his face.

"Not since your last update."

"You know where Mizrahi or Glass are now?"

"Yeah, they're back on thirty-six, talking. They're in front of the elevators. Why?"

Hmmm....

"Here's what I want you to do," Arnold said, standing up from the toilet and tossing in the sodden wad of paper.

Chapter 40

GLASS ASKED MIZRAHI, "Why keep hanging around up here, Itzhak? Why not go down to the lobby to wait? He has to show up there sooner or later. There's no other way out of the building. Unless, of course, he waits until morning when the lobby opens up and his odds of getting out improve. And I doubt he'll do that."

Mizrahi was still gazing at the ceiling, wondering, *Could the little fucker still be up there?* Was the picture of Goofy sent by a team member nothing more than a diversion? Was another of Gold's team in the building? If so, could they have opened that door instead of him? Had he and Glass both swallowed the bait by jumping to the immediate conclusion that Gold had opened that door?

Were they making a huge mistake? Were they falling for a trap?

Yeah, that would be just like that little shit: suck him into an endless spinning spiral of a mind game...

"Itzhak?"

"Huh?" he said, turning back to her, seeing her standing a few feet away, hands on her broad hips, giving him a strange look.

"I asked why don't we go down to the lobby to wait for him?"

"Are you serious? We don't know if he's taken the pictures yet."

"What pictures?"

Mizrahi blew a breath and began massaging the back of his neck, rocking his head side to side. For the love of God, questions-questions-questions.

A never-ending diatribe of questions.

"The pictures he's supposed to take to prove to Collier that he actually made it into his office."

Glass's look of curiosity intensified.

"Why his office?"

Mizrahi blew a sigh of frustration. Always questions.

What's with her?

"Because that's the proof they agreed on."

Soon as the words left his mouth, he realized he just said too much, assuming she was bright enough to catch it. Which he doubted.

"Really?" Head cocked, she began tapping her cheek with the handheld radio antenna. "And how, pray tell, do you know this?"

"I know this because it's my business to have superior intelligence."

She continued tapping her chin.

"So, it *is* true. You've bugged most of the firm?"

"That's a lie!" He recoiled in shock. "Who told you that?"

Smiling at his indignation, she paused a beat before speaking.

"I make it my business to have superior intelligence."

ARNOLD STOPPED ON the turnaround landing between the second and first floors to make sure he was holding the correct keycard, the one for the guy who worked on twenty-two. Before continuing down the stairwell, he'd slipped that card into his left front pocket to keep it separate from the others. No room for error on this next move.

No, this was crunch time, baby.

He radioed, "All set?"

"Roger that."

"Okay, let's do it."

He started down the final flight of stairs to the lobby door.

"Hey, boss, our cameras just picked up Gold getting on an elevator on floor fifty."

"Say again? Floor fifty?" Glass replied, shocked, shooting a surprised look at Mizrahi. Who continued a smoldering burn.

"Roger that. Fifty."

"How the hell did he get up there?" she asked without thinking.

How did he circumvent so many cameras?

The guard in the main CCTV monitoring room hesitated, then said, "Sorry, boss, but I'm just reporting what the camera picked up."

Fifty?

The number reverberated through Mizrahi's mind like an echo machine.

"Wait just a goddamn minute," Mizrahi radioed back. "You're telling us the camera picked up Gold in the *elevator lobby?*"

"Yes, exactly. That's what I said," came the rather snippy reply.

"Don't give me any *attitude*, asshole. Stop and think about what you just said."

Silence.

Eyeing him with wariness, Glass backed up another step, raising both hands, one of which was still holding the radio.

He eye-skewered her.

"Think about it for one goddamn minute, Glass. If Goofy's picture shows up on your system, we know that Gold's stolen your network." He paused to let that bit of logic permeate her dense brain. "Now we get a report that he's up on fifty. Clearly, he's found a way to bypass your brand-new whoop-de-do facial recognition software and is now fucking with us."

"Sure, I get that, Itzhak," she replied, arms across her chest. "But I really can't see where you're going with this?"

"Where I'm *going* with this, Glass, is that we'd be fools to believe that your hacked system had miraculously become accurate. Or, to put it in simple terms you might even have a chance to comprehend, we can't trust a goddamn thing it reports about Gold."

"That's exactly what I was trying to hammer into your thick skull," she said, throwing up her arms in frustration, "when I suggested we move to the lobby. Staying here will accomplish nothing. Or have you not heard a word I've said?"

He'd heard every word of her hysterical rant but opted to tune her out while he desperately searched for a way to minimize the damage this rapidly enlarging clusterfuck would inflict. Gold not only wormed his way back into the law office but was now making a mockery of him by gleefully playing with North Sound's new security enhancements.

"Come on, Itzhak," Glass urged as she moved to the elevator bank.

"And do what, exactly?"

"At least confront him."

For all the good that will do.

Mizrahi began punching his left palm. The pivotal question was whether Gold already had the shots required for proof of penetration. He carefully began to work back over the events that unfolded since the little shit vanished—presumably into the ceiling.

And he was now one hundred percent convinced that's exactly where he'd gone. And after checking every office on that floor, there was no evidence he'd been able to climb down yet. Meaning there was no way the test could've succeeded yet.

Could he now salvage the evening by calling Collier to report that he had Gold trapped in the ceiling?

Would that demonstrate just how effectively he did his job? That in spite of Gold's cunning, he and Glass, in a seamlessly collaborative effort, had kept the invader at bay.

Yes, a preemptive strike would allow him to declare the test a failure.

In so doing, he could claim that any evidence Gold produced

was taken *after* the fact.

Might that work?

It was worth a try. In fact, it seemed to be his only chance for survival.

He heard Glass radioing, "Concentrate the lobby detail at the elevators."

"I think it's time to bounce if you have a shot at it," Lopez radioed.

"Copy that," Arnold said, opening the door from the stairwell into the lobby.

About a hundred feet away stood a guard next to the only lobby door out of the building at this time of morning. The guard did a double take as Arnold came strolling out of the stairwell doorway.

Then Arnold took off running for the stairwell to the garage, and the guard yelled, "Stop!" as if he actually believed Arnold would be stupid enough to comply.

Arnold blew through the door, began jumping stairs two at a time, left hand sliding along the tubular railing for balance, hit the first parking-garage level, shot through the EXIT door. He jogged across a row of yellow parking-stall stripes, cut around the red-and-white guard arm, then out onto the sidewalk with its crisp, salt-scented, deliciously refreshing night air.

Out of the building now, there was nothing Mizrahi nor North Sound could do, so he took a moment to savor the cleansing feeling of fresh air flowing through his nostrils and down into his lungs.

Finally refreshed, he started the uphill slog to their parking spot on Eighth.

He radioed.

"Anyone up for a burger and beer at the 5 Point?"

Chapter 41

THE TEAM WAS shoehorned into an impossibly small booth, Arnold and Prisha facing Lopez and Vihaan, having just yelled their orders for beers and burgers to a heavily tatted and pierced, anorexic-looking waif in well-worn denims, and gray Georgetown sweatshirt with amputated sleeves.

After packing into the booth, they'd spent a moment doing nothing but collecting their thoughts and unwinding after so many intense consecutive hours of figure skating atop wafer-thin ice.

As Arnold surveyed his team, he couldn't keep from radiating intense gut-lifting pride for successfully pulling off another Larkin Standish creep.

A major David and Goliath one at that.

A coup.

Jesus, what a high.

After another minute of decompression, Arnold decided it was time to refocus everyone on the job they still had to finish.

He leaned toward the center of the table, the others following suit, forming a huddle to be able to converse over the waxing and waning cacophony of blaring music and conversations.

"I texted Mr. Collier during the drive over," he told them. "So, at this point, the ball's in his court. We can all just relax and wait for the final act."

The final act occurred at 8:35 AM the next morning when Arnold's phone jarred him from a deep dreamless sleep. Despite the haze of being half asleep and not having his glasses on, he could make out Mr. Collier's name on the screen, so cleared his throat, ran his tongue over desert-dry teeth, and swiped Accept.

He croaked, "Good morning, Mr. Collier."

"I apologize about waking you, but I'd like us meet with Frank this afternoon in my office at five thirty. I hope this works for you. I'll make a point of being free at that time. Frank has already agreed to be there."

In other words, declining wasn't an option.

Knuckling a granule of sleep from the corner of his right eye, Arnold said, "Absolutely, sir. Prisha and I will be there."

He blinked.

After disconnecting the call, Arnold dictated a reminder to himself before carefully replacing the phone atop its charging disk, pounded his pillow back into his preferred shape, slumped onto his right side, let his muscles relax, and slid back into dreamland within seconds.

5:15 PM

Mizrahi and Glass huddled in his office scratching around the What-If sandbox for a strategy to minimalize the anticipated blowback from last night's disaster. There was no way to sweep the outcome of Gold's pen-test under the rug, even though Mizrahi had gone to great pains to adjust Collier's fucking picture of his wife just-so on the desk after Gold set it down.

He'd done this after the lobby guards notified him that they saw the little fucker run from the building through the garage, leaving little doubt that Gold's mission had succeeded. At this point, he and Glass were facing a horrendous damage-control situation.

Their radios broke squelch with, "Hey, boss, be advised that both Gold and Patel just came through the lobby on their way to thirty-four."

Earlier in the day he'd mentioned to Glass to expect a meeting late this afternoon—in the neighborhood of five thirty or so—between their bosses and Gold. She didn't bother to ask how he'd obtained the specific information, just nodded.

Glass squeezed the button on her epaulet mic, said, "Copy that," while flashing Mizrahi a conspiratorial here-we-go expression.

After a resigned nod of confirmation, he adjusted his desk chair and angled his monitor slightly to give them both a view. He figured what the hell, she'd made a point of letting him know she was aware of his clandestine surveillance system, so why pretend it didn't exist. Might as well demonstrate how vital it was to the security mission of the firm.

He said, "We can see which conference room they go to and then listen to the damage report. Any problem with that?"

He would be surprised if she did.

Before she could answer their radios broke squelch again.

"It now seems that Mr. Smith's headed up to the same floor."

"Copy that," she answered, then muttered, "Shit," while sending Mizrahi another knowing glance.

They watched Collier meet Arnold, Prisha, and Frank Smith in the Larkin Standish lobby, then followed the group up the north stairwell to thirty-six. Once they exited the stairwell, Mizrahi switched to the webcam view from Collier's monitor.

For the meeting, the lawyer had added an extra guest chair to his usual ensemble of two.

After they were all in the office, he closed the door, saying, "Please," with a sweep of his hand toward the chairs. Smith, Prisha, and Arnold were already sitting as Collier slid into his padded desk chair, his single computer monitor to his right. Leaning forward, forearms on the desk, fingers knitted together, he held eye-direct contact with Arnold and said, "Thank you for coming on such short notice, but Frank and I have several questions concerning the events that transpired during the night." He paused to glance at a note pad on his desk. "Primarily, we want to clear up some confusion about the precise sequence of events." After checking his notes one more time he leaned back in his chair, crossed left leg over right knee, then, "At approximately one-fifty-five this morning I received a phone call from Mr. Mizrahi saying that he and Ms. Glass discovered that you were hiding in the false ceiling." He pointed to the overhead tiles. "Is this true?"

With a nod, Arnold said, "Yes sir, I was up there."

Collier gave Smith a nod.

Smith asked, "How'd you get up there?"

After Arnold's explanation, Smith just shook his head.

"Unbelievable. How were you able to gain access to the room?"

"Those specific details will be included in our After-Action report, sir."

"Regardless," Collier said, leading the discussion back on point. "Mizrahi claims you weren't able to access my office. However, when I explained that both of us received copies of the evidentiary photos you took, he alleged they were digital images Photoshopped from the prior test and so didn't prove you actually made it into my office." He quickly raised a hand, cutting off any reply. "Furthermore, when I entered my office this morning, Gretchen's picture was in its *normal* position and not the one we'd agreed upon. How do you explain this discrepancy?"

Arnold shot Prisha a quick side-eye, then said to Mr. Collier, "Please bear with me for one moment," and pulled his phone from his pocket.

As he was doing this, Prisha said, "He's about to send you a link to a video clip we believe will help clear up any confusion."

"Ah, there we go. You should have it any second now," Arnold said to Mr. Collier.

A second later, Mr. Collier said, "Here it is," then motioned to Smith. "Frank, why don't you come around so we can watch this together."

He motioned to the side of his chair.

Frank Smith took up a position to Collier's left while Arnold and Prisha stood to his right, all eyes on the monitor.

"Everyone ready?" Collier asked.

"I am," Smith answered.

"Play it," said Arnold.

The video was a wide-angle shot of Collier's desk at night as evidenced by the darkness outside the floor-to-ceiling windows. A moment later, Mizrahi could be seen approaching the desk with his phone in hand, then dropped into Collier's desk chair, glanced from the silver-framed picture of Collier's wife to the phone, reached over to carefully reposition the portrait. He stood, consulted his phone once more before making another slight adjustment. He backed up a step to check again. After carefully scrutinizing the position of the picture, he walked out of the camera's field of view.

Collier glanced up at the assembled group, then motioned them to retake their seats. They did so as a heavy silence hung over the room.

Sitting back in his chair, right leg over his left, Mr. Collier cleared his throat, pressed his lips tightly together before saying to Arnold, "The time stamp clearly shows this was taken last night. Is this correct?"

"Yes sir, that *is* correct."

"And it appears that the video is from the webcam on my monitor in my office. Is this also correct?"

"Yes, sir."

Collier took a moment to smooth his tie along the front of his crisp white shirt.

"And from the time stamp on the pictures you sent us, isn't it true that this appears to happen *after* you were in my office? he asked in a tone of a lawyer cross-examining a witness.

"That appears to be the case."

The lawyer appeared deeply perplexed for a moment, but then suddenly reared back with wide-eyed astonishment and said, "This raises several questions. First, how did Itzhak know that the proof of penetration involved Gretchen's picture?"

Arnold, Prisha, and Smith silently exchanged questioning glances as if completely baffled.

"But clearly Itzhak didn't know that we'd agreed on not putting the picture back in its original location."

Arnold nodded.

"And who was recording from my webcam?"

Arnold sat silently, looking back at Mr. Collier as Mr. Smith fidgeted in his chair. Prisha remained inscrutable.

With a gasp, Mr. Collier stared directly into the webcam and said, "My God, does this meant that Mizrahi did not dismantle his monitoring system as instructed?" The lawyer then leaned forward in his chair, moving closer to the webcam in the monitor: "Itzhak, perhaps now would be an excellent time for you to come to my office to discuss this. *Now*."

Chapter 42

AS ITZAK LISTENED to Collier's biting words a tingling sensation sprouted inside his anus, suffusing rapidly through his body, burning his face with prickly heat. He could feel Glass's eyes boring into him like bayonets.

What was there to discuss?

That he had the firm's security foremost in his mind? That he had—until they stabbed him in the back by hiring that little fuckwad to purposely try to make him look like a clown—kept the firm incredibly secure? Was this how they planned to treat one of their most devoted and faithful employees? Well, fuck them!

But he really did need the job. He turned to Glass for support but was confronted by an incriminating stare.

"What?" he demanded as harshly as possible. "You just witnessed how effective this system can be for maintaining security. After all, we knew exactly where that little shit was."

She pushed out of the chair.

"Tell you what, Itzhak, why don't I get out of your hair so you can go have a chat with your boss. Good luck, by the way."

Then she shot out the door like a rocket.

"Wait!" he yelled, moving past the threshold.

She stopped and turned to face him, but said nothing, just

stared at him with questioning eyes. Mizrahi swallowed hard. Hated to grovel.

"Well?" she finally asked after several seconds of very dead air.

"If the worst comes of this and Collier" —he swallowed again— "terminates me…"

Terminates me, sounded so…fatal.

Glass didn't respond to the non-question. Rather, she raised her eyebrows and shifted her heft from one foot to the other, waiting.

Mizrahi went on to say, "I was wondering if North Sound would hire me?"

His voice carried a slight note of pleading, which he hated. It should be the other way around; she should be asking him.

Without hesitating, she shook her head with the finality of a hanging judge.

"No."

Mizrahi recoiled at how emphatic and final her single word rang out. As if she had the power to determine a decision yet to be made, a decision she really had no say in. It would be up to North Sound's HR department. Then again, she might have suction with them…what had he ever done to that cunt to deserve such shameful treatment? After all, he'd given her advanced warning on both pen-tests. Wasn't that worth some gratitude? The more he pondered this, the more he knew she'd always disliked him because he controlled the six floors leased by the firm. Not only that, but she'd always been jealous of him for his total command of his staff.

Despite knowing this, he couldn't help but ask, "Why not?"

"Why not? Let me think about that for two milliseconds: for starters you're a flaming misogynistic homophobic asshole, and a despicable example of a manager. But if you want me to go into details, I can and will. Yes?"

As Arnold, Prisha, Smith and Collier waited for Mizrahi to

Allen Wyler

materialize at the door, Arnold motioned Mr. Collier and Mr. Smith closer, then whispered, "If there's any chance that Mizrahi will be terminated today" —as if that possibility was actually up for serious debate— "I suggest that North Sound deactivate his keycard. Like, immediately."

"Excellent suggestion, Arnold," Smith said, turning questioning eyes to the lawyer.

Collier appeared to weigh the suggestion for all of a half second before nodding at Smith.

"I suggest you call from the men's room."

"Another good suggestion," Smith said, rising out of the chair to scoot out the door.

Suspicions validated, Arnold said, "While he's doing that, do you mind if I have my team deactivate his password to the firm's network?"

Mr. Collier made the Anjali Murda hand gesture.

"*Thank* you, Arnold. Another excellent suggestion. And while you're at it, I assume you'll take care of the other matter?"

Arnold nodded and stood.

"That's ready to go. I'll give the word when we take care of this other matter." Amazingly, Mizrahi backed up data to only one external hard drive, so wiping both the laptop and storage hinged on just two commands. Once issued, his recordings of various conferences and discussions within the law firm would be gone. "I'll be right back."

His phone was already out of his pocket as he raced off to the men's room to join Smith.

Prisha remained seated, legs crossed, looking totally chill as she casually perused CNN headlines on her phone. Ms. Unruffled.

A moment later there was a knock on the door as Mizrahi breezed in, saying, "You wanted to see me" with an overly confident tone.

Defiant, almost. Certainly, without the slightest hint of remorse.

As he started to sit in the chair Smith had vacated, Collier

278

said, "Sorry, Itzhak, that seat's taken. So is the other, by the way. Regardless, no need to sit. This won't take but a moment."

Mizrahi glanced at the vacant seats as if intending to point out that they looked empty to him, but instead mumbled, "Yes, sir."

Leaning back in his chair, the managing partner washed the firm's Head of Security with a slow once-over and, in so doing, dropped the room temperature at least ten degrees. Thick silence enveloped them. Even the air felt as if it had stopped circulating.

A moment later, Smith hustled back in, broke pace for a fractional second as his eyes locked onto Mizrahi, then silently slid back into his chair.

The dead silence continued. Then, as if on cue, Arnold scurried in to join the group and reclaim his seat. Lowering her phone, Prisha redirected her gaze to the lawyer.

With the players now reassembled, Collier began by tapping steepled fingertips against his chin for several heavy moments, before saying, "Well, now that we're reconvened, let's move to the primary topic of our agenda." Then to Mizrahi: "Do you wish to say anything in your defense, Mr. Mizrahi?"

After a quick scan of his inquisitors, Mizrahi shot a nervous over-the-shoulder glance at the open door and hall beyond.

"Oh, no need to concern yourself with privacy at this point, Itzhak," Collier said, "since it doesn't seem to have concerned you before now. And besides, we're all on the edge of our seats waiting to hear how you justify ignoring the managing partners' directive. So, please..." he said, extending a palm to him. "We're all ears."

After appearing to steel his nerves, Mizrahi said, "I hope you realize that I've always had the firm's security front and center in my mind while working here, Mr. Collier. You can't fault me for that."

He added a note of indignity to his tone.

Although Arnold knew this interchange was really between Mr. Collier and Mizrahi, he couldn't help but ask, "In that case,

Allen Wyler

how do you justify surveilling my house? I know it wasn't you the first three nights because it was a woman with vibrant sapphire eyes. But the other night it was you. Was that protecting the firm?"

Collier glanced from Arnold to Mizrahi, then with raised eyebrows said, "Ah, yes, I knew there was something I was forgetting." He turned back to Arnold: "Thank you for jogging my memory." To Mizrahi again: "In reviewing Lauren's time sheets I noticed that she was apparently working for us on the same evenings that Arnold's security cameras documented a disguised female matching her body type and eyes watching his house from the back alley. Is there anything you'd like to tell us about this?"

Mizrahi's face slowly segued from blustering defiance to anger, both hands knotting into balls of white knuckles.

He stabbed a finger at Collier, saying, "Know what? Fuck you!" He turned to Arnold. "That includes you and your fucking Swami Bindi bitch. For the record, fuck all you assholes."

He swept the extended finger to include Frank Smith before storming into the hall and toward the stairwell.

Arnold stood and followed Mr. Smith to the office door where they watched Mizrahi repeatedly try to open the north stairwell door with his keycard.

Smith called out, "Sorry, Itzhak, but your card's been deactivated."

He turned to Collier who, by now, was also at the doorway.

Collier called to Mizrahi: "You can collect your personal items at the security desk in the lobby, at which point Lorna Glass will escort you from the building. I hope you have a better rest of your evening."

Arnold watched Lorna Glass step into the elevator alcove from the side hall and join Mizrahi at the elevators. Without a word, she reached over and pressed the Down call button.

Mizrahi turned to Collier.

"Don't say I didn't warn you assholes."

Out the side of his mouth, Mr. Collier asked Arnold, "Please

280

tell me you took care of that issue."

Arnold said, "Checking on that now" as he thumbed Lopez a text.

They continued to watch in silence as the elevator swallowed Mizrahi and Glass, then returned to their chairs. As Arnold was sitting down, his phone dinged. A reply to his text: *Taken care of.*

He told the lawyer, "That other matter's been taken care of."

A wave of relief flashed briefly across the lawyer's face before Smith could pick up on it.

Now that the group was reassembled, Mr. Collier calmly set his hands just so on the desk in front of him and said to Arnold, "I believe we still have unfinished business to discuss."

At which point, Smith pushed up from his chair saying, "Excuse me for interrupting, Webster, but this is probably an appropriate time for me to let you folks discuss these other matters in private." Then with a sad headshake, "Not a pleasant business, this one, but one in need of doing. And for what it's worth, I think you handled it appropriately."

Arnold suspected he knew what was coming. If so, Frank Smith's presence would expedite his proposal—at least, one part of it. There was still an enormous obstacle to deal with.

He said, "Actually, Mr. Smith should remain to hear what I'm going to propose since it will direct impact North Sound."

Clearly caught off-guard, Smith glanced questioningly at Collier.

With a shrug, the lawyer said, "I have no problem with that, Frank." To Arnold, he said, "I believe this brings us back to our phone conversation from a little over a week ago. Except now the circumstances are more critical. How do you propose we cover Itzhak's responsibilities?"

And there it was. Arnold felt everyone's eyes on him, waiting to hear his answer. After all, Larkin Standish was not only their prime client, but a major status firm in the city. Problem was, Gold and Associates' workload was presently maxed. He became aware that his palms were wet, so dried them on his jeans, shifted in the chair, cleared his throat, and wondered why—since he'd known this moment was barreling down on him like a Kenworth eighteen-wheeler—he hadn't prepared for it. The topic, after all, didn't arise in a vacuum. He also knew that he'd been subliminally processing the issue because he couldn't believe for one moment that Mizrahi complied with the Board's directive.

"So, here's the thing…" he said to Mr. Collier, mind now going like crazy fitting pieces together. "His job description is to oversee the firm's physical and IT security. Is this correct?"

"Correct," agreed Mr. Collier.

"Well, to be honest, I've never understood the rationale for that. What I mean is, far as I can tell, the firm's physical security is taken care of by North Sound. Even more so now that the new enhancements are in place. So, unless I'm missing something, my first suggestion is to eliminate that part of the job description." He shrugged. "I mean your major access points are maximally controlled, so realistically, what more can that person do to secure your physical offices?"

Leaning back in his chair now, Collier slowly raked his front teeth over his bottom lip several times before nodding.

"Put in that light, I have to agree. Thinking back on it, when I assumed the responsibilities of managing partner, his job description was just one of the many things I inherited from my predecessor. I have to admit that a few times it crossed my mind to take a closer look at that role, but there've always been other, more pressing issues to distract me from pursuing it. Having said this, given the present turn of events, you're absolutely correct. This is the perfect time to address the issue. However, that still leaves us asking how we manage our IT staff. Now more than ever, we'll need your help handling that for us."

Arnold glanced from Mr. Collier to Prisha's inscrutably impassive expression, then back to the lawyer.

"We need a minute, okay?" Arnold asked, despite it not really being question, especially since he was already pushing out of his chair.

"Of course," Mr. Collier called after him. "Frank and I have a few items to discuss in the meantime."

Arnold motioned Prisha toward the open door. Without a word or change of expression, she followed suit and silently boogied out into the hall and over next to the door to the men's room.

Finger-combing his black curly hair, Arnold asked, "Thoughts?"

Looking at the ground, forehead clamped in her left hand, she said, "I need a minute to process this."

"I mean," Arnold prattled on, "it isn't like we didn't know this was coming. And besides, it just feels like we owe him. At least to me it does."

"Dude!" she said sharply with a look of exasperation. "Give me a moment to think."

Probably best to just shut up and focus on their good-news, bad-news situation, Arnold decided. Increasing business was generally good news. But the flip side was that layering more work on an already maxed workload would wipe out any remaining elasticity in the system for accommodating unanticipated requests. Admittedly, this present conundrum was unique, but....when they accepted this case, he'd toyed with the idea of recruiting another team member, but for an ill-defined gut reason, he'd flat-out rejected the idea.

What was it that gave him pause? What was his gut trying to tell him that he wasn't hearing?

In his young life, he'd learned from several hard lessons to not argue with his gut.

"Know what I think?" Prisha said, jarring him back from his internal debate. "It's totally insane to accept a job we know diddly-squat about." She shot an over her shoulder glance toward Mr. Collier's office. "I mean, what do we actually know about their routine IT workflow, staffing, or present staff capabilities? Or am I overlooking something?"

And there it was: she just nailed his gut's mystery message.

A message he'd been too busy with planning the pen-test to pay attention to. Something so elemental that he was embarrassed to have missed it.

After a sigh, he nodded.

"Naw, you're absolutely right, So, what're you saying?" he asked, already moving past the immediate issue toward the long-term strategy for the company, the one that had been simmering on a back burner for over a month now. One he realized also factored into the gut message.

She cocked her head.

"Thought I was very clear. We'd be nuts to take the job without knowing a ton more about the particulars. And maybe when we do, we should take a pass. Hell, I don't know," she said, throwing up her hands and shooting another glance at Collier's open door. Knuckling the tip of her nose, she said, "But we also have a direct responsibility to bail him out of a rocky situation." Pause. "What I'm saying is we're in a massive bind."

Arnold began to knead the knuckles of his right hand, shuffling his feet, scrambling to nail down a new plan, one that wasn't just a solution to their immediate problem, but a solid strategy for achieving his vision for Gold and Associates. And for the first time since that vision began stewing in the back of his mind it became clear enough to verbalize.

But would Prisha buy it?

"Yeah, yeah, you're right about the Mr. Collier thing, but what I'm concerned about is what's coming up down the road." He glanced from her to the open door to Collier's office. "Part of me is like super thrilled Mr. Collier trusts us enough to essentially give us access to a load of highly sensitive records." He paused for a breath. "This offer's also a double-edged sword because we'd be totally overextended. But his offer should also tell us we're building an extremely valuable cachet within our niche clientele." He shuffled in place, selecting his next words cautiously. "It seems to me, we're at an inflection point and can go one of two ways. If we accept the job, we'll have to hire someone to help manage our routine workload and continue rocking along. But before too long, we'd be facing the same situation and be forced to repeat the process. Because you know that's exactly what's going to happen, right?" He jettisoned kneading his knuckles and started rubbing his hands together, as if warming them. "So, here's what I think we should do. We need to take our company in an entirely different direction." He paused to polish his words to sell the vision he'd begun hammering out since Frank Smith dangled becoming North Sound's go-to pen-testers as an incentive. Looking her dead in the eye, he said, "The five of us have become a great team, right?"

She responded with a wary nod, as if anticipating a prelude to a more complicated proposition than just assuming Larkin Standish's IT supervision.

"We trust each other, know each other, and have each other's back. And it's precisely because of this that I'm in no huge rush to hire someone we don't really know all that well. We could be just asking for problems. We've been lucky so far." Arnold paused, scrubbing his palms together more vigorously, gazing down the hall at nothing in particular but in the direction of the lawyer's office. "What I propose we tell Mr. Collier is that we'll have Vihaan supervise his present techs *only* as long as it takes to make a realistic determination of their actual IT needs rather than some self-serving Mizrahi-bullshit excuse. Once we know what those are, we'll be in better shape to give them a final recommendation. Could be they need to hire a replacement for Mizrahi but it's actually more probable that it may be unnecessary. My gut says that Mizrahi's position can be handled by one of their present techs—especially now that North Sound will be covering their physical security."

"I dunno, dude, Vihaan's been keeping us afloat with the routine—"

"Yeah, yeah, yeah," Arnold said, swatting away the remark with a hand wave. "Our present workload's super maxed. I get that. But this will be only temporary. Vihaan can probably come up with a reasonable assessment in less than two weeks." He held up his hand, indicating he wasn't finished. "Yes, it's going to strain the system, but I think we can do it for a short period of time. And to take some of the sting out of it, we make Lopez and Vihaan full partners. Hell, we've been intending to do this for weeks now but just have been too busy with other things, right?"

"Okaaaay...but?"

"Yeah, I know what you're thinking. We'll have other requests for work, so here's the kicker: starting now, we don't accept new jobs that can't be *comfortably* accommodated with our present personnel while giving priority to our present accounts. This means that sooner or later we'll be forced to tell a prospective new client we simply don't have the bandwidth to accommodate them. Yeah, yeah, I totally get that we risk pissing them off, but in the long run I believe it'll only increase our prestige. I don't know about you, but I want to see us become an exclusive, highly-sought-after, boutique company known for delivering a quality product."

Arms folded across his chest, he radiated a look of solid determination. He was relieved to finally crystallize and lay out his long-term objective for the company that was born when he removed a virus from Mr. Davidson's computer.

Which now, seemed a lifetime ago.

"So," he said. "What do you think?"

Chapter 43

COLLIER WAS TYPING on his keyboard and Smith was pacing ovals around the guest chairs when Arnold and Prisha came sauntering back into the lawyer's office with Cheshire Cat grins plastered across their faces.

Turning from his computer monitor, Collier cast them a questioning look as they tucked back into their seats.

"Please tell me you're not going to leave us in the lurch."

"No sir, we won't do that, but our answer isn't so simple, so please bear with us. We need to clarify a few items before we can give you a definitive answer." Arnold was sitting forward now, legs crossed, fingers knitted over his knee. "For starters, we know nothing of Mizrahi's actual job description as it pertains to IT oversight. Can you outline them, please?"

Lips pursed in a sour lemon expression, Collier sat back in his chair, drumming both hands on the respective arm rests in a portrait of a man scrambling for an answer.

After a moment he said, "I'm embarrassed to admit I have no idea, but that information should be in his HR file. I'm sure I can have it for you in the morning."

"Okay, good, then that's the first issue we need to sort out,"

Arnold said in a tone that he hoped would relieve some of Mr. Collier's obvious embarrassment. In truth, Arnold would've been surprised if the lawyer could spout those details off the tip of his tongue. "I believe three IT techs are under Mizrahi's supervision. Is this correct?"

Collier's expression relaxed.

"This I do know, and you're correct. Three technicians."

"Good," Arnold said. "So, here's our suggestion. For starters, our team's presently working at maximum capacity, so our bottom line is that we can only help out on a *temporary* basis to stabilize the situation. We propose to begin by assessing your actual staffing needs to determine what, if any, additional changes need to be made. However, it's entirely possible that your firm may work perfectly well by promoting one of your present techs to a supervisory role and hiring one additional tech. If this turns out to be the case, we'll help you with that selection process. But to be clear, our involvement can only last through this process. In other words, once we get this settled, we'll no longer be involved with the day-to-day management of your IT department. Both Prisha and I hope this proposal is acceptable to you."

Collier appeared to process this information while sucking an incisor.

"What you just proposed makes a great deal of sense, especially *if* Mizrahi's position was inflated. That's another aspect of the firm I inherited as managing partner but never felt qualified to question. Which now, in the clarity of retrospect, wasn't particularly good diligence."

"Short of hiring a consultant to evaluate that for you, it's impossible for you to make that determination, Mr. Collier," Prisha offered. "A staffing realignment may well end up being one of the benefits to having done the pen-test."

"She's right, Webster," Smith offered with a sympathetic note and smile.

On the elevator ride down to the lobby, Prisha asked Arnold,

"Does this mean you're going to hang around town while Vihaan sorts this shit out?"

Arnold had started rolling that question around in his mind the moment Mr. Collier gave a thumbs-up to their plan. Valid arguments could be made to stay or return to Honolulu, but truthfully, he was anxious to see what might or might not develop with Noriko.

"Naw, I think after you drop me off, I'll see what flights I can snag. I have some unfinished business to attend to there. Which, now that you've brought up the subject, I have a proposition for you."

HONOLULU

Chapter 44

Four Weeks Later

ARNOLD CARRIED THE stack of warm boxes of twelve-inch medium pan pizzas—two Da Sumo Specials and one pepperoni—out to the table on the back deck where he'd already set up a roll of paper towels and a stack of paper plates.

The ice chest was stocked with Bikini Blonde for those who just wanted a nice smooth brew to wash down the pizza, but also some Big Swell IPA for those who were bound and determined to get their buzz on.

"Pizza's here," he announced to Brian Ito, Prisha, Vihaan, Lopez, and Noriko.

The team—now all full associates—had voted to blow through most of the $25,000 bonus to fly Prisha, Vihaan, and Lopez over to Honolulu and put them up at the Hilton Waikiki for a week.

A sort of team building experience, Arnold rationalized.

And besides, it wasn't like they were hurting for work. In fact, their work orders were increasing. Not only that, but Gold and Associates had locked down a contract with North Sound Security for a series of pen-tests on the properties they guarded. But dealing with those issues was for another day. For now, the most important point of the evening was for everyone to relax, feed their faces, and enjoy their mini-vacation.

Of course, they still had to grind out some routine work every day, but those jobs could be handled remotely from the comfort of their hotel room or back here on the deck with their laptops.

Vihaan had determined that Serge Valchenka could be promoted to IT manager, but that there was no rush to backfill his spot. This decision had yet to be presented to Mr. Collier, since the firm was presently taking applications for the open position and all candidates who had passed Serge's screening would be interviewed by Vihaan once he was back from vacation.

Mr. Collier and the Board of Governors were delighted with the recent personnel changes as well as the positive effect it had on their annual budget. They were also thrilled with the job that Gold and Associates had done in locating and destroying Mizrahi's recordings, which it turned out, were not that many.

However, those he did have were highly sensitive. Apparently, he had a good nose for what was explosive. No one was quite sure what happened to Mizrahi. Well, except Arnold did destroy the hard drive of the stolen laptop along with the external drive. Eventually he planned on replacing his present Inspiron with a new one and delegating the old one to decoy status, which meant leaving it out in the kitchen.

Arnold set the boxes of pizzas on the table, then backed up to admire the Gold and Associates Tiger Team as they started scarfing the eats and popping bottle caps.

He smiled at Noriko.

She caught it from the corner of her eye, turned, returning the smile.

Yes, life is good.

Allen Wyler

DIGITAL science

Acknowledgement

JT Gaietto, CISSP, ISCFE, TPN.
Principal, Chief of Staff, Digital Silence, LTD.

Printed in the USA
CPSIA information can be obtained
at www.ICGtesting.com
LVHW042015260724
786517LV00005B/1007

9 781960 405357